In Love with a Rude Boy:

Renaissance Collection

In Love with a Rude Boy:

Renaissance Collection

Nika Michelle and

Racquel Williams

www.urbanbooks.net

Urban Books, LLC
300 Farmingdale Road, NY-Route 109
Farmingdale, NY 11735

In Love with a Rude Boy:
Renaissance Collection

ISBN 13: 978-1-62286-679-3
ISBN 10: 1-62286-679-7

First Trade Paperback Printing March 2018
Printed in the United States of America

10 9 8 7 6 5 4 3 2 1

This is a work of fiction. Any references or similarities to actual events, real people, living or dead, or to real locales are intended to give the novel a sense of reality. Any similarity in other names, characters, places, and incidents is entirely coincidental.

Distributed by Kensington Publishing Corp.
Submit orders to:
Customer Service
400 Hahn Road
Westminster, MD 21157-4627
Phone: 1-800-733-3000
Fax: 1-800-659-2436

In Love with a Rude Boy:

Renaissance Collection

Nika Michelle and

Racquel Williams

Chapter 1

Kadijah

"Damn, DiDi, your man got some explaining to do, bitch," my girl Tamia stated as she stared at me with wide eyes.

I shrugged my shoulders indifferently. "It ain't nothing for him to explain." With that said, I walked into my two-bedroom condo to pour myself a glass of Merlot.

Her nosy ass was right on my heels as she closed the door behind us. "I'm your best friend, and I had no clue that Daryn was fucking with some other chick. Did you?"

I made my way to the kitchen as I thought about my boyfriend . . . well, as far as I was concerned at that point, my ex-boyfriend Daryn. His side bitch had shown up at my crib, talking cash shit about how I had stolen him from her. I had told that bitch to kiss my ass, just like he had been doing for the past two years and three months. Shit, I couldn't wait for that nigga to show up and try to explain that messiness away. One thing about me was the fact that I did not, and I repeat did *not*, need to depend on a man. I always made sure that I was good, for the simple fact that if I relied on a man for shit, I'd be left with *nothing*, because a man was never consistent.

A man always talked a good game and did what he felt he had to do until he got you in his clutches, and then that shit would come to a complete halt. I was sick of the same old, same old. When it came to relationships,

I felt that I was just doing what everybody else around me expected. I took a man's bullshit out of fear of being alone, but why? I mean, a bitch could do bad all by her damn self, but from where I was standing, my shit looked like it was all good. I was holding my own and doing a damn good job at it. Not one man could take credit for my success, not even my father. He had disappeared a long time ago. It was just me, my mom, and my older brother, Jameel.

Jameel was older than me by three years. He was the typical older brother, because he was overprotective as hell. All I could hope was that he wouldn't come running to my rescue if my bestie decided to call him. I had to make her back down, because I didn't want any more drama.

When I found the bottle of Sutter Home Merlot in the fridge, I popped the cork out and poured Tamia and myself a glass. "I didn't know, either. Look, I can handle Daryn. Just go home and let me do me. I'm a grown-ass woman. You know I got this. I'm gonna just let him get his shit after I tell him where to go. You don't have a thing to worry about." I handed her one of the glasses of merlot.

She looked at me and shook her head as she sipped her wine. "Heifer, who the hell do you think you foolin'? I can literally hear the wheels turning in your head. You plotting on that nigga."

I couldn't help but laugh as I took a large gulp of the dry red wine. Damn, I needed that drink. "No I'm not. I'm simply gonna pack his things and cuss him out in the process. That's it. Besides, it's probably best that I leave his boring ass alone, anyway. Did you see that bitch he's fucking? He cheated on me with that?" I shook my head.

Tamia started laughing too. "Hell, yeah. She looked like a black Mary Poppins."

"Right. Talking 'bout, do you know Daryn Marshall?" I mocked her. "Um, yeah, bitch, I've been fucking him for the past two years. Get the fuck outta here. What? Is he your husband?" I shook my head, trying to defy the tears. I couldn't believe that fool had played me like that. The nerve of him.

I was a catch and a damn good one at that. Fortunately, the bitch had claimed that they weren't married, but they had been together for four years and were engaged. What the fuck? I had something for his ass. I couldn't wait until that black motherfucker used the key that I had given him a few months ago to walk inside my spot. Oh, I had something for him to catch, and it certainly was not some of my good pussy. Hell, nah. I was college educated, but I had been raised in the hood. Like they said, "You can take the chick out of the hood, but you can't take the hood out of the chick." Damn right!

Not only was I proudly hood as hell, but I was also smart. With the help of my common sense, I had refined my book sense. Therefore, I was the perfect combination of beauty and brains. The thing was, I knew how to keep the street side of me at bay. I'd learned over the years that, that ignorant-acting mess got me nowhere. I had a foul mouth, and I cursed like a sailor. Daryn's trifling ass had often told me that cursing wasn't ladylike. Little did he know, but I didn't give a damn what was ladylike. I definitely carried myself like a lady, but I handled my business like a nigga. I knew how to talk and carry myself despite how and where I'd been raised therefore, I had managed to make a good living for myself at the age of twenty-five.

"You gonna be okay?" my bestie asked, concerned.

We had been close since the first grade, and although I'd been brash with her, I was actually glad that she had been there when that heifer rolled up. However, the plain-Jane ho was gone, and Daryn was on his way over.

As much as I loved Tamia, I felt the need to handle the situation on my own. It was up to me to get to the bottom of my own relationship issues. As far as I was concerned, the heifer who came over to tell me all about her long-term relationship with my man had had enough evidence. She'd shown me pictures of them together, text messages, and all types of shit. I'd even heard a few voice mails, and it was his voice. I had not one shred of doubt about it.

I had hoped that old girl would stick around for the showdown, but she had claimed that she would confront him later and wanted only to let me know because it was weighing on her heart and mind. Turned out that she had been investigating his social network activity, being that he had become less and less available to her. He'd been claiming that he had to go out of town for business. Daryn was an event promoter and a law school student who did spend a lot of time working, but his lack of availability had probably been because of his affair with me. When I looked at the bigger picture, I realized that *I* was the side chick. Daryn had been cheating on that average-looking bitch with me.

"Yeah." I nodded as she finished her wine and put the glass down on the granite-top counter.

"Okay. You sure? 'Cause—"

I cut her off. "Yes. I'll call you and fill you in after he leaves."

She reluctantly walked toward the door before turning around to look at me. "I can stay and—"

"No," I said, cutting her off again, as I literally pushed her out the door. "I got this."

"A'ight, if you say so, but make sure you call me."

"I will."

I stepped out into the hallway and watched as she disappeared around the corner to get to the staircase. When I got back inside and closed the door, I finally broke down in tears.

***

In less than two hours, Daryn was sitting at the dining room table, ready for me to serve him, like usual. The candles were burning, and the lights were all low and romantic. Talk about setting the mood right. I was looking all erotically hot and inviting in a sexy-ass red silk lingerie set by Frederick's of Hollywood. The color made my smooth bronze-toned skin look like it was glowing. My MAC lip gloss was popping, and the black red bottoms on my feet had my calves standing at attention. That sorry-ass nigga loved that sexy-ass shit.

I narrowed my already slanted copper-brown eyes at him and then puckered my thick lips to blow him a kiss. My five-foot-ten-inch, 165-pound frame was enticing him, and I could tell by how he was staring at me. I stood at the stove, carefully placed his favorite meal in a bowl, then placed the bowl on a plate. He was from New Orleans, and gumbo was his shit. I also served him some rice and mixed veggies on the side, along with a few toasted Hawaiian rolls. He loved them. I figured I'd remind him of everything that he would be missing.

"Damn, baby girl. You got it smelling all types of good up in here," he said as he rubbed his hands together.

I didn't know if he was hungry for the food or for me, because I was looking damn good. As I tossed my bouncy shoulder-length hair over my shoulders, he simply stared hungrily.

"You want me or the food?" I asked slyly as I glanced back at him.

I hoped that the smile on my face was convincing, because I needed him to feel it. He had to know that he'd attempted to play the wrong bitch. With my back turned to him, I made the face that I really wanted him to see. I damn sure wasn't fucking smiling. What the hell did I have to smile about? The man I thought I'd be spending the rest of my life with had planned his future with another bitch, and she had the ring to show for it.

"I love your cookin', sexy, but you know I'll always choose your fine, thick ass over food." His smooth dark brown skin was literally radiant as he fed me more bullshit.

His sexy dark brown bedroom eyes, close-cut wavy hair, and thick lips made me weak, and so did the aroma of his True Religion cologne. I stared at his handsome face and wanted to go ahead and reveal what had been made known to me. Instead of spilling the beans, I held my feelings in.

With that fake-ass smile on my face again, I made my way over to him, carrying his food on a tray. A tall glass of sweet tea with lemon was balanced on the tray as well, and he looked like he was so ready to grub. That shit made me want to laugh, despite my hurt.

"Well, for now you'll have to settle for food. I'm savin' the best part of the night for last, baby," I said.

I smiled down at him as I swiftly picked up the bowl of steamy, hot gumbo. I dumped it in his lap, and he yelped in pain. Before he could shoot up from the table, I dumped the rest of the food on him and then the tea, to cool him off a little.

"Shit! Fuck, yo! Why'd you do that?" His eyes were on fire, but I didn't give a fuck.

"What? You thought you were gonna just play me and shit, nigga! Yeah, your average-ass bitch popped up over here today. So, your ass is engaged, huh? You better be glad I ain't do what the fuck I wanted to do to you. I should've let your ass go to sleep and set your dick on fire, like I saw this bitch do on Facebook. You ain't worth me catching a charge over, though, nigga! Get the fuck out!" I went off and removed my heels, just in case I had to box his ass.

"Baby." He held his hands out. "Hold up. . . . What the fuck you talkin' 'bout?"

That nigga had the audacity to play dumb about that shit. It was a good thing I had my evidence. His fiancée had sent me pics of them together and a video of the damn proposal and all.

"Oh, really? You gon' act like I'm makin' this shit up, nigga!" My iPhone was in my hand, and I was strolling, ready to show him what I had on his lame ass.

The look of shock on his face spoke volumes, but I didn't want to hear any more of his lies. He was clearly a liar, and I was so fucking done with him.

"Di, baby, I can explain. Look, she doesn't mean shit to me. Her father is a partner at the law firm I want to work at, and I have to deal with her to get where I want to be. I was going to break it off. I promise you I was planning to tell her the truth about us," he explained.

Well, his explanation wasn't worth shit. He had no credibility with me, and that shit didn't matter either way.

I laughed mockingly in his face before I walked toward the front door. When I opened it, I used my hands to emphasize my point. "If you don't get your lying ass outta here, I'm gon' send you outta this bitch on a stretcher or in a body bag. Straight the fuck up. Oh, and give me my fuckin' key!"

I threw the bag with his things in it that had been sitting beside the door, and then I put my hand out.

The stain on the crotch of his pants reminded me of the mess I had to clean up, but I couldn't give two shits about that.

"I'm sorry, baby girl. If you give me a chance, I can make this up to you." He looked all pitiful, but I wasn't falling for it.

"Key please." I wiggled the fingers of my extended hand for emphasis.

He sighed before reaching in his pocket and retrieving his keys. He removed the key to my place from his key ring and placed it on my outstretched hand. I tried the key out just to be sure it worked. It was the right one.

"Baby, look—"

I cut him off real damn quick. "Bye, Craig! Yeah, *look* at it one more time, nigga, and salivate over the good-ass pussy your dick'll never have the pleasure of feeling again. Miss me with the bullshit, just like you gon' miss me, nigga! Get the fuck out!"

He walked past me and gave me a look of longing. "You'll be back to your senses tomorrow, DiDi. You already know that I'm a catch, ma. Don't play yourself."

"What? Nigga, are you serious right now? You played *yourself*. I can do so much better than you. Besides, I was with you only 'cause I thought you were going to be a successful lawyer. The dick is wack as fuck!" With that said, I slammed the door in his face.

"Fuck him," I said out loud and walked back toward the kitchen.

I put some of the gumbo in a bowl and sat down at the dining room table. After tasting it, I couldn't help but give myself credit for how good it was. Too bad I was looking all good and shit for nothing. Shit, after that, I had that "fuck a nigga" attitude. Love wasn't shit but a setup for a bitch to be all fucked up. From this point on, it was money over niggas. My career and my funds were going to be my focus. I didn't have time for love, nor did I have any patience for a lame-ass man. It was all about me now, and so . . . I was going to do me.

Chapter 2

Omari

Jah know star, the sun was blazing on the field as we played our regular Sunday evening football game at the ball field. I heard the chicks screaming my name as I kicked the ball into the goal. I smiled at the crowd of females, who made it a ritual to watch us every time we played.

As I jumped on my Suzuki Hayabusa 100R motorcycle, I looked around and smiled, because it was a big come up from the ghetto that I had grown up in.

I was born and raised in Cockburn Pen, one of the poorest ghetto neighborhoods in the rural area of Kingston, Jamaica. Shit, we were poor as hell, and being the oldest of eight children, I had to help Mama out. I knew that once I got older, I had to get away from that life. There were days when we didn't have anything but water and a piece of bread to eat for our dinner.

Killing and robbing were everyday things. Even as a young *yute*, I used to hang around the bigger dons of the area, watching and learning. It was then that I made a mental note that I was going to get out and make a better life for myself, and it didn't matter how. I was going to get mine by any means necessary.

I was about fourteen years old when I decided I had had enough of being poor. So, I got up, kissed Mama on the cheek, and bounced. Life was rough in them streets, and for the first couple of months, my homeboy and I robbed drug dealers and used the money to get bags of ganja. Selling drugs wasn't what I wanted, though. It was only a means to survive.

Being on the streets gave me different opportunities, and one of them was music. Ever since I was young, I had been fascinated with reggae. Me and my brethren would gather around and battle each other with songs that we made up. News traveled fast, and I became one of the hottest deejays in Cockburn Pen. It didn't take long for me to reach my true potential, and before you knew it, I was given an opportunity to deejay on a well-known sound system called Killamanjaro. See, Killamanjaro was mashing up the place and shutting down every sound it clashed with. I accepted the offer, and the rest was history.

I didn't mean to brag, but I was one of the hottest deejays in Jamaica right now, and with that came fame. Bitches started to throw themselves at me. Every night after the show, I could expect to leave with a different woman. I wasn't trying to settle down, but fucking pussy was definitely bragging rights among me and my brethren.

I was a *gallist*, a player, until I met my beautiful wife. It still sounded weird to me, when I said the word *wife*, because I had never thought that I would be married and would have two beautiful kids. Those kids were the only good thing that had come from me being tied down for the past three years.

I parked my bike in the driveway and opened the *grill*, the door, to the five-bedroom house that I had bought in the Stony Hill area of Kingston. It was a big come up from the ghetto, because only people with big money could afford to live up in this area.

"Daddy's home! Hey, Daddy," my youngest daughter exclaimed. She jumped on me as soon as I walked inside.

"A wey you did dey? You si mi a call your rassclaat phone?" Angela said, confronting me about where I'd been.

"Aye, watch yo' mout'. Mi a big man, and mi nuh haffi check in," I said. I was pissed as hell that instead of greeting her husband, all she did was fuss all the damn time.

"Mi know you cheating, but mi a tell yuh and dat bitch, she better go find her own man. Mi done talk," she said before she walked off into the room.

I took a seat on the couch. I was really tired of coming home to this bullshit. For once in my life, I wasn't fucking nothing else, and all she could do was sit on her ass and complain and accuse me of cheating. Jah knows those bitches out there be throwing pussy at me on the regular, but after I got caught cheating over a year ago, I'd been laying low. Shit had got sticky between my wife and the bitch from Waltham Park Road that I was fucking. Somehow, I had left my phone at home by mistake, and Angela had gone snooping around. All hell had broken loose when she read the text messages between the bitch and me. She had called the bitch, and they had met up and had got to fighting. It was so bad that Angela cut the bitch's face up. She got locked up that day, and later she was given probation. I was angry when I found out about it, because Angela was a wife, yet she was out in the streets, behaving like she was a *matey*, a side chick.

Ever since that incident, Angela had been accusing me of fucking everything with a pussy. I had to stop her from coming out to the dances that I kept, because she did not know how to act, especially when she saw other bitches.

I wasn't going to lie. The relationship was wearing me the fuck down. I was ready to get away from her and her old, miserable ass.

Chapter 3

Kadijah

It was my final class with my favorite professor, Chef Cunnings. A tall, husky, dark-skinned man from New Orleans, he had an array of recipes, from French to Italian, that he taught us, but his specialty was Southern cuisine.

"Kadijah . . ." His eyes rolled back in pleasure as he tasted my risotto. "This is perfect. It's fantastico!"

Beaming, I looked back at my jealous-ass classmates. I'd been a standout in my culinary arts classes from the beginning. No, I wasn't perfect. I was just a natural cook, and I enjoyed putting recipes together.

"So, explain what you have to accompany this delicious risotto." His eyes lit up as his eyes took in my delicious display.

"I have an Italian seafood stew with shrimp, scallops, clams, and mussels. Also, there are roasted vegetables, which consist of zucchini, bell peppers, eggplant, onions, and asparagus."

As he picked up a forkful of the vegetables, he literally salivated. Then he popped it into his mouth.

"Mmm . . ." Taking in the savory flavors, he chewed slowly and finally swallowed. "The entire dish is perfect. You are definitely graduating at the top of your class. If you need a referral, I have the letter already written up."

"Thank you so much, Chef Cunnings."

As he moved on to the next student, all I could do was envision myself walking across that stage to get my credentials.

One thing about me was I could cook my ass off. Although my brother was older than me, I was the woman of the house when Mama was working, and I made sure that we ate. The job she had at a warehouse had her out of the house for at least thirteen hours a day. Because of her hard work for minimum wage, I had had to learn how to cook early. Another thing I had learned from her was the fact that I didn't want to work as hard as she did.

That was why I had decided that I wanted to be a chef. Cooking was something that I was good at, and I enjoyed it, so why not make money from it? Two weeks had passed since the fiasco with Daryn, and I was just ready to move on. What better way to do that than to go into the next phase of my life? I was going to graduate from Le Cordon Bleu today, and I was ecstatic. Unlike commencement ceremonies at traditional colleges and universities, my graduation was being held in August. My mother and brother were so proud of me, and I had to admit that I was actually proud of myself.

"Oh my God, baby girl. You look amazing," my mother said, with tears glistening in her eyes.

"Thanks, Mommy," I said gratefully before planting a kiss on her cheek.

"What you thanking me for? I'm your mama. The only parent you got. I did what I was supposed to do." There was a huge smile on her face. "You know I'm proud of you, right?"

I nodded, trying to keep my own tears at bay. "Yeah, I know, Mama. You tell me all the time."

"Okay. Let's go. Your brother's gonna meet us there. He got li'l man with him." She rolled her eyes. "His mama claims she got some business to handle. What that is, I don't know, since the trifling heifer ain't never worked nowhere in her life."

The mention of my nephew, Cameron, made my day. He was three years old, and his mother, Imani, was a straight up thot who had no class whatsoever. I hated her ass, but I kept the peace because of Cam.

"Forget that heifer," I told her. I wasn't going to let the thought of bashing that bitch's face in ruin my mood.

"You're right about that." My mother let out a snicker before grabbing her black clutch bag.

"Let's go, Ma. I got a graduation to attend."

She nodded. "Right. Yes, you do. This is my child! She's a chef!"

I couldn't help but grin, because she was telling everybody she saw that I was graduating from culinary arts school. Two of my professors had written reference letters to the restauraunts I was interested in working for. I'd consistently been a proficient student, and over time, they had noticed. Being that both of them were top-notch chefs with reputable careers, I was sure it would look good that they had vouched for me.

When I was eighteen, I got pregnant by someone who I thought at the time was the love of my life. College had been in my plans before that, but I didn't want to leave my baby. Me and Derrick broke up when I was seven months pregnant because I'd caught him with a bitch I couldn't stand named Tarsha. To make a long story short, not long after that, I lost my baby. I had to give birth to my little girl, name her, and then fill out her death certificate.

The trauma from that experience really made me retreat and shut down. Any future that I may have thought about seemed dim and nonexistent then. But while the experience was hell, it made me stronger in the end. After losing the baby, I thought I'd get back with her father, but

I didn't. It was time for me to move on, so I did. After years of working hard, I saved enough money to go to school. And now here I was, getting my associates degree in culinary arts at the age of twenty-five. Despite my past and all the hurdles I'd jumped over, I didn't lose my strength. Damn, I was one strong-ass bitch. Nothing could bring me down, and I felt invincible.

After the ceremony, I sat in my seat in the auditorium and savored the moment. When I saw my besties, Tamia and Nicole, I was ecstatic. They walked over to me, and we all joined hands and squealed in excitement.

"Congratulations!" they said in unison.

"Thank you." I couldn't hold back the tears any longer.

Shit, I was just so glad that they were there. The two of them had gone on to college after high school and had graduated four years ago. I had been able to hold my own while they were in college: I had had my own spot, as well as a good job as an office assistant at an affluent law firm in Atlanta. I had even had a part-time gig as a bartender at the Wet Willie's on Piedmont Road in Buckhead. Shit, I'd managed to drive a nice-ass ride too. My 2014 silver Beemer was in my name, and I had made my payments on time every month.

Now that I'd graduated, I could follow my dream of cooking at a five-star restaurant or hotel. Wow, I'd come so far, and I was ready to conquer the world. Okay, the endorphins were kicking in with my thoughts of success, but as far as I saw it, the sky was the limit.

Tamia passed me a bunch of balloons that said CON-GRATULATIONS, GRADUATE, a bouquet of lilies, and an envelope. Lilies were my favorite flower, by the way.

"Thank you," I gushed.

"That's from both of us, bitch," Nicole whispered.

I cut my eye at her and smiled. "Thank you, Cole."

There was a satisfied look on her face. "You're welcome, boo."

"Open it," Tamia urged.

I tore the envelope open, and my eyes almost bulged out of their sockets. "A plane ticket to Jamaica for . . . seven days and six nights!"

"Yes, an all-expense-paid vacation at a nice five-star resort. Oh, it's on and poppin', boo!" Nicole yelled dramatically.

Tamia shook her head at our friend's antics. "Girl, we've been saving up for this for a while. You ain't gotta worry about nothing. All you have to do is pack tonight and be on that plane with us tomorrow, at two p.m."

"Aw, thanks, y'all." My boos hugged me, and then we made our way outside, with my small family in tow.

When I spotted that fuck nigga Daryn standing by my car, my heart dropped, and I let out a sigh. "This'll only take a minute," I threw over my shoulder as I walked away from my group.

My brother gave me a hard look. He knew what was going on, and he wanted to beat that nigga's ass. "You want me to handle that mufucka . . . ," he called.

I stopped walking and turned around. "Nah. I got this," I assured him. "Just go to your car, bro."

When I reached my car, I just stood there and gave Daryn a hard stare.

"Congrats, baby," Daryn said with a white, toothy smile.

I rolled my eyes. "Don't 'baby' me, and I don't need your sorry-ass congratulations. Why are you here?"

He looked down before passing me a gift bag, which I hadn't noticed in his hand. "I, uh, I broke it off with . . ."

I didn't take his gift. "No thanks, and I don't give a fuck. Please get away from my car so I can leave."

There was pitiful look on his face. "I understand that you pissed and shit, but damn, don't act like we ain't have shit."

"We didn't have shit, nigga. What the fuck you mean? You played my face the whole damn time. Don't ruin this moment for me, Daryn. Just take your gift and leave please."

I glanced over at my family and friends, and they were all wearing screw faces.

He must've noticed, because suddenly he backed down. "Okay, I'm gonna go, but I'll call you later. I'll hold on to your gift. You can get it whenever you want it."

"Uh, don't hold your breath waiting for that, and there's no need to call me. I'm good on you."

Suddenly, Daryn's hand was on my waist. My brother was just a few yards away at that point and was ready to fuck that nigga up, despite the fact that he had his son with him. I gave Jameel a look, so he grabbed Cam and walked off.

"I just wanna make shit right with you, baby," Daryn told me.

I pushed his hand away. "Just go. Please." The look in my eyes must've let him know that I was serious.

He sighed and removed his hand. "A'ight, Ma. We'll talk later."

Instead of defying his wishes again, I just nodded. All I wanted him to do was leave me the fuck alone so that I could leave. I was ready to celebrate, and I wasn't going to let him ruin my good mood. *Fuck him.* After getting drunk as hell, I was going to get up early in the morning and pack for my trip to Jamaica.

I'd always wanted to visit that beautiful island, with its reggae music and some of the best food in the world. Damn, I needed that shit, and my girls were right on time. A vacation was just what I needed after finally earning something that I'd worked so hard for. It was also on time being that I'd been through so much shit. I was ready to relax and have some drinks while lounging on the white sand. A bitch was ready for some sparkling turquoise water, palm trees, and that beautiful tropical sun.

Chapter 4

Omari

I got up bright and early and tried to sneak out before Angela or the kids woke up. This weekend was big for me. Matter of fact, it was my chance as a deejay to show my skills on a major platform. It was August, which meant it was Appleton Special Dream Weekend in Negril, Jamaica. It was our eighth year, and we definitely expected it to be flooded with locals and foreigners from different countries. My sound system was playing, so me and my other deejay planned to be on the turntable all weekend long.

I took a long shower as my mind raced off to all the previous years that the festival had gone on. All kinds of bitches had swarmed Negril. I wasn't going to lie. If Angela hadn't been with me, I would've flirted or probably even fucked a couple of dem Yankee *gyals*. This year I planned on leaving her ass at home. There was no need to take her with me, because I was working, anyways.

My thoughts were quickly interrupted when I heard the shower curtain move.

"Wha happen?" I quizzed as she stood in front of me, naked.

"Wha you mean? Mi wan' some dick. Last night yuh sleep 'pon di couch and pretend like you nuh wan' mi pussy."

I really don't. You fuss too much, I thought.

I didn't say that, though. Instead, I pulled her into the shower and started kissing her. I rubbed on her breasts, and she moaned. I wasn't in the mood to make love. Honestly, I just wanted to fuck. I snatched up her little size three body and wrapped her legs around my waist as I sank my wood deep inside of her.

"Ow, fuck mi, baby!" she screamed.

"Yo, easy nuh. Yuh no wan' wake up da yout' dem."

I sank my wood all the way in. She sank her teeth into my shoulder, which made me thrust harder. I felt my veins getting bigger, so I prepared to bust.

"Cum inside of me, baby. Please cum inside of me," she pleaded.

I totally ignored her and pulled out. I put her down just as the thick cum shot out into the tub, mixed with the water, and went down the drain.

"What is your problem? You act like it's a crime to bust in me," she said, with an attitude.

I didn't say anything. I just grabbed my washcloth, soaped it up, and started to wash off my wood. She stood there cussing until she had dried off and put her house-dress back on. Then she stormed out of the bathroom and slammed the door behind her.

I shook my head. "Yo, this bloodclaat gyal never happy yet," I said to myself.

I turned the water off and stepped out of the tub.

I ironed my clothes, got dressed, and grabbed the bag with the belongings that I had packed. I was going to be in Negril for a few days. I walked into the kids' room and stood there, watching them as they slept soundly. I loved my children with everything in me, but I didn't know how much longer I was going to stick around.

Angela's behavior was getting more out of control, and I didn't want to hurt her. I kissed both of the kids on the cheek and then walked out of their room.

I made my way toward the kitchen, where Angela was.

"I'm going to Negril. Won't be back till Monday. There is money in the drawer, if you need anything," I announced.

She turned to face me, and I could see that she was crying. "Money? You tink money can fix every damn ting. I 'ave my own money. Mi want a man dat care 'bout me. I don't need a man dat throw money at me. Yuh tink I don't know it's Dream Weekend, huh? Yuh gyal must be there. Why yuh didn't tell me about it? Omar, yuh not fooling anyone but your damn self."

I could stand there and try to argue with Angela, but I had been raised to believe that a man couldn't win an argument against a woman. I turned around and walked out.

"Yo, my yute, the place is packed," my linky Garey said to me.

"Hell, yeah. I'm loving the vibes right now for real. Yo, let's go blow one real quick."

We both walked out of the hall where I had set my music up. It was loud, as Vybz Kartel's song "Freaky Gal" was playing. On the way out, I noticed that the females were dressed to the teeth. Shit, most of them barely had any clothes on. A few tried to grab my arm as I made my way through the crowd.

I rolled up a big spliff, and Garey and I started to smoke. I took a few drags of the ganja and started coughing.

"Easy nuh, man. Mind you kill yuhself," he joked.

"Nah. This shit's good shit," I joked back.

I passed him the spliff and turned around to face the crowd that was going inside. I looked and thought the weed had me seeing things, but nah. There was this bad-ass bitch walking in. We locked eyes, and I couldn't stop staring.

"Yo, brethren, you a'ight? Look like yuh just see a ghost." Garey tapped me on the shoulder.

I looked at him. I was about to say something but decided not to. I just took a few more pulls on the spliff and decided to go inside. I wondered who the fuck she was and whether she was there by herself. There was only one way to find out, and that was to find her!

I went back to the music, but my mind was not on that. That was the first time a woman had ever looked at me like that. It was like she had looked deep into my soul. I knew that I was married, but at that moment, none of that really mattered. I was a man who knew what he wanted, and that chick whom I just saw had definitely grabbed my interest.

Chapter 5

Kadijah

"I'm in love with Jamaica already, bitches," I squealed to my girls.

We'd been there for only about three hours, but I was already drunk. Shit, I'd been drinking since the night I graduated. A bitch even had a few drinks on the plane, and I was still sipping. The celebration was nonstop, as far as I was concerned, and I was going to be a lush. I deserved to relax and unwind a little.

After chilling in our luxurious hotel suite for about an hour, we ventured out to the pool in our itty-bitty bathing suits. The Olympic-sized pool was packed with tourists and hotel staff. I wasn't shy at all, so I went and asked one of the islanders what was popping. I knew not to ask a tourist. How the hell would they know? The dude I did ask had on a bellboy uniform.

"It's Appleton Special Dream Weekend, so it'll be music, food, and every ting," he said, trying his best not to use the native patois as he spoke. His accent was thick, but it wasn't hard to understand him.

"Is that, like, a festival or something?" I asked, sipping my drink.

He tried his best to be professional, but his eyes kept drifting down to my thickness. I smiled, because the male attention wasn't offensive at all to me. To be honest, he was kind of cute with his smooth dark brown skin.

"Yes, it is . . ." His voice trailed off. "It's not too far from here. You can catch a taxi and get there in thirty minutes."

I nodded and looked at his name tag. "Thank you, Colin."

"You're welcome. . . ."

"I'm Kadijah, but everybody calls me DiDi." I shook his hand.

"Okay. Nice meeting you, DiDi." He smiled. "Where are you from?"

"I'm an American girl. Born and raised in Atlanta, Georgia."

He grinned. "Ah, a Georgia peach. I've been there a few times. Family there. I love Yankee gyals."

I smiled back, but I was confused. "Yankee . . . ?"

He laughed. "We call American women Yankee gyals here. I'm aware that in the States, it has a different meaning."

"Oh, okay." I knew that in Southern American culture a Yankee was a white Northerner. When I looked in the mirror, I saw a black Southern gal, so that Yankee comment had thrown me off. "Well, thank you for your help."

"You're welcome," he said, with that smile still on his face.

I walked over to Nicole and Tamia and told them both about what I'd found out from Colin.

"So, y'all down?" I asked. I was tipsy, and I wanted to experience the authentic side of Jamaica. That tourist shit was for the birds. When I looked around, I saw too many white, bourgeois-ass motherfuckers.

Nicole spoke up first. "Hell yeah. You already know my single, horny ass is ready to see some hunky-ass black men. Let's go."

Tamia laughed. "Let's go change and see if we can get a taxi."

"Let's do it," I said excitedly. "Maybe we can find some ganja."

"Hell, yeah," Nicole agreed.

"I need to smoke," Tamia added.

The crowd was thick, and I could feel the pulsating beat of the reggae music all over my body. We'd been at the festival for about ten minutes, and I needed some water.

"All that drinkin' got me dehydrated. Y'all want some water?" I asked as I looked around to locate a place to get beverages.

Nicole was winding her waist as she shook her head. "Hell yeah. It's hot as shit."

Tamia laughed. "We're in Jamaica, bitch. What the fuck you expect?"

I spotted a table with a tall, lanky dude standing behind it. He was selling food and snacks, so I figured he was selling water too.

"Okay," I said and started to walk in the direction of the table with the food.

"We're comin' with you." Tamia's overprotective ass was on my heels.

"It's right there, Mia," I said, pointing at the table. "You two can see me. I'll be fine." I shook my head.

"You know how I am, bitch. We're in a foreign country. I'on care if everybody around us is black. Anything can happen," Tamia explained.

"Calm down, Mia. She's not going that damn far." Nicole shook her head and pulled her oversize shades down from her head to cover her eyes.

I couldn't help but laugh as I walked off. My besties were total opposites. Nicole was wild as hell and didn't give a fuck what she said. She was the general manager at the Macy's in Lenox Square and made really good money.

She was the perfect bitch to run a company, because she was cutthroat.

Tamia was a little bit more laid back than Nicole, but she was no angel, either. She worked as a radiologist at Emory University Hospital. The bitch was smart as hell and was the only one of the three of us who was a mother. Her two-year-old daughter, Madison, was so adorable and made me think of the daughter I had lost. Tamia was also the only one in a long- term relationship that seemed to be going well. She and her fiancé, Markus, had been together for almost five years.

I had the bottled waters in my hands, and when I looked up, I laid eyes on pure sexiness. When I say the man was fine, he was fine. Honestly, he was more than fine. He was also sexy. We locked eyes for at least ten seconds before he finally broke our eye contact.

It felt like I was stuck, because my eyes were still on him. He looked up at me again, exposing straight white teeth. Did he just smile at me? I looked back to see if there was some chick behind me who was staring him down too. There wasn't. That made me smile. When I looked again, his eyes were still on me.

Just go talk to him, I thought.

He was obviously interested, because he couldn't take his gorgeous slanted dark brown eyes off me. His coffee-toned skin looked like it was literally gleaming in the sun. I watched as his biceps bulged beneath his white shirt. His chest was wide, and from where I was standing, he looked to be at least six-one. It was obvious that he was very athletic. Damn, I really loved his long, sexy dreadlocks.

When he finally looked away from me, I finally snapped out of it and walked back over to my girls so that we could make our way inside. I handed Tamia and Nicole each a bottle of water.

"Damn, bitch. What's wrong with you?" Nicole asked as she took the bottle of water from me.

"Nothing." I looked back over at the handsome specimen who'd taken my breath away. My girls' eyes followed mine.

"Ohhh," Tamia said before taking a sip of water.

"What?" I couldn't help but grin.

"You were checkin' that fine-ass dude out. Don't front, heifer," Nicole spat.

"I wasn't. . . ."

"Stop lyin'. You know you like what you see. We followed your eyes to him, chick. When you came back over here, you looked like you'd just chemically combusted and shit," Tamia said with a laugh.

"Shut the fuck up." I couldn't help but laugh too. "He's fine . . . but I can't . . ."

"You better sample some of that dick. I heard Jamaican niggas be packin'. I know I'm gon' get fucked while I'm here. Shit," Nicole chimed in and then licked her lips.

I shook my head. "I don't know."

My thoughts drifted to perhaps having a one-night stand. Shit, you only lived once, and I wanted to live life to the fullest. Whoever the sexy stranger was, I just knew that a man had never, ever looked at me like that before. It was a must that I saw him again before I left that island.

Chapter 6

Angela

I had no idea what had gotten in Omari's head lately, but I knew he was on some bullshit. See, this *bwoy* thought I was a fool, but I, Angela, was far from being a fool.

When I first met Omari, he was everything that a woman dreamed of, or so I'd thought. He was tall, dark, and sexy. The kind of man that made your pussy tingle at first sight. I met him at a Beenie Man dance one night. That was before he started making money. Back then, he was just another around-the-way bwoy. I didn't care that he didn't have any money, because I was already a gal with her own house and money. All I needed—or wanted, for that matter—was a man who could fuck me really good.

I remembered that when I first met him, I pretended like I wasn't digging him, because I knew the crew he rolled with, and those dudes were known to be gallists. They weren't faithful to no one woman. As a matter of fact, they had multiple bitches. I wasn't trying to be no bwoy's side bitch, so I was reluctant to start something with Omari.

"Gal, wha deh 'pon yuh mind?" my homegirl Paula asked me as we dined at a well-known restaurant on Red Hills Road soon after I met Omari.

I smiled at her. That chick knew me too damn well. Maybe it was because we'd been friends since elementary school. She was two years older than me, but that hadn't ever mattered. We were inseparable. Whenever you saw me, trust and believe she wasn't too far behind.

"Girl, I am feeling that bwoy Omari, you know."

"So, if yuh like him, what is stopping yuh from going wit' him?" she quizzed.

"Girl, I 'ont know. I am too grown to be playing games with these dudes that only want to screw around. I want to marry and have a few babies running around the house."

"I hear yuh, but how will yuh know if yuh not willing to take a chance on him? I know dem bwoy deh have a bad reputation, but the way I see he pursuing yuh, I think he is really digging yuh."

I knew that Paula barely approved of the dudes I talked to, so for her to sit here and try to convince me that Omari was a good catch was very surprising. I looked at her and smiled.

We finished up our lunch and parted ways. The entire ride back downtown, I couldn't seem to get Omari out of my mind. I remembered him giving me his number when we first met. I called him soon as I stepped foot in the door. My heart was beating fast, and my palms were sweaty. I'd been with plenty of niggas before, but there was something about him that had me feeling nervous.

The following day we met up, grabbed a quick bite, and got to talking. I was surprised to find that he was so different from the public persona he gave off. He was a street dude, but he went to Campion College, which was one of Jamaica's prestigious high schools.

After a few dates, we ended up fucking. That dude had a wood the size of an arm. At first, I wanted to say, "Hell no," but I was a bad gyal, and I had a reputation to keep.

I couldn't let it get out that I couldn't take the wood! So I put on my big girl panties and straight bruk off his wood head. With the sound of reggae music playing in the background, I tic-tocked, slow wined, and dutty wined on his wood.

"Cho, gal, this pussy good as fuck," he whispered in my ear. At that moment, I knew that I'd accomplished what I'd set out to do.

After that day, we became inseparable. I was his woman, and he was my man. I made sure he was straight, and he made sure my pussy was good. I wined and dined him, and he made sure my pussy was serviced.

Months later, I found out I was pregnant with our daughter. He was more excited than I was, because truthfully, though I knew we had been fucking raw, but I wasn't ready for no kids yet! Shit, my body was hot, and I didn't want to mess it up with no stretch marks. Plus, I ain't want no baby daddy. I wanted a husband.

"Hey, babe. I was thinking, we need to make it official," Omari blurted out around four months into my pregnancy.

"Wha yuh just say to me?" I popped my head up from his lap.

"Chill out! Mi wan' make you mine, so it's only fair mi give you mi last name."

I rested my head back on his lap. Taking a few minutes to think, I let the words marinate. I loved him, I wanted to be his woman, but the nigga needed to make more money. At first, I'd been fine with footing the bill, but things had changed. I had changed. I needed more than wood. I wanted it all.

"So, what yuh tinkin' 'bout?" he said, interrupting my thoughts.

I swallowed hard and then replied nervously, "Mi would love to marry you, babe. You don't tink we moving too fast?"

"Nah. Yuh carrying mi child, and I want to be in his, or her, life. Mi no have my pops in mi life, and Jah know, it was hard for mi mudda. Mi vow to be there for my yute. You si mi?"

I sighed and then spoke. "Yes. Well, then, we have a wedding to plan, don't we?"

We ended up having one of the biggest weddings in Kingston. Everyone and anyone who was somebody was present. Our wedding was the talk of the entire town, and I loved it, because all the bitches who were jealous of me had something to talk about.

Things started progressing for Omari right after our daughter was born. He finally started selecting different sounds, and his name started ringing bells. His big break came when he started selecting on a much larger platform. It was a dream for him. In no time, he bought us a nice mini-mansion uptown and a new car. Everything was *irie*, good, at first, because he was contributing to our household and I didn't have to put out as much. I had taken a break from higglering after my child was born, so my money was kind of slow.

I should've known that Omari's fame meant that hungry bitches would be lined up, with their hands out. At first, I paid that shit no mind, because I was the wife. I lived in his house, and I had had his child. Things started going from bad to worse when his phone started ringing late at night. He would pretend as if he didn't hear it, but I knew better. Shit finally hit the fan when I found out that he was fucking this bitch from the ghetto. I was devastated at first, but I quickly dried my tears. I wasn't going to stress myself out over his ass. Instead, I did the ultimate get back and started fucking around with his right-hand man, Garey.

I thought it would be hard for me to get Garey, but it was so easy. Came to find out, he had liked me from day one. He had just been too scared to approach me. Well, I made it easy for him after that day. Every time Omari claimed he was traveling to the country area to select, his boy would fill his space. Before you knew it, Garey was my part-time lover.

The sex was good, and he threw money at me. Shit, I was living the ultimate double life, fucking my man and his homeboy. It kind of gave me a rush that Omari had no idea. See, two could definitely play the game, and I was sure that I was the better one at playing it!

Chapter 7

Kadijah

The vibe of the festival had changed by the time the sun started to set. It seemed to become more grown-up and sexy as the crowd thinned of children and only adults lingered behind. The native women were decked out in sexy short shorts and bra-like tops. I felt overdressed in my tank top and Bermuda shorts, and my body had started to overheat. Nicole had discovered a small bar that sold mixed drinks. Adding to the already high volume of alcohol in my system just made me want to get naked even more.

"Damn, I'm *so* fucked up!" I yelled over the sound of Lady Saw talking about getting on a big ninja bike.

When I looked up at the stage, that sexy-ass deejay that I'd first spotted outside wasn't there anymore. Instead, some other dude was standing behind the sound system, with earphones on. Damn, he'd been gone for at least a good hour, and I wondered if he was coming back.

"You ready to fuck ole dude, ain't you?" Tamia asked as she shook her head at me, a smile on her face. "I wonder where he went."

I sucked my teeth. "Girl, bye. I ain't tryin'a fuck that nigga. I'on even know him." My words were slurred as I lied.

Shit, if he said the word, my horny ass was going to be on him like fish grease. I was so overdue for a good nut, it was ridiculous. My body felt like mush, because I was so intoxicated. I ground all nasty like to the beat pulsating from the huge speakers. The crowd was thick as hell, and it was like people were literally standing on top of each other. I tried to move out of some chick's way as she sprayed champagne in my direction.

"What the hell?" I asked as my shirt and hair got soaked.

My eyes locked on the thick chick with long, curly bright red hair and a white short set that fit her like a bodysuit.

"Wha yuh lookin' at?" she asked as she walked closer, with the bottle pointed at me.

"I'm lookin' at you, bitch! You got champagne all in my hair and shit!"

"Bitch? Mi got yo' bitch! Dis champagne cost more than that cheap-ass weave, yuh Yankee ho!" There were three chicks with her, and they were cosigning with laughs.

"Fuck that shit. We came here to have a good time, not for no drama. C'mon—" Tamia said, but she was shut down real quick by Nicole.

"Oh, hell, nah. She ain't 'bout to disrespect my girl. Unlike yo' fake, fucked-up-ass lace front, her hair's one hundred percent real . . . ho." One hand was on Nicole's hip, and the other was in the air, emphasizing her words.

Tamia sighed. "Really, y'all. This ain't the time or place to—"

"Shut the fuck up!" I snapped. "I don't give a fuck where we at. I ain't 'bout to let nobody get my fuckin' hair wet. Shit, do you know how much I paid to get my damn shit done? And now I gotta be here for six more days, lookin' like this?" I lifted my ruined hair, ready to go upside that bitch's head.

I was all natural, and my hair was thick and coarse. It took a lot to get it just right. I knew that it was going to get fucked up, but I didn't expect it to happen on the first damn day I was there, and especially not when I was nowhere near any water.

"Heifers," the strange bitch hissed to her friends. "Mi no have time for this shit. Mi no mean to get that shit 'pon yo' funky-ass hair! If you wanna do some ting 'bout it, do it. . . ."

I lunged for her, and then I felt somebody grab me around my waist and lift me up effortlessly. When I looked to my left and right, Tamia and Nicole were both standing there, so I knew that it wasn't them.

"Calm di fuck down, and no ruin di fun for everyone else," a deep voice with a thick Jamaican accent said in my ear. "They'll shut tis ting down real quick. That goes to y'all too. Get outta here."

The chicks walked off with pissed looks on their faces. When my feet were planted back on the floor, I turned around and was face-to-face with the fine-ass deejay I'd locked eyes with earlier.

"What, you went from deejay to security guard or some shit!" I snapped at him.

"No, but mi can tell yuh not from round here, and yuh don't wanna get locked up here. When yuh get champagne sprayed 'pon yuh, don't take it as disrespect. It's a different culture here in Jamaica. Sure, yuh hair got wet, but yuh can get it done ova. No worries. No reason to trow yuh life away." His eyes were sincere as he tried to reason with my drunk ass.

Tamia shook her head and walked off to dance with some dude. Nicole just stood there, making sure that I was good. Tamia had always been the one who didn't want to fight. I got it, but damn, I wasn't one to let a ho just say or do anything to me. My mama didn't raise me like that.

"Can mi talk to yuh gyal . . . alone?" the fine stranger asked, with his eyes on Nicole now.

I looked at her too. "It's cool."

She nodded and walked toward the bar.

"Mi noticed yuh earlier, before the sun set, and mi couldn't help but notice how beautiful yuh are. Mi used to women, and mi no stranger to beauty, but yuh, yuh captured my soul or some ting." His eyes seemed to penetrate mine, they were so intense. "Mi had to see yuh again, but mi didn't expect to see yuh about to fight. Mi like fiery women. Mi can't lie. It kinda turned mi on to see a Yankee gyal who no scared of no island woman." His smile revealed deep dimples in his smooth, dark skin.

His locks were pulled back, and I tried not to stare at his handsome face. The smell of the tropical air and his cologne seemed to take over my senses. *Damn.* Suddenly, I felt nauseous as hell, and before I knew it, I was throwing up all over his shoes. *Fuck!*

"I'm so sorry," I managed to choke out from embarrassment. All I wanted to do was disappear real quick, but where the fuck could I go?

"It's okay," he said sweetly as his hand moved up and down my back. "Yuh irie? Do yuh need a ride to ya hotel?"

I nodded and heard Nicole's voice behind me.

"DiDi, you good?"

"Yeah," I said faintly.

"Hold tight and gimme a few to clean up and get yuh a taxi back to di hotel," the stranger said.

"What's your name?" I heard Tamia ask.

"Omari," he simply said. "Make sure she's okay for now. Mi be right back."

"Oh my God. I can't believe I did that," I sighed.

Tamia fanned her face as she frowned. "You smell horrible. Yes, bad first impression, boo. Not only were you actin' ghetto as hell, but you also threw up all over the man. I'm sure he wants you now."

"Oh, please shut the hell up, Mia. A little throw up and a fight ain't never turned a man off," Nicole threw at her.

I couldn't help but laugh, despite the fact that I agreed with Tamia. "Fuck it. It doesn't matter. When it comes to men, I'm cursed, anyway. There's plenty of dick on this island, and I'll get some before I leave."

Nicole and Tamia laughed as they held on to me. I didn't throw up again before Omari got back, but the nausea hadn't eased up.

"Okay, ladies. Yuh ride awaits. Follow mi," he said, and then he led the way to a taxi.

Tamia and Nicole both got in first.

I turned to Omari. "Thank you so much, and I apologize again for . . ."

He waved me off. "Mi told yuh already. It's okay. Shoes can be replaced. Mi almost done for tonight, anyway. Go sleep it off and give mi a call tomorrow."

I pulled out my phone and tried my best to look at the screen. He laughed as he pulled his phone out of his pocket.

"How 'bout mi get yuh number? Mi know a place yuh can get your hair done up."

"Good idea." I giggled before reciting the digits. "I hope that's right."

He smiled down at me. "Let me check wit' yuh gyals. Mi not lettin' yuh go wit' out yuh number."

He peeked his head inside the car as I climbed in. "Good night, ladies. Mi hope yuh enjoyed yuhselves, despite what happened and shit. Uhh, mi just wanted to make sure yuh gyal give mi di right number."

"Oh, it's 404-786-9919," Nicole confirmed.

"Okay, that was correct. Thank you." He grinned.

He turned to me. "Mi will call yuh tomorrow, gorgeous."

After he closed the door, my girls squealed in excitement.

"See, bitch?" Nicole said, fucking with Tamia. "That mufucka still want that ass."

I couldn't help but laugh as I tried my best not to throw up again.

Chapter 8

Omari

I stood outside the venue, kicking it with some of my other niggas for a little while. Garey was on the sound system, since he was just as good as I was when it came down to playing hot tunes. I could always count on him to have the crowd going. Finally, I decided to head back to inside.

I was on my way back in when I noticed a bunch of bitches standing in a crowd. I quickly realized that some drama was about to be popping off. I wasn't trying to have that up in there, not when my sound was playing. One thing about the Babylon bwoy them, they loved to turn off the music, and what I was watching would definitely give them a reason to do so.

I inched closer to the crowd and noticed the same chick from earlier. I also saw a group of women stepping toward her aggressively. She stepped closer to one chick, and I knew shit was about to get real up in there. I pushed through the crowd and grabbed her up before she got the chance to throw a blow.

I could tell she wasn't feeling me grabbing her like that, but I had to let her know that this wasn't what she wanted. When she spoke to me, I realized she was a Yankee gyal. Even though it wasn't the time to be feeling any kind of way, her accent sent a thrill through my body, instantly giving me an erection. While she stood there pouting,

I admired her physique. Baby girl's skin was smooth, like a newborn baby's ass. Her face was cute, and her shape was one to die for. In my book, she was an all around bad bitch.

After diffusing the situation, I put them in a taxi, but not before getting her number. I wanted to see her again for sure. I wasn't sure how long she was going to be on the island, but that didn't matter. I was determined to get to know her before she left.

After the taxi drove them away, I walked back in the venue. Before I could get to where our sound was located, a big fat bitch approached me and stepped in my path. I realized she was one of the bitches who had been fussing with the Yankee chick earlier.

"Yo, selector bwoy, is what kind of idiot thing that you pulled earlier?" she said.

"Yo, B, watch yo' pussyclaat mout'. Who you a dis, gyal?"

"You one of us, but you show your ass off in from of dem Yankee gyals. I thought you was a real nigga, but I see you not."

"Yo, B, get the fuck outta my way." I didn't wait for a response. I walked away from that gorilla-looking bitch and headed back over to Garey. He was ready to take his break, and it was my time to make the crowd go wild.

It was the wee hours of the morning, and it was time to cut the music off. I drove to the hotel where I was staying for the night. It was damn near seven in the morning by the time I showered and got into the bed.

I pulled out my phone to check if I had any missed calls. As I lay on my back, all sorts of thoughts of shawty invaded my mind. That was strange for me, because I had seen bad bitches before, but she was different. I sat there pondering what it would be like to just hold her in my arms, to massage her breasts, and to slide my wood all the way up inside her. *Fuck that.* The anticipation was killing me, so I searched through my phone and found where I had stored her number.

I pressed the button to call her, but then I started to get cold feet. I wasn't scared or nothing like that, but I wasn't into sweating no bitch. I almost hung up, but she answered before I could.

"Hello." Her voice sounded like a sweet melody in my ear.

"Hello. This Omari . . . the dude you met yesterday at the venue," I said, almost choking up.

"Oh yeah, I remember you. How are you doing?"

"I'm good. Just getting in."

"Damn, that's crazy. Y'all know how to party out here," she giggled.

Damn. Why did she do that? My wood was starting to pay attention. I adjusted it in my boxers.

"Yeah, well, you know Jamaica's di party capital of the world."

"Well, tell me, Omari. Why are you on my phone this early?"

"Well, to be honest, I know you wasn't feeling good, so I decided to hit you up to see how you are feeling," I lied.

"Aw, that's so sweet," she said sarcastically.

We ended up talking for a little while. I learned her name was Kadijah, DiDi for short, and she was from Atlanta, Georgia. I'd never been there, but I had heard it was a great place for entrepreneurs to live.

"Yo, what you got planned for later?" I asked as our conversation wound down.

"I'm not sure. I have to check with my girls to see what they want to do. They are skinny-dipping right now in the pool."

"Got you. Well, I'm about to rest my eyes for a little. I'll be up round one. Hit me and let me know what you got planned. I wanna to see you, DiDi," I said in a serious tone. I was trying not to overdo it with my native tongue, because I wanted her to understand everything that I was saying.

"All right, Omari," she said in a sexy voice before hanging up the phone.

I ended the call with a big smile plastered across my face. I got up, turned the phone off, and plugged the charger in to get a little juice. When I jumped back in the bed, my eyelids were closing on me. I lay there until I dozed off, thinking about the beautiful Miss Kadijah.

Angela

There was no reason for me to sit around and mope. Omari had thought his ass was doing something when he left for Negril without me. Yes, I had fucked him good before he left, because he was a whore, and I had wanted to make sure that he was satisfied and he wouldn't have time to be worried about fucking another bitch.

See, I was cheating on him with his bwoy, but I didn't want my marriage to be over with. I wasn't in love with my husband anymore, but I'd be damned if I was going to let another bitch get him. I was the one who had picked his ass up when he didn't have a pot to piss in, and there was no way another one of these dutty, careless-living gyals was going to come in the picture and snatch him up.

Soon as he was out the door, I called my side piece to let him know that he could stop by.

"Hey, baby," he answered.

"The coast is clear. You can come ova now."

"Okay, cool. I'll be there in another hour."

I hung up the phone.

See, that nigga was no Omari. His dick was a regular size, but he'd been deported from New York, so he knew how to eat my pussy out. I had decided to keep him around, because he let me know what my husband be doing, and he kept me satisfied when my husband was running the streets with his other bitches.

I got the children ready and called my mother to come pick them up. It was their weekend to spend with their grandmother. Within an hour, she came by and I kissed them good-bye. Once they left, I was happy that they were gone, and decided to straighten up really quick. After making sure that I changed the sheets, I jumped in the shower, washed Omari's scent off me, and shaved my pussy clean. My side nigga loved when my pussy was bald, so he could dive right in.

Soon as I got out of the shower, I heard my phone ringing. I ran to grab it, and it was Garey letting me know that he was outside. I wrapped my towel around me, walked to the back door, and opened it.

"Hey, baby," I greeted him as soon as I opened the grill.

"What a gwaan, Ma?" He pulled me closer to him and stuck his tongue down my throat.

"Come on. Let's go in here." I pulled him away from the back door, closed it, and led him into the house. I made sure the door that led to the living room was properly secured. I knew where Omari was, but I was still kind of paranoid.

"You want something to drink?" I asked.

"Yeah. You 'ave a Guinness?"

"Yeah. Follow me."

We went into the kitchen. I walked over to the fridge, took out a cold Guinness stout, and passed it to him. He went into the living room and took a seat on the sofa, and

I walked back into the bedroom, so I could lotion myself down. I rubbed some baby oil between my legs. I wanted to make sure he could slide right in.

"Damn, babe. Yuh sexy as fuck," Garey said as he crept up behind me. He started kissing my neck, which instantly aroused every sexual emotion in my body.

"Stop, boy," I joked, because God knows I was loving every bit of it.

He picked me up, took me over to the bed, set me down, and started kissing me all over my body. He then took my legs and spread them apart. He put his head in position and inhaled my sweet, fresh scent. I gasped for air as his tongue made a connection with my clit. That man was a pussy artist and knew how to make love to that shit by using his tongue. He stuck his tongue all the way inside me and then swirled it around. I grabbed his head and held it down. My legs trembled as I yearned for more.

"Suck mi pussy, baby!" I screamed out with everything inside me, letting go of his head.

The sound of my moans sent him into an uproar. He latched onto my clit and sucked harder.

"Aw, baby, awwee!" I yelled out.

My legs trembled more, and the veins in my head started getting tighter, like they were about to burst. I grabbed his head again as I exploded in his mouth.

He wasted no time and licked up every drop of my pussy juice. He then flipped me over aggressively and entered me from the back with force. He hit every corner and every inch of my body, satisfying me in every way imaginable. I buried my head in my pillow and tooted my ass up like the bad gyal I was.

He grabbed my hips and pulled me back to him. I wined my ass all over his wood as he ground into me.

"Damn, I'm about to bu . . ." Before he could finish his sentence, he exploded all up in me.

Fuck. I'm not on the pill, I thought.

We just stayed there for a few minutes, while he rubbed my hair. I was sort of irritated because he'd busted inside me, knowing damn well I was married.

"Hey, babe. I was thinkin' 'bout something," he said before he sat up in the bed.

I sat up and looked at him. "Wha happen?"

"Yo, I find myself falling for you deeper and deeper every day. Wha mi trying to say is, why don't you get rid a di bwoy Mari and just be wit' me?"

I was hoping I hadn't heard that fool right. Did he know what he was saying? Just because he fucked me good and ate my pussy didn't mean I wanted him. He was good as a fuck buddy, and I intended to keep it like that.

I knew then that I would have to break it off with Garey really soon, because he was talking recklessly. There was no way I could risk Omari finding out about our affair. Not because I was scared of what he might do, but, as I said before, because I didn't want to lose my husband to any of those other bitches.

"You know I can't do that. I love my husband, and we got kids together," I said, trying to reason with him.

"Wha the bloodclaat you mean? Yuh love dis nigga, di same nigga dat is fucking round on yuh, disrespecting you and shit. How can yuh love him?"

"Garey, yuh need to chill out. Yes, we 'ave our problems and shit, just like every other couple, but I can't just walk away like that."

I rubbed his shoulder, trying to diffuse the situation, because the last thing I needed was for him to be upset with me. He had been in my corner while Omari ran these streets, but my heart wasn't with him. I might not have been in love with my husband, but he was the only man I intended on being married to.

After reasoning with him for a little while, he finally calmed down. I even put the icing on the cake when I fucked him in the shower. We got out, and then he got dressed and left. He had errands to run and promised he would be back later.

I was kind of glad he had gone, because I didn't know what had gotten into him. He knew that he was only my fuck partner, and that I was staying with my husband. I was so worn out from fucking that I straightened the sheets out and sprawled across the bed. I needed rest bad.

Chapter 9

Kadijah

That nigga Daryn was blowing my phone up, and I kept sending him to voice mail. After call number twenty-six, I added that nigga to my block list. What he didn't know was that once I was done, I was fucking done. There was no going back, and I meant that shit. Especially after the way he'd lied and tried to play me.

Then the thought of Omari's sexy-ass voice and accent made me smile. Damn, he was so fine. I'd been embarrassed as hell about throwing up on him, but he hadn't seemed to mind at all. Me and my girls had skinny-dipped in the pool and had got full on some Jamaican cuisine, and now we were back in our hotel suite and on the prowl to find something to smoke on. It was a little after three o'clock in the afternoon, so I called Omari to see if he could get us some ganja. I still wanted to see the "real side" of Jamaica, not just the tourist part. I was hoping he could help with that too.

"Hey, beautiful," he said, with a smile in his voice, when he answered.

Damn, my pussy was instantly wet. I reminded myself to put on a panty liner after I took a shower. Shit, if he was going to be around me later, I was going to need it.

"Hey, I don't mean to bother you, but . . ."

"Oh, no, you not botherin' mi at all. As a matter of fact, mi was just tinkin' 'bout you. Mi wanna see you."

My heart leaped. "Okay, but you know I can't leave my girls."

"That's fine. Mi know you don't trust me . . . yet. Mi got shottas to entertain them too," he said with a chuckle. "But mi expect to spend some alone time wit' you before you leave."

I smiled. "I can do that."

"Cool, cool. Mi soon come scoop you, so be ready."

"Oh, I know you can get something to smoke on," I threw in. I wasn't really trying to drink anything after how sick I had felt that morning.

"You know dat. Mi gotcha. Mi call when mi in route to you. Okay?"

"Okay." I hung up.

"He 'bout to come scoop us," I said, filling in Tamia and Nicole.

"Girl, he wants you, but I hope he got some sexy-ass friends," Nicole said as she looked through her suitcase for something to put on. As she did, she pulled out a roll of Magnums. The shiny gold foil shimmered in the light. "I'm getting me some dick, and I came prepared."

We all laughed.

"He said he got some homies for y'all to kick it with," I told her as I shook my head.

She was a trip, but I felt her. After the shit that had gone down with Daryn, getting some dick that had me climbing the walls would be on point. The thing was, I wasn't the type to just fuck a random nigga. I was that chick who was always in a relationship. However, with my track record with men, shit had to change. It was time for me to get my rocks off and not give a fuck. I wanted to try Omari out, and if he played his cards right, he was going to be knee-deep in my pussy real fucking soon.

***

I was dressed more appropriately now in a pair of cut-off jeans shorts and a midriff top. My thick ass cheeks were hanging out, my belly ring was showing, and I was loving the attention and stares that I was getting from men and women. Hell, yeah. A bitch was bad, and I knew that shit. It felt good to be able to be confident after learning that my ex was fucking a five when I was a certified ten. *What the fuck?*

"First tings first," Omari said as he stopped the car in front of a shop. We'd been riding and smoking in his black Mercedes convertible for thirty minutes or so.

His ride was nice as hell, and he smelled even better. My girls kept giving me the eye in the rearview mirror.

Nicole mouthed, "You better fuck him tonight, bitch."

All I could do was shake my head. I didn't want to react in front of Omari.

He opened the car door and then looked back at me. "C'mon, sexy. Mi promised to get ya hair done."

I looked over and read the sign on the shop. It was a hair salon and spa. Damn, he was aiming to impress me, and that shit was working.

"Wow. I almost forgot about that." I smiled at him. "Thank you."

"Oh, hell, yeah, I like you, Omari," Nicole said and winked at him. "After this, just get me to one of yo' niggas who got a body like yours."

Omari laughed. "Mi got just the nigga for you. It won't be long before we head out."

We all climbed out of Omari's whip and made our way inside the salon. The setup was nice, and it smelled of jasmine incense. The sound of waterfalls made the ambience peaceful and tranquil. I loved the place already.

He waited patiently while I got my hair done and my girls got manicures and pedicures. They didn't need to get their hair done, being that Tamia had a sew in and Nicole had Senegalese twists. When I thought about it, it would've been smart if I had got braids or a sew in too. Still, I was satisfied with the blow out that old girl had done for me.

"Thank you," I said gratefully as Omari paid her.

"You're welcome," she said and smiled.

We headed to the car.

"Wow, mi didn't tink you could look any better, but you're even more gorgeous." Omari held the car door open for me to get in.

"Such a gentleman," Tamia chimed in as he opened their doors too.

I agreed with that. I'd heard rumors that Jamaican men were rude and aggressive, but Omari seemed to be the opposite of that. Maybe he was closer to his mother than the average man. Either that or he was just trying to get in my panties. The thing was, that shit was working.

"Thank you," Omari said politely as he climbed behind the wheel. He pulled off.

"Mi love my mama so . . . ," Omari declared, his voice drifting off.

I decided to change the subject. "That weed got me hungry again. I'on know about y'all."

"Shit, I could eat," Nicole said.

"Some stew chicken would be so good. If it tastes the way it does in the States, I can imagine what it tastes like here," I threw in.

"Hmmm. Mi might be able to make dat happen fa you." He smiled and flashed deep dimples.

Suddenly his phone rang, and he looked down at the screen in disdain. Instead of answering it, he pressed a button and then placed the phone in his lap. I figured he'd ignored the call. Was it another woman? Shit. It wasn't like it mattered. I'd be gone in a few days, and we would both be going on with our lives.

"Where are we going?" I asked as I watched the scenery change.

Suddenly, we were obviously in the slums. Although I had said I wanted to see the authentic side of the island, I didn't think I was quite prepared for this. After seeing poverty in the United States, I thought I'd seen it all. I had experienced the downtrodden side of society first-hand and had promised myself that I'd never go back to that way of life. However, the small, broken-down shacks and disheveled children made my heart stir.

"Mi homeboy's spot. No worries. He no live near here." He pulled a blunt from the ashtray and lit it. "Sit back. We gon' be ridin' for a while."

He passed me the blunt and then picked up his phone. When he put it to his ear, he said, "Yo, Don, put on some stew chicken. Mi be there in 'bout another hour. Irie."

When he hung up, he turned the music up full blast. Reggae blared from the speakers, and although I couldn't understand shit the artist was saying, I moved my body to the pulsating beat. Damn, I loved that music. It made me just want to climb in that nigga's lap, pull out his dick, and ride him until my pussy exploded. Mmm, I was so hot.

I passed the blunt back to Tamia, and as I did, my arm grazed Omari's. He looked over at me with longing in his bedroom eyes. Shit, I wanted to reach out and grab his locks. I could imagine him on top of me and my fingers wrapped around his hair. I had heard from a few chicks I knew who dated Jamaican men that they didn't eat pussy. Hmm, something had me thinking that I could get that nigga to eat mine. I knew how to seduce a man, and his tongue would be all up in my pussy before my feet touched American soil again. You could put money on that.

Omari's boy Don lived in a huge house right by the water. It was definitely a far cry from the houses in the impoverished neighborhood we'd ridden through.

The images were still in my head, but after more ganja and some good food, my mood was better.

Don was a chef who worked at a five-star resort in Montego Bay. He was twenty-nine and single, so Nicole was on him. It was cool to meet a fellow "foodie," as I liked to call folks who loved to cook. Plus, he seemed to be living good. As we all sat outside, I filled him in on the fact that I was also a chef and had just graduated.

"Congratulations," Don said. "Have you ever thought about workin' at a resort here? I'm tellin' you, the American dollar is worth a lot more than Jamaican money. You could live even better here."

He didn't talk like Omari, although he still had an accent. I figured that was because of his profession and the fact that he came into contact with all types of cultures. The way I saw it, he was just adjusting the way he talked so that we would understand him better.

"That food was so good, Don." Nicole was smiling all up in his face.

"Thank you. You ladies want a drink? I got some Jamaican rum in there," Don said, being hospitable.

"Nah. I've had enough to drink," I said, declining.

Omari was rolling another spliff, and my head was already swimming.

Tamia was dozing off in the recliner she was sitting on.

After a few more minutes of vibing, I could feel the sexual tension in the air. Don had fixed Nicole a drink, and she was winding all in his lap to the low sound of the reggae music that was playing.

Omari got up and grabbed my hand. "C'mon."

I stood up and followed him inside the house and then down a long, dimly lit hallway. Despite the low light, I could see the beautiful art on the walls.

"This is a nice place," I commented. I wondered why we were at his friend's house instead of his.

I'd filled him in on the fact that Tamia had a man back home, and so she wouldn't appreciate him introducing her to someone. Still, I had thought we'd go to his spot. Maybe he had a woman or something that he lived with. Although it wasn't supposed to bother me, it kind of did.

"Yeah. Don's done good for himself." He nodded as we walked into a bedroom.

I questioned why I was brave enough to be with a man I didn't know in a strange country. Part of me wanted to ask him why we weren't at his place. Then I thought about it. All I wanted to do was live for once. It was the last time for me to make a reckless decision before real life kicked in. *Fuck it.* He seemed to be a high-profile deejay. I doubted he'd risk everything to hurt me.

As if he had read my mind, he said, "Relax. Mi not here to hurt you."

"So, where do you live?" I asked, feeling the weed making me relaxed.

"Mi know ya wonderin' why we here instead of my place. It's far out, so this spot was closer to where ya ladies stayin'. The festival's one more day, so . . ."

I nodded. "No, it's cool. I mean, you don't owe me an explanation. I'm havin' a good time."

"Good." He nodded. "This is just chill time, though. Mi plan to show you an even better time later. Mi just wanna have some time wit' you . . . alone."

His eyes were on mine, and then his lips were on my neck. "Mmm," he moaned. "Mi been wantin' to do that since the first moment mi saw ya. Ya smell so good, star. Jah bless."

Damn, my body was on fire. In no time the blunt was nowhere to be found, but his hot mouth was all over me.

"Mmm," I moaned, feeling my skin getting all feverish from his touch.

"It's just some ting 'bout ya, DiDi."

The low sound of a reggae love song played in the background.

"What's that?" I asked in a sexy whisper.

His hands were moving up and down my thigh, and then he unbuttoned my shorts. "Mi don't know how to explain it. It's like . . . mi wanna do tings to you mi ain't never wanted to do."

I hoped eating pussy was one of them. It was time to turn on the seduction, so I lightly pushed him away. He looked at me like his feelings were hurt, but he just didn't know that I wasn't about to reject him. His eyes lit up when he realized that I was removing my clothes.

"Is the door locked?" I asked.

He nodded slowly, with his eyes glued to my body. His mouth was literally wide open as I stood, buck-ass naked, in front of him.

"Oh . . . Jah . . . blessed you. Yuh perfect." His eyes roamed my body as I walked over to him. I grabbed his hand and led it to my freshly waxed pussy.

"You like how that feels?" I asked as his fingers grazed my smooth skin and then drifted to my wetness.

"Hell yeah," he whispered, pushing his fingers inside me slowly. "The pum pum's so fat, wet . . . and tight. Damn."

There was a contemplative look on his face as he stirred my hot pussy up. Damn. I didn't realize how much I needed to be fucked until that very moment. My whole body quivered.

"Well, it tastes even better," I said.

My eyes were on his as I waited for his reaction. He looked at me like I'd lost every ounce of sense I'd been born with, but the look changed when I spread my glistening pussy lips open for him.

"Ya got the fattest clit mi ever seen, yo. Fa real. Some sexy shit."

I used my pussy muscles to push his fingers out of me and then started to wind and grind to the music that was playing. As I bent over in his face and twerked my thick ass cheeks, I made sure that he had a rear view of my fat pum pum, as he called it. I turned around, then dipped and bounced, and as I did, my titties jiggled. He was mesmerized.

"If you wanna feel this sugary-sweet Yankee pussy, you'll suck this fat clit first. I mean, I am an American woman, and I like gettin' my pussy ate out before I fuck." I leaned over as I spoke and grabbed his dick through his pants. "Like I thought. You got an anaconda in your pants, and you ain't fuckin' me till you get this thang super wet."

He licked his lips and contemplated it. "Shit, the way that pussy was grippin' mi fingers, mi down to suck on that mufucka. Fuck it. Put it 'pon mi face."

My pussy was positioned over his face in no time, and he sucked on my clit like he knew what he was doing. Fronting-ass nigga.

"Mmm . . . shit . . . ," I moaned. It felt so fucking good. Especially when he started fingering me with those long, thick fingers.

When I felt like I was about to cum, I started rotating the pussy in his face.

"Ahhh . . . fuck . . . ," I moaned.

Before I could explode in his face, that nigga moved out of the way. But it was cool; I had got my nut. I guessed he was scared to get that shit in his mouth. That was okay. If he was going to be fucking with me while I was there, he'd get over that shit.

I watched his sexy, ripped body as he undressed. His body was magnificent, but his dick, that shit was a different story. Not only was it long as hell, but it was also as thick as my damn arm. Fuck! I'd never felt anything close to that big inside me, and I was nervous.

"No worries, sexy. Mi be gentle wit' it. Mi promise. Besides, it's clear that ya pum pum's good, and it should be savored."

Damn, the way that nigga talked made me shiver. He slid the condom down that huge dick and then positioned himself on top of me. As I spread my legs wider to receive that big shit, the head was pushing its way in.

"Fuck . . . ," I breathed as I closed my eyes. That nigga's dick was spreading my walls out like it was my first time.

"Mmm. Dis pussy's so tight. . . . Oh shit, star . . ."

I grabbed his ass as he moved and ground inside me. In no time that shit was feeling good as fuck, and I was screaming that nigga's name as he explored my pussy with that massive-ass dick.

"Fuck! Omari . . . shit! Get that pussy! Damn! Aargh . . . mmm . . . ahhh . . . fuck! Omari!" I was so loud, and I didn't give a fuck.

"Ahhh, DiDi, baby. Dis pum pum's like heaven. . . . Jah . . . fuck . . . Best pussy mi ever had."

He suckled on my breasts and touched my G-spot like we'd been fucking for years.

"Shit! I'm cumin'. Ohhh, fuck!" I yelled.

He was so deep inside me, and I was having back-to-back orgasms. Shit, I had five more days to take advantage of that good-ass dick, and damn it, I planned to have it every way possible. Hell yeah, a bitch was gone over the "d."

After we lay there for a minute, I got a text from Nicole, letting me know that she and Tamia were ready to leave. As tired as he was, Omari got up to take them back to the hotel, anyway. I guessed Nicole wasn't feeling Don. We would definitely talk about it later.

"Ya comin' back with mi?" he asked before we got in the car. "You can keep mi awake."

"Yeah," I said, with a nod, knowing that I'd do any damn thing he wanted me to do.

Chapter 10

Omari

I knew I would end up fucking shawty, but I never imagined it would be that damn easy. I knew that she was all into me by the way she looked deep into my eyes when we talked. The sound of her voice sent chills up my spine and gave me an instant erection. I wanted to fuck this Yankee gal really bad.

I knew I couldn't take her to the crib, and the hotels around here were all booked because of the events that were taking place. After trying my best to come up with something, I remembered that my homeboy Don lived close by and that there had been times when he allowed me to bring my bitches to his crib to smash. I grabbed my phone and dialed his number after I ignored Angela's third call.

When we were at Don's house, DiDi's scent pulled me in instantly, and my mouth gathered water. My wood started to rise, and I glanced around to make sure no one else saw that. I quickly adjusted myself.

I'd always considered myself a shotta, or bad boy, and sucking pussy was a no-no in my world. In Jamaica we didn't promote that kind of foolishness, and niggas that sucked pussy were often clowned, especially in my circle.

All that shit changed, though. DiDi's scent had been driving me fucking crazy, and when she suggested that I suck her pussy, I didn't resist. It was my first time, and truth be told, I had no idea what I was doing. I'd watched lots of blue movies, and I'd always considered myself the pussy doctor.

I slowly sniffed her freshly shaved pussy. A whiff of her fresh powdered scent hit my nose. I then took my fingers and opened up the pussy. I think I was only trying to make sure the pussy was clean. I started licking the clit, and I used my fingers to massage her at the same time. Her pussy was wet, and I was anxious to taste the sweet juice. I closed my eyes, dug my head deep in, gripped her clit, sucked on it like it wasn't my first time. She started moaning, which boosted my confidence, and then she gripped my head. Shit, I must've been doing something right if she was gripping my head like that. I felt her grip tighten, so I knew that she was about to cum. I quickly moved my head away.

I didn't waste any time when I saw the look she gave me. Shawty was ready for the wood, and I was there to deliver. I parted her legs and entered her slippery, wet pussy. I took a few seconds to breathe. . . . Her tight, fresh pussy's grip on my wood felt more like she was sucking it up. I made my way through her walls and deep into her soul. Seeing how she looked deep into my eyes, I slow fucked her, all along staring into her eyes too. This Yankee gal's pussy was definitely high grade, and I planned on leaving a mark on it.

After pounding her walls down, I finally pulled out and busted. I swear, shawty's pussy was so fucking good, I wanted to hop back on asap, but I was fucking drained. I lay on my back as she walked to the bathroom to wash off. I was feeling like a brand-new man. I only wished this feeling would last and DiDi would be mine.

Angela

I was getting ready to lie down when my cell started ringing. I was irritated as fuck because I hadn't heard from my husband in over twenty-four hours. That nigga had lost his fucking mind. Ever since he left, claiming he was going to Dream Weekend, I hadn't heard one fucking word from him.

I snatched up the phone from my dresser and answered with an attitude, without looking at the caller ID.

"Hello," I answered angrily.

"Damn, bitch. What's wrong wit' yo' ass?" Paula quizzed.

"Sorry, boo. Didn't know it was you," I said, lowering my voice quickly, as I lay on the bed.

"Well, bitch, are you sitting down?"

"I'm lying down. Why? What's going on?"

"You know I don't try to get into your and Omari's business. . . ." She paused.

I sensed this was serious, and wished she would just hurry the fuck up and tell me whatever it was she was going to tell me. Whatever it was wasn't good.

"Well, I was down here at the event, and I saw Omari and a few females walking together, so I decided to be nosy and saw him all up in this one bitch's face. I believe she is a Yankee gyal."

"Okay, you know that he playing music, and all them bitches be on him like that. It ain't no biggie." I shrugged. Even though I was sideways bothered.

"Bitch, you better listen to what I'm telling you. You know I be talking to his boy Don, so last night I asked him about Omari and the bitch I saw him with. That's when he spilled everything while I ride his wood. Bomboclaat, gal, 'im tell mi, say a di gal weh Mari meet the otha night. Him also tell mi dat dem dey ova at his house."

I jumped up off the bed. I pressed the phone closer to my ear. I wasn't sure I had heard her right, but she continued talking, and I hung on to every word she was spitting out. The veins in my head were getting bigger, and I had an instant headache.

"Gal, why yuh suh quiet? Yuh need to bring yo' ass down here and see what the fuck is going on," she said.

"I'll see you lata."

I didn't wait for a response from her. I hung up. I then dialed Omari's phone number, but his phone was turned off. I decided not to leave a message, because I didn't want to alert him of my intentions. I called him a few more times, but the result was still the same. I then dialed my mother's phone.

"Hello," she answered in an upbeat tone.

"Hey, Mama. I need a favor from you."

"What yuh want now?" she responded, like I was bothering her.

"I need you to watch the kids real quick. I got a run to make."

"You know it's the weekend and mi 'ave some run around to do. Cho, man."

"I know, Mama, and I'm sorry. Some business just come up, and I need to run to Ochi real quick."

"All right, but yuh need to drop them off, because mi is polishing this floor."

I was sick of her rudeness, but I really needed her right now, so I gave her a pass.

"Thanks, Mama."

I hung the phone up and walked outside to get the kids from next door, where they were playing with the neighbor's kids. I quickly got them dressed and took them to Mama's house.

After that, I went home and searched my closet for a pair of shorts, a wife beater, and a pair of worn-out J's.

I grabbed my ratchet knife and a pack of razor blades. I had no idea what I was walking into, but whatever it was, I was ready for anything and everything. That nigga had lost his pussyclaat mind.

I stepped outside, locked up the grill, and jumped in my car. Backed out in a haste, because I knew I needed to hurry. I was getting on the highway, and if I was lucky, there would not be any traffic and I'd be there in an hour, tops. I stopped by the gas station, filled up the tank, and soon I was on my way.

My heart was hurting and tears filled my eyes as I thought of my husband disrespecting me in the worst way. I knew that I was cheating on him, but at least I kept that shit discreet. Nobody could tell him that they had seen me around town with his boy.

I turned on the radio, and "She's Still Loving Me," by Morgan Heritage, was playing. Tears flowed down my face as I gripped the steering wheel.

Honk! Honk!

The sound of a bus horn startled me back to reality. I swerved and then got back in my lane. Glancing at the time, I saw that I was almost there. My phone started ringing. I picked it up, looked at the caller ID, and noticed it was old boy calling me. I wished he would leave me the fuck alone right now. See, I couldn't stand an old, clingy-ass nigga.

Nigga, you the side piece, so please play your position, I thought.

Finally, I saw a sign that said WELCOME TO OCHO RIOS. My heart started racing more as I envisioned how this might turn out. I'd been to his boy's house numerous times, so I knew exactly where I was going. I thought of calling Paula but quickly changed my mind. She was my right hand and all, but she was fucking Don, and I'd known bitches who betrayed their friends over some dick. I didn't want to risk anybody tipping Omari off.

I pulled up at the residence and immediately saw Omari's car in the driveway. I started having second thoughts about going to the door, even though I was a bad gyal, and I didn't fear no one or nothing. I pushed those thoughts aside. I parked my car, grabbed my purse, got out, and walked up the marble driveway. After I rang the doorbell, I waited impatiently. I heard movement on the other side of the door, so I knew that someone was inside the house.

I heard the lock snap, and the door opened. . . .

"Yo, wh-what the bomboclaat . . . ?"

"Hello, husband." I wasted no time greeting my husband, who was standing in front of me in his boxers and a white wife beater, with his tongue hanging out of his mouth.

"Yo, Angie, what's going on? How you know I was here?"

"The question is, who the fuck you here with, nigga?" I tried to push past him, but he quickly blocked my path.

"Yo', you trippin'. Where're the kids at? And what the fuck you doing here?"

"Yo, Omari, yuh tink mi a play? Which gal yuh 'ave inside of there?"

"B, yuh trippin'. Ain't no girl in here. I played all night, and I was tired, so Don let mi come over here to get some sleep."

I looked at that lying-ass nigga with rage in my eyes. I knew how his nose flared up when he was feeding me bullshit.

"Omari, is everything okay?" I heard a bitch's voice ask before she walked to the door.

When she got closer and saw me, I could tell that she was just as shocked as I was, but I maintained my composure. There was no way I was going to let that bitch see me sweat.

"Who is this, Omari?" she asked in her American accent.

"Hello, bitch," I snarled. "You must be the one that I got the call about. This here is my husband, and if you were fucking him, your dirty ass was fucking a married man."

Her mouth dropped open. Before she could reply, I leaped over Omari and grabbed that bitch. I didn't even think he saw that coming, but if he really knew me, he would have known that I barely argued with bitches. I'd lay these hands on them first, then ask question later. That bitch was petite, but her blows hit hard. She was definitely matching each of my hits.

Omari tried to grab me upas I fought my way inside, but I started kicking and scratching him. "Let me go! Yuh need fi hold yo' bloodclaat gyal before I hurt her," I shouted. Then I sank my teeth deep down into his arm.

"Fuck, B!" he yelled and let go of my ass.

I started running back toward the bitch, who was just standing there, trying to question Omari. I could tell that he was not trying to hear all of that right now.

"Yo, B, you need to leave up out of here!" he yelled at me, fire spitting from his eyes.

I was kind of shock that *my* husband was standing there, dissing me for a bitch that he'd obviously just met. My eyes started to tear up, but I used everything in me not to display any sign of weakness.

"I didn't know you were married," this bitch stated.

He turned his attention away from me and toward that home-wrecking bitch. "DiDi, I can explain," he said.

"I'm standing here, and you catering to that bitch? What kind of bloodclaat shit you on?" I grabbed my husband's arm.

He stepped closer to me. "Angela, I say, go home!" he yelled as spit flew out of his mouth and onto my face.

I could no longer hold back the tears, and my heart started racing as I struggled to gain an understanding of what was really going on. I looked at the man standing in front of me, and I didn't recognize him. How could he treat me like that? I had no idea what the fuck was going on, but I was married to him, and there was no way I was going to walk away from him.

In the midst of the chaos, I heard the door behind me open. It was Don and my bitch Paula.

I walked over to Don. "Don, this is how you do me? Yuh kno' mi and Omari is married, and yuh let 'im bring dis nasty gal up in here!"

"Angela, mi nuh 'ave nuttin' fi do wit' dis," he said and then walked away.

"Are you okay?" Paula quizzed as she stared at me.

Then Paula turned to Omari. "Omari, a fuckery dis. How yuh fi dis har like this?" She poked him in the chest.

"Yo, B, mind yuh bloodclaat business. Dis don't concern me," Omari growled.

"Go suck yuh muma, dutty bwoy. A my friend dis, so it concern me," Paula told him.

By that time, the bitch had walked off and grabbed her stuff, I guessed, because by the time I tried to get in the middle of Omari and Paula's argument, she was heading out the door with Don. I tried to run up on her, but Don pushed me back.

"Man, chill out wit' all this. Shawty just trying to leave," he said.

"Man, fuck you and that bitch!" I yelled.

"Nah, you stupid ho, fuck you. If you were such a good wife, your man wouldn't be out here screwing around on you!" the bitch yelled as the door closed behind them.

I was devastated as I looked at Omari, who was putting on his clothes.

"Yo, I swear this over. Get the fuck outta my house and out of mi fucking life!" I yelled as I walked out the door.

Paula ran behind me. "Why yuh didn't tell mi yuh was coming? We could've whup that bitch ass together. Mi can't believe a so Omari a deal wit' yuh so, star."

"I got to go! Mi ago call ya lata."

I walked off, and tears continued rolling down my face. I couldn't believe what had just happened. I jumped into my car and drove off. I was devastated and couldn't think straight. *That nigga Omari and his bitch will pay for what they did to me,* I thought as I hit the steering wheel.

Chapter 11

Kadijah

After almost fifteen minutes of driving, Don pulled over to the side of the road and Omari's familiar black Mercedes pulled up behind us. I rolled my eyes, hoping that his crazy wife wasn't pulling up too. The last thing I needed was to catch a charge for murdering a bitch in a foreign-ass country. I couldn't believe that nigga was married. Why hadn't he just told me that? Shit, I would've fucked him, anyway, being that I would be back in the States soon. Damn. At least he could've warned me.

"Why are you stopping?" I asked Don, knowing that we had a good forty minutes of driving to get to my hotel.

His girl Paula was pissed that he was taking me back to my hotel, but he had told her to calm her nerves about it. It wasn't like they were in a relationship or anything, according to him. It was clear now that Nicole had wanted to leave because Paula had popped up. It was funny that I hadn't noticed an extra car in the driveway when we left. It was also weird that Nicole hadn't mentioned that to me. I'd just figured that Don had gone to bed. I guessed she didn't want to ruin my time with Omari. Shit, I was also sure she had no clue that the bitch who had popped up to see Don also knew Omari's mystery wife.

"He wants to talk to you," Don said as he looked over at me.

"How did his wife even know I was there? Did that chick you were fuckin' tell her? Did you tell her?" I interrogated him, being that I didn't see Paula until I saw Omari's wife.

"To be honest, I didn't know Paula was comin' over. I'm sure Omari didn't, either. She got a different whip, so I don't think he knew she was there."

"Or he wouldn't have been brave enough to take me back to your spot," I added. "Can you please just drive off? I don't want to talk to him. I'm good. I just want to enjoy the rest of my time here. I'll pay you."

Don was fucking Omari's wife's best friend. *How convenient.*

Don shook his head. "Keep your money. I know my boy Omari. He wouldn't give a fuck about talkin' to any other woman after that, but for some reason, he wants to explain himself to you. Him and Ang been havin' some problems for a while, and while he ain't perfect, he ain't a bad guy, either. Something's tellin' me he's feelin' you . . . on some real shit."

"I don't give a fuck about none of that. He's married, and I don't have time for this shit. I just got into a fight with his wife, and that's not what I envisioned as a highlight of my island vacation. I could've stayed my ass home and fought my ex's girlfriend. Shit!" I shook my head. "Please, just get me out of here," I begged, knowing that Don's loyalty didn't lie with me. That nigga was probably ready to leave me there with Omari, so that Omari could deal with that shit, while he ran back to Paula.

All I could do was watch as Omari walked over to the passenger's side of Don's car and opened my door.

"Let mi apologize for that please. Jus' let mi explain," he began, with a regretful look on his face.

I shook my head. "I don't need an apology or an explanation from you. You're not my man, or anything close to that. Shit, you should be explaining and apologizing to your wife, not me."

"Please, please, DiDi. Just give mi da time it'll take to get you back to your hotel to explain myself to you. I'm beggin' you." Suddenly, he seemed to want to throw out the patois that I was used to him using, and now he was talking more like me.

I guessed he felt that this was one way to get through to me, but all it did was help me understand what he was saying better. It didn't make me care one way or another about what he was saying. Yeah, he had banged my back out and given me the orgasms I needed, but to hell with him. After what Daryn had put me through, I could give a fuck about a lying-ass man, good dick or not.

When I glanced over at Don, he looked like he would rather be anywhere but there with us, trying to help diffuse a fucked-up situation. It wasn't like he had asked for any of this, but he still had given his boy a place to cheat on his wife.

"Just to let you both know, I'm pissed the fuck off because that bitch jumped on me without even attempting to get the whole fuckin' story. I'm from the streets, so I ain't new to that shit. However, if she'd stopped and asked me one question, she would've known that I didn't know she existed," I said. I looked at Don. "Still, how the fuck you gon' let your boy do some shit like that at your spot? You just as bad as him." Then I looked at Omari. "And you, what the fuck? How could you put me in a position like that? Damn! In that case, I could've just stayed at the hotel with my girls. What if those bitches would've jumped me? What then? Shit, I'm thousands of miles away from home. That didn't matter to you, though, I'm sure. All you wanted was some Yankee pussy." I paused for a moment. Then I mocked his accent when I added, "This is some fuckin' bullshit. Ain't no dick worth this!"

Omari shook his head as he held his hand out for me. "Please, just let me get you safely to ya hotel. That's not up to Don to do. Mi fucked up, mi know, but just let me do that."

I refused to take his hand, but in a way, he was right. Don wasn't the one who had picked me up and taken me to his house. It was Omari's responsibility to make sure that I made it safely back to the resort. Without saying another word to Don, I got out of the car and walked back to Omari's Mercedes. He stayed back to talk to Don for a second, and I got in the car.

After I buckled my seat belt, I looked out the window and waited as Omari walked back toward his car. *Fuck.* Why did he have to be so damn sexy with all that swag? His walk, the way he talked, and even the way he smelled all fucked with my head. There was just something about him. The poetic way that he talked and how he looked at me. It was like he could see right through me, and we'd just met.

Then the thought of him being married crept back into my mind and brought me back to reality. Although it was only a sex thing, the chances of it being more had been a thought of mine. Well, that was until his fucking wife knocked on the door and changed everything. Then again, who was I fooling, anyway? I was on vacation, and that shit with Omari was just a fling. Why the hell was I reading more into it? He really didn't owe me anything. I was just some American girl he had fucked, nothing more and nothing less.

When he got in the car, I looked straight ahead without saying one word. For a good five minutes, he didn't say anything. Instead, he let Sizzla explain how much he needed his woman. Before I'd ever visited the island of Jamaica, I was a reggae fan, and I had always loved Sizzla. At the moment, I wanted Omari to turn that crap off. I wasn't his woman; that bitch who had jumped on me was.

Why wasn't he going after her instead of pursuing me? Was it because I was leaving soon and she would still be there? Was the pum pum that good that he just had to have a little bit more before he made up with his wife?

"Mi apologized to you, but now I'm at a loss. Mi really have nothing else to say to make it up to you. To be honest, mi neva t'ought you'd let me . . . make love to you."

"It wasn't love. . . . It was sex. We fucked," I reminded him in a harsh voice.

"Either way, it took mi by surprise. Di way I felt, it was different than what . . . I'm used to."

I rolled my eyes in annoyance, because Jamaican men were just as bad as American men when it came to lying. That shit just sounded better.

"Please, just stop. Stop the lies please. You have a wife, and I'm sure y'all have children," I told him.

He didn't say anything.

"How many?" I asked in a low voice. The shit was just getting worse.

"Two." He cleared his throat. "I won't lie, DiDi. I love her because she had my children, but I'm not in love. If I was, I wouldn't cheat."

"So, you cheat a lot?" I knew that I wasn't the first, but damn. "Why the fuck are you married, then?"

"Mi have cheated a few times, but tis is the first time mi felt anything other than lust. When mi first laid eyes on you, it was something mi can't describe. I can only say it was a first . . . ya know. It made mi feel like maybe I'm wit' da wrong woman. Like mi said, mi love Ang 'cause she gave mi my yute, but . . . she . . . she ain't mi soul mate, ya know?"

"Yeah, whatever." Not knowing Omari didn't keep me from being a straight asshole. At that point, I wasn't afraid of what he'd do to me, shotta or not.

I turned the music up full blast to drown out that redundant shit he was spitting out of his mouth. His accent made the fuckery sound good, so I really wasn't trying to hear it. All he could do was shake his head as I pretended to be entertained by the scenery and the sounds of the bass that were vibrating into my back. After a few minutes of letting me have my way, he turned the music back down, and I sighed in frustration. His sexiness was getting on my nerves, and the sooner I got away from the lying-ass bastard, the better. I couldn't wait to fill my girls in on what had happened. I was also ready to cuss Nicole out for not warning me about the bitch who had shown up.

"You have a right to be pissed, but ya should know that I never meant to disrespect you or to lie to you. Mi didn't expect to feel any—"

"Please." I put my hand up. "Just give it up, already. I only wanted to fuck you, anyway, so you're makin' this way deeper than it is. The dick was good, and I got what I wanted. I'm leavin' soon, and I wanted to try some Jamaican dick. So what? It is what it is. Just like you wanted to fuck a Yankee gal. Don't flatter yourself. I could give a fuck that you're married. Okay. Whatever. Make up with your wife. I just didn't expect to get into a fight over some dick that I only wanted to fuck while I'm here."

My nonchalant attitude must've gotten to him, because his expression was priceless. It was like he wasn't used to such bluntness, although his wife was clearly a nutcase who had no class whatsoever. Then again, by the way that he looked at me, what I had just said to him seemed to be a turn-on.

"Really? You just wanted to fuck?" There was a smirk on his face. "It's more than that. You just mad, B. I can tell. C'mon. Mi sucked ya pum pum. Mi no even do that shit to mi wife. Bambaclatt!"

"Well, ain't that 'bout a bitch?" I shrugged my shoulders and turned the music up.

We probably had a good thirty minutes to go before I got back to my hotel. As good as the sex was, and as intriguing as Omari seemed to be, I just needed to separate myself from him for the rest of the time I was here. I had actually entertained the thought of a nice, exotic romance, but that was just a fantasy. In the real world, sexy, lying-ass men existed, and I'd fucked one of them. Oh, well. It wasn't the first time, and I was sure that it wouldn't be the last.

Just like I'd hoped, Omari didn't say anything else to me for the remainder of the ride. He did roll up a couple of fat-ass spliffs, which took the edge off a little. I couldn't wait to go to the bar and get a few drinks. After that, all I wanted to do was get my mind off that good, thick-ass dick that I'd never again have the pleasure of feeling against my G-spot. It was just my luck to find a man who could fuck but who was also married.

Daryn had just fucked me over, and now I'd been fooled again somewhere else on the globe. It only further proved to me that all men were dogs. It didn't matter the race, background, or climate. How could I ever trust a man again, knowing that a man who had no reason to keep the truth from me had done that shit, anyway?

Omari pulled up to the resort hotel, and I opened the door without saying anything to him. He grabbed me by a belt loop on my jean shorts and kept me from getting out of the car.

"Don't just leave mi like dat, B. Say sumthin' to mi, mon. It's a reason we met, and mi no give a fuck what ya say, star." His eyes were blazing with passion, but I didn't want to give in to it.

"You're married, Omari." I shook my head and sighed. "Anything we could've possibly had is out the door.

We met, we fucked, and I enjoyed it. Let it go and let *me* go. Bye."

When I looked down at his hand, it was clear he got the point, because he released his grip on me.

"You're beautiful, DiDi. If mi was a single man . . . Hmm, let's just say you'd be di one mi wed under Jah's blessin'."

Mmm-mmm-mmm, he was fine. "Well, Jah blessed you and another woman, so that's irrelevant," I replied.

I grabbed my purse, stepped out of the car, and walked away quickly. As I made my way inside the hotel, my footsteps sped up. Damn, all I wanted to do was see my girls.

"Shit, bitch! I didn't know," Nicole gasped after I told them every detail of what had happened.

"I'm sayin', though. You didn't even mention that bitch!" I snapped at her.

Tamia spoke up. "I was knocked out 'cause that nigga's food gave me the itis. Nicole didn't even mention that chick to me till we got here."

Nicole rolled her eyes. "I didn't think shit of it. I figured they were two single men who could fuck who they wanted. Shit. Don't blame me," she said. "I didn't think Don's bitch would be your problem. At first, I was gonna fuck him, but she started ringin' the doorbell. He let her in like it was nothing, and then they went in his room. After that, I texted you. When you decided to go back over there with old boy, I figured what the hell. After what you went through with Daryn, you needed to get some dick." She shrugged her shoulders. "I just wish I'd been there to help you fuck that bitch up."

Tamia shook her head and was the voice of reason. "Oh, well, Di, you didn't know. If the dick was good, at least you got your rocks off. Now, let's enjoy the rest of our time here. Fuck him and his bum-ass wife."

I shook my head as I opened my suitcase. "You're so right. Oh, well. I found out I've been lied to twice in two weeks, but it's all good. At least he ate my pussy, but I ain't suck his dick!"

My girls and I laughed, and they slapped me fives. I stopped laughing before they did, because that shit with Omari kind of stung a little bit. As much as I tried to downplay it and pretend like he was just a piece of dick, my gut told me something else. *Shit! Fuck it.* All I needed to do was take a shower, wash that nigga off me, have a few drinks, and enjoy Jamaica for the last few days I was there. *Fuck a nigga.*

Chapter 12

Omari

Jah know star, I couldn't believe what had popped off earlier. I was shocked as fuck when I opened the door and it was Angie standing in the doorway. I wanted to slam the door shut, but I knew that would be a big mistake. The best move for me was to stand there and face the music. I was hoping DiDi would stay her ass in the bedroom, but all hope diminished when I heard DiDi's voice asking me what was going on. I thought of a quick way to diffuse the situation, but I was a minute too late when Angela popped off. I tried to keep them apart, but it was like two savage animals going at each other. Angela was a beast with her hands, but I thought she had finally met her match, because DiDi's little, thick frame was matching her blow for blow. It was almost was comical . . . if the situation wasn't fucked up.

Eventually, I managed to pull them apart. I didn't want it to go any further. After I got them apart, DiDi was cool, but Angela was still popping off. It was in that second that I realized how different both women were. DiDi wasn't no punk, but she was laid back. Angela, on the other hand, was loud and drama filled.

Angela tried to convince me to leave with her, but there was something about DiDi that wouldn't allow me to leave just then. The way she made me feel was enough to risk losing my marriage to Angela. I saw the pain in

Angela's eyes when I refused to leave with her, but there was nothing I could do to ease the pain that she was going through. I had no idea if DiDi and I were going to be anything more than a fuck, but it was a risk that I was willing to take.

Begging a bitch to be with me wasn't my thing, but there was something about this Yankee gyal that grabbed me. I had been with plenty bitches with good pussy, but it was more than the pussy. I felt something deep inside that made me want her even more. After I caught up with her and Don, I begged her to let me take her to the hotel. At first, she kept shooting me down, but being the nigga I was, I wasn't going to give up. She must've sensed that, because she finally gave in. She argued with me for the entire ride, while I begged her to hear me out. I had a feeling that I had fucked up, and it was going to be real hard to get back in her good graces. DiDi seemed like she was a no-nonsense woman!

After I dropped her off, I decided to stop by a spot to meet Don. We had a big show tonight, and I had to make sure we were ready, because it was the last night, which meant it was sound clash night. We were playing against sound out of St. Elizabeth. I wasn't tripping off them country niggas; I planned on killing them pussies and taking the crown tonight. I pulled up at the bar where Don and the rest of the fellas were hanging out. I parked and got out.

"Wha gwaan, brethren?" Don greeted me as soon as I walked in.

"Ain't shit, nigga." I took a seat by the bar.

"My nigga Omari, what's good yo?" Mikey said. I could tell by his smile that Don had been running his mouth about what had happened earlier. Those were my niggas, and that was how we rolled. We often joked around.

Tonight was different, though. I was tight as fuck. I waved for the bartender, who was standing on the side, talking to the brethren Howey.

"Hey, Omari," Patrice, the bartender, said seductively. See, Patrice and I went way back. I used to smash that ass, but she wasn't about nothing outside of being a gold digger, so I had had to cut that ass loose.

"Let me get a glass of Hennessy White."

"Yo, my nigga, it look like you got the world on your shoulders. I hope everythin' worked out, 'cause, nigga, yo' ass is in some serious shit," Don joked.

"My nigga, I got this. I run bitches, not the other way around." I took a big gulp of the liquor. I then pulled out a pack of Rizla and the bag of weed I had in my pocket. I quickly rolled the blunt and took a long pull. I waited a few seconds for the smoke to illuminate my brain. I took another drag of the high-grade ganja.

I tried to clear my head, but I couldn't get DiDi off my mind. I put the glass to my head and drank it all. When I was finished, I placed 350 dollars down on the counter and got up.

"Yo, mi genna, I'm about to bounce," I announced.

"Damn, dawg. You ain't even say two words to us," Don complained.

"Man, I got to go. I'll catch up wit' you niggas lata."

I walked out of the lounge. The warm breeze hit my face, and I gladly welcomed it. Something had to give, because I couldn't shake the feeling.

Angela

To say I was hurt would be an understatement! I couldn't believe that I had just been disrespected in the worst way by my so-called husband and his ho. I jumped on the highway; I was heading back home. I grabbed my phone and dialed my side piece's number. He picked up on the first ring.

"Hey, babe. Where you—"

"Did you know Omari has been cheating on me again?" I said, cutting him off.

"What you talking 'bout?"

"Well, I just caught him at that fuck nigga Don's house with a Yankee bitch."

"Bomboclaat! Mi neva know 'bout that one deh." He sounded alarmed.

"It gets worse. That nigga disrespect mi for this bitch."

"Yo, B, I been telling you to leave dis nigga 'lone. Yuh 'ave a nigga that love you, but yuh keep on fucking wit' dis nigga that don't fuckin' love yuh."

I was angry that this nigga would use this time to profess his fucking love to me. Did this pussy hole hear a word that I just said, or he was too busy trying to put in his bid?

"Yuh know what? I'll talk to yuh lata, 'cause it's pure fuckery yuh a talk 'bout now."

I didn't wait for a response and quickly hung up the phone.

The tears started flowing again as I sped through town. I was no longer crying because I was hurt; this was my anger inside. Hate engulfed my heart, and I spent the rest of the ride planning and plotting.

I got back to Kingston in no time and stopped by my mom's house to pick up the children. I really wasn't in the mood to deal with them, but I knew that my mother would be calling and arguing soon if I did get them.

"Hey, Mama," I greeted her as I walked onto the porch.

"I was just goin' to call you. Why the hell yuh look like yuh been crying?" She took a closer look at me.

"Mama, I just catch Omari and a gyal down a Ochi." I broke down.

"Say what?" She looked at me with a surprised expression plastered across her face.

By that time, I was bawling and couldn't stop myself to explain to her what I meant.

"I always tell yuh, I don't like that bwoy. He was only using yuh for your money, and soon as he start making a few dollars, he give yuh his ass to kiss. I say leave his ass and tek yo' kids."

It was true. Mama had never liked him. She had been screaming the same thing about him ever since she met him, but I had dismissed her concerns and had gone on to marry that bastard. I really didn't want to hear her "I told you so" speech.

"Well, I got to go. Where are the kids?"

"They next door, over Miss Dolly's house. Sit down. I need to chat to yuh."

I looked at her and saw the seriousness on Mama's face. I took a seat on the porch seat and placed my purse next to me.

"I can't tell yuh how to live yo' life. Regardless of how I feel 'bout him, he's your husband, and if yuh really want him, yuh need to go see that man in St. James."

I looked at Mama, shocked by what she had just said, because I knew exactly who she was talking about when she mentioned that man in St. James. See, Mama had never kept it a secret that she was into obeah, or voodoo. We used to get teased by other kids when we were growing up because of the fact that Mama was "into witchcraft," as they said. I didn't believe it until I got older and saw firsthand that she was deep into that obeah business.

"Mama, yuh know I'm not into all that bullshit. It's to God alone, mi a pray."

"Open up your eyes and stop acting like yuh don't know what's going on. That gyal have her paws in yo' husband, and sooner or lata, he is gonna leave you and dem kids high and dry. Stop being a fool, gyal. All yuh doing is holding on to what belong to yuh."

"I got to go, Mama. I'm going to call the kids. Thanks for watching dem."

I got up and grabbed my purse. I walked out the grill and made my way over to the next-door neighbor's yard. I picked up the kids and got them in the car.

On the way home, I couldn't help but think about what Mama had said to me earlier. Even though I wasn't into that kind of foolery, it might not be a bad idea to go see that man so he could give me some insight into what was really going on! After all, I had no intention of walking away from my husband and everything that we had built. If there was a way for me to get rid of that ho and hold on to my husband, I was willing to go the extra mile to get it done!

I got the kids home, fed them, got them ready for bed, and tucked them in. I was happy when I was finally alone. I poured me a glass of Red Label wine and got into bed. I checked my phone, but Omari hadn't called or texted. The only ones who had called were Paula and my side nigga, and I didn't want to talk to either one of them right about now. I turned the light off and closed my eyes, and then I dreamt of ways to pay my husband back in full.

Chapter 13

Daryn

"Nita, I can't do this anymore." Finally, I'd manned up and told her. "I'm leaving you."

It had been almost a week since DiDi's graduation, and she was all that I could think about. Her gift was sitting in the glove compartment of my car, and I was waiting for the right time to give it to her. The only thing was, she wasn't answering my calls. It seemed hopeless, but I wasn't giving up. I was even willing to lose my chance of being a lawyer at one of the most lucrative black-owned law firms in Atlanta.

"What the fuck do you mean, you can't do this anymore?" Nita shot back. Her eyes were narrowed as she stared up at me.

The fiery sting surprised me when she slapped me in the face . . . hard.

"What the fuck?" I stared down at her as I rubbed my cheek. "Now you're acting psycho." First, I'd been attacked by DiDi, and now her. Shit. I was wrong, but she needed to keep her hands to her damn self.

"Fuck you! I can't believe you're dumping me after I forgave you for cheating on me with that common, ghetto-ass bitch! What? Are you in love with . . . her?"

The hurt in Nita's teary eyes was apparent, but for some reason, I wasn't really moved by it. If anything, her weakness only showed that she wasn't the woman for me.

Why the hell would she forgive me for cheating? I mean, it wasn't the first time, but it was the first time I'd actually fallen in love.

I'd never been in love with Nita. She was just a means to an end, to get hired by her father. When I met her, I knew exactly what I was doing, and my plot had back-fired on my ass. Loving a strong, independent woman like DiDi had changed my priorities. After I dumped Nita, I was sure that her father would not want me to work for him. Not that I would want to. But I figured I could get hired at another law firm when I passed the bar.

"I'm sorry. . . ."

Nita lunged at me and started slapping, punching, and kicking me. I tried to hold her down, but she was a feisty little thing. As I grabbed her arms and tried to subdue her, she bit my hand, and I let go. After that, I made my way across the room.

"Look, I don't want to put my hands on you, but you're pushing it right now." I was mad as fuck. "Now, just let me leave, all right? At least I'm being honest with your ass."

"You're being honest with me? You asked me to marry you, and now, all of a sudden, you want to call it quits? Since you're being honest, motherfucker, be completely honest. Why the fuck is this happening, Daryn? Huh? I love you. . . ."

"I don't love you, Nita. I never have, and I never will. I love DiDi and—"

"You fucking bastard!"

When a vase flew toward my head, I ducked really quick, and it crashed against the wall.

"Nita, calm down, baby—"

"I ain't your baby, nigga! Don't you fuckin' call me that. I ought to chop your fuckin' dick off!"

Oh, shit. She had never talked like that. She had always been so soft spoken and high sidity. All I could do was try to figure out a way to get past her and out the door. I'd come back to get my shit after she had time to cool off.

"I know you're mad at me, Nita, and I do apologize for misleading you for so long." As she glared at me with sheer aggression in her eyes, I slowly moved toward the front door.

"You scared?" She taunted me with an evil grin, although tears were streaming down her face. "You worried about what I'll do? You thought I was weak, huh? But I love you. That's all. You took advantage of that, though, and I can't let you get away with breaking my heart."

The crazed look on her face had me shaken. I held my hands out, as I didn't want her to jump on me again. Knowing that I could beat her didn't make putting my hands on her a plausible response. If I put my hands on her, her pops would put me under the jail. There was no way. I just needed to get out of there before she went off and grabbed a knife or the nine that she kept in the closet in our bedroom.

"I told you that I'm sorry for hurting you, Nita. What more do you want from me?" My eyes pleaded for her to just be rational about the situation.

"I want you to want me! I want you to undo the hurt! What the fuck do you think, you asshole!" she screamed at the top of her lungs. Her face was bright red as she looked around the room.

"What are you doing?" I interrogated her as I used the opportunity to move closer to my escape route.

When she grabbed the small fish tank that was on a shelf, I was glad that the door was only a few steps away. I reached the doorknob, opened the door, rushed out, and pulled the door closed before she could hit me with the heavy glass object. From outside, I heard the sound of the fish tank shattering upon impact as it hit the door.

As I shook my head, I rushed toward my car. Of course, she ran out to continue talking shit.

"Fuck you, Daryn! I hate you, and I'll never forgive you for this! I'm going to get my daddy to get somebody to kill your cheating-ho ass! He's a lawyer, so he knows plenty of criminals! I hate you and that bitch you're fucking, and I hope she dies slow too! I'll get both of you back, you bastard! I promise you that shit!"

Ignoring her threats, I hopped in my car and pulled out of the driveway just as her crazy ass jumped on the hood of my car. All I could do was shake my head at her shenanigans.

"Get off my car, Nita!" I didn't want to hurt her, but deep inside, I wanted to speed off so she would fall off my shit.

"No, don't leave me like this, Daryn! I love you!" She stared pitifully at me through the windshield, and I actually felt sorry for her.

Suddenly, I slammed on the brakes, and her grip on the hood slipped. She hit the concrete, but her fall wasn't hard. When she stood up, I knew that she was okay, so I drove away from her ranting and raving. It was the best thing to do. Shit, I had to leave, because I was miserable. DiDi constantly consumed my mind as well as my heart, and I wasn't going to stop until I got my woman back.

A taxi dropped DiDi off while I sat in the driveway, waiting. I'd been there for over three hours, hoping she'd finally show up. Her car had been in the same spot for days, but when I saw her luggage, I realized that she had been out of town. That was a relief, because I knew that she hadn't just been avoiding me. Maybe she had been rejuvenated on her vacation and would let me make it up to her.

She rolled her eyes when I got out of the car to help her with her bags.

"What are you doing here?" Her voice dripped with animosity, but I ignored it.

"I'm here because I love you, Di. Let me help you with your bags."

She sighed. "Nigga, I don't need your help. All I need you to do is get back in your car and get the fuck up away from me."

"Look, Ma, I broke it off with Nita, and I want to be with you."

DiDi let out a sarcastic laugh as she shook her head at me. "Daryn, you got some nerve. I don't give a flying fuck what you did. I couldn't care less, nigga. I'm so fucking done with you and the entire situation. I wasn't joking when I said that we were over. Did you see a fuckin' smile on my face? Huh?" Her face was curious as she stared me down, with her hand on her hip.

"No, but I can make it up to you."

She didn't seem convinced. "I doubt that very seriously." She let out a breath and pulled her suitcase on wheels toward her house.

"I can, and I will, baby. Just let me."

DiDi turned on her heels, and the look she flashed at me was sour as hell, like she'd just bitten into a lemon.

"There's not a motherfuckin' thing your sorry ass could do or say to make it up to me. I'm so sick of y'all niggas just doing whatever the fuck you want and thinking a bitch is supposed to just forgive and fuckin' forget. Y'all are so damn delusional, it's ridiculous. Those niggas on reality TV done got y'all twisted. You think all of us are stupid. Well, I got news for you, nigga. You ain't special. Not by a long shot. Honestly, you ain't all that. Your dick game is tired, so you gotta eat pussy. That's 'bout all you did to impress me. Now, please, get the fuck outta here before I call my brother. He wants to beat your ass, anyway."

I just looked at her. I knew that anger was talking, so I didn't even take her stinging words to heart. Her insults and threats didn't stop me from reaching in my car to retrieve her gift. Once I had her gift in my hand, I looked up and saw that she had turned her back on me again and was walking toward the steps of her crib.

"Hold up, DiDi."

That time when she turned around, I was on one knee, with a black velvet box in my hand.

She shook her head. "What are you doing, Daryn?"

"I know I fucked up, but damn it, I love you." My eyes burned with tears as I cleared my throat in an attempt to hold it together. "All I want is to spend my life with you, Ma." When I opened the box and revealed the two-and-a-half-carat princess-cut diamond engagement ring, DiDi's hard eyes didn't even soften.

"Will you marry me?" I asked, anyway, before taking the ring from the box to place it on her finger.

She let me slide the ring on but still didn't give me an answer. Instead, she stared at me and then at the ring as it sat sparkling on her ring finger. With a menacing glow in her eyes, she took the ring off and threw it across the street. Without saying a word, she turned and left me outside to simmer on that shit. My pride was all fucked up as she closed the door on me and my proposal. With my heart on my sleeve, I went to retrieve the ring. One thing I wasn't going to do was give up. I loved DiDi, and I knew that she was hurt. It would take some time for her to forgive me, but I was determined to convince her to do just that.

Kadijah

Sipping my wine on the sofa, I had to laugh at Daryn's trifling ass. After dealing with him and that nigga Omari, I was numb to the bullshit. The fuckery was real, and I realized then that any man other than my brother wasn't even worth my time. Yet I still loved a fine-ass chocolate man. *Mmm.* That shit was my weakness. I couldn't let it consume me, though. It was time to face reality and start my career. My vacation was officially over.

The sound of my phone ringing made me take my eyes away from the TV screen. I was watching *Scandal*, and although I liked that show, I resented the side chick role. Some of us didn't choose to be the chick on the side. Sometimes sorry-ass men made that choice for us. It was that nigga Omari, and although I wanted to block his number, I hadn't done it yet. Instead, I pressed the IGNORE button.

After that, he called three more times. Finally, there was silence, and I leaned back on the comfortable sofa. When my phone rang again, I realized that it was Tamia, so I went ahead and answered.

"What's up, *chica*?" I asked after pressing the TALK button.

"Shit, chillaxing. Nicole's on three-way. What's up with you?"

"Sipping and watching *Scandal*. Y'all won't believe what the fuck just happened."

"What, bitch?" Nicole chimed in, ready for the tea.

I told them all about that nigga Daryn's bogus-ass proposal, and they fell out in a fit of laughter.

"Was he serious?" Tamia asked, surprised.

"Hell to the yeah," I said.

"And you really threw the fuckin' ring?" Nicole asked. "I would've kept that shit and sold that mufucka."

"Shit. Fuck him and his ring." I sipped my drink.

"You talked to Omari?" Tamia had to bring up the dreaded subject of the rude boy I was smitten with.

"No, and I don't plan to. He's a gazillion miles away. Life goes on."

Nicole cleared her throat. "I noticed how sad you looked the last few days we were there, boo. You like him more that you're admitting."

"It ain't that. I just . . ."

"Like him more than you're admitting," Tamia said, cosigning.

They laughed, but I didn't join in. "Fuck y'all. Let me get back to my show."

"Well, damn, you salty bitch," Nicole snapped.

"I know," Tamia agreed.

I felt bad, because it wasn't their fault that niggas weren't shit.

"I'm sorry. I'll hit y'all up tomorrow," I said.

We ended the call, and I went back to watching TV, but I wasn't really paying it any attention. The next day I'd get back to my job search. That would be my focus, not a man. It was time to get on with my shit, and love wasn't part of the plan. The only thing was that damn Omari was heavy on my mind.

Chapter 14

Omari

As I pulled up to the house that used to be my safe haven, I sat there shaking my head and thinking. I wasn't prepared to go in there and face Angela. I had played out different scenarios in my head while I was driving. I had even thought about begging for her forgiveness but had quickly dismissed that idea. Truth of the matter was, I hadn't been in love with Angela in years. I would be lying if I said she wasn't a beautiful woman. Matter of fact, she was a bad-ass bitch. But that was all she had to offer, and I needed more.

I wanted a woman who respected her man, and Angela had no respect. She could be the sweetest person, but the minute we got into an argument, she would tell me to suck her asshole or suck my mother's pussy. So many times, I had got so close to smacking the fuck out of her ass, but she was my yutes' mother, and I had tried hard not to take it there with her. I knew that there was no excuse for the way I'd behaved the other day, but I honestly was done and just wanted out of the marriage.

I got out of the car and opened the gate, then got back in the car and pulled into the driveway. I parked, turned the music down, then turned the car off and got out again. My heart was beating heavily, not because I was scared of my wife, but because I was scared of what I might do to her if she popped off at me. I opened the front door and walked in. The house was quiet, which was strange, because normally the kids would hear me pull in and rush to me. After I took a few steps, it hit me that today was Monday and the kids were in school. I let out a sigh of relief, because at least I could shower and get my thoughts together before I talked to them.

"Where the fuck you tink you goin'?" Angela stepped in my path before I could walk into the kids' bathroom.

"Yo, B, get outta my way."

"Get outta yo' way? What kind of shit is that? You spent the weekend wit' your rassclaat whore, and now you walk yo' ass up in here, telling me to get outta your way?" She lifted her hand.

Slap! Slap! Slap!

"What the fuck you doin'?" I grabbed her aggressively and threw her against the wall.

"Get off of me, you old, stupid-ass nigga!" she yelled as she tried to get loose from my tight grip.

"Calm yo' pussyclaat down. I don't want to hurt you, B."

"I swear to God, you better let me go!" she said as tears rolled down her face. The feisty Angela wasn't looking so feisty, after all. I could see the hurt in her eyes. I couldn't take it, so I let her go.

It was a stupid idea to do that, because the minute I turned my back to walk out, I felt an object hit my head, and I stumbled. I caught my balance and looked up to see her coming at me once again with a broomstick. I jumped out of the way, then grabbed her little body up, and that time, I slammed her on the floor.

"Nooo!" she screamed.

"What the fuck yo' problem is? I told yo' ass, I don't wanna hurt you, B. Why do you act like this, Angela?"

"I fucking hate you. How could you treat me like this? All because of some bitch you don't even fucking know. I hate you! I swear, you will never see my fucking kids again," she spat, her venom spilling out.

"Aye, pussyclaat gyal, you threatening me wit' my kids?
Don't you ever threaten me! Before I lose my kids, they'll
find yo' ass at the bottom of causeway. You hear me,
bitch?"

I was done for real. It didn't make any sense to stand
here arguing with a bitch who had hate toward me.
Everybody that knew me knew my kids were my life, and
threatening me was the last thing she should've done.

I left the house, jumped in my car, started it up, and
backed up out of the driveway. I needed to go before I
ended up killing that bitch!

Angela

For days I had waited for Omari to walk in the door
and apologize for cheating on me. I just knew that he had
made a mistake, and that there was no way my husband
and best friend was going to choose a Yankee gyal over
me.

I was dozing off when I heard the grill open. I wanted
to jump up and meet him at the door, but the voice in my
head uttered, "Bitch, stop tripping," so I played it cool.
But after a few minutes I figured he wasn't planning on
facing me. I didn't wait; I got up and confronted that ass.
This nigga thought he was gonna walk up in here like shit
was sweet between us.

I was never the kind of bitch to be scared of no fuck
nigga, so I stepped to that nigga and slapped his face
off. I knew he was no punk, but I also knew how he felt
about putting his hands on a female. So I knew there
was no way he would hit me back. That fuck nigga had
me fooled, because he threw up against the wall while
squeezing my arm. I tried to get out of his grip, but I
couldn't get my arm away. I was furious once he let

me go. I swear on my mama's soul, I wanted to grab a kitchen knife and cut that nigga's dick off clean. That way, that ho—or any other ho, for that matter—would not be able to enjoy it anymore. I glanced at the broom and then grabbed it. Without hesitation, I knocked him in the head with it. I watched as he stumbled. That was my cue to run, but my legs wouldn't move.

I wasn't scared of that nigga, so I stood there. A fucking mistake, because that nigga grew some motherfucking big balls. He picked me up and slammed me onto the tiled floor. I cringed as my small body frame made contact with the floor. A single tear fell from my eye as I noticed what that fuck nigga had just done. I grabbed my side as an excruciating pain ripped through me. I wasn't sure if I was hurt, but I tried not to show a bit of fear. I watched as he walked out, without even checking to see if I needed medical care. So much for him being a loving husband. I heard him pull out of the driveway, and I then broke down. By no means was I crying over that bitch-ass nigga; I was crying because I had really thought that no matter what, he loved me. I had really been hoping that it was only a phase, but I had seen the coldness in his eyes, and I knew that he had no love left for me.

After crying a fucking river, I picked myself up off the floor. I walked into the kitchen, poured a glass of ginger wine, and swallowed it in one gulp. I poured me another glass and did the same as before. I quickly dried the tears that were left. My mother had always told me not to cry over spilled milk. That nigga had done fucked with the wrong bitch's heart, because when I'd taken those vows, for better or worse, I meant every goddamned word, and my husband would soon understand what 'till death do us part' meant.

***

After not being able to sleep the night before, because of all the shit that was on my mind, I was up bright and early. I ironed the kids' clothes and made them breakfast. It was crazy how this nigga had fucked me and made these babies but could walk out on them in the blink of an eye. Which part of the fucking game was that for real?

"Mommy, when is Daddy coming home?" one of my babies asked.

Her question kind of caught me off guard, and I really wanted to say, "Your daddy is out being a ho," but I looked at my innocent little child and knew she wouldn't understand any of it.

"Baby, Daddy is working really hard. He will be home soon." I smiled at her.

"Okay. Can I call him?"

"Listen, you have to eat and go to school right now, but yes, you can call him later."

It broke my heart that my kids loved that bastard that much and he would allow a piece of pussy to come between him and his family.

After I got the kids on the bus, I decided to stop by Mama's house. I'd been thinking long and hard about what she said to me the other day. I didn't believe in obeah, or voodoo, but I was desperate, and I needed help holding on to my husband. I knew that it was early and that Mama would probably cuss me out, but I needed the info for that man she always bragged about.

I got to her house, banged on her grill, and waited to hear her big-ass mouth yelling.

"What the hell you want this early? Is something wrong with my grandbabies?" she said when she opened the grill.

"No, Mama, your grandbabies are fine, but I need that man in St. James's number," I answered as I walked in the house.

"What man yuh talkin' 'bout, dear?"

"The obeah man," I said, kind of annoyed, because I felt like she was being sarcastic.

"Oh, okay. I see you finally come to yo' senses."

"All right, Mama. I don't need no speech. Just gi' mi the address and 'im number."

"Child, lower your damn voice in my house."

I didn't bother to respond; I just rolled my eyes and waited for her to give me the info.

After she gave me a piece of paper with the obeah man's name, address, and phone number, I thanked her and rushed out of the house. I hurried home so that I could take a quick shower and get on my way. I didn't want to waste another second, because time was of the essence. I wasn't sure how good the man was, but after hearing my mother brag about him for years, I was pretty sure he was good at whatever he did. I just hoped he could change my husband's mind and bring him home to his family.

I was already feeling better as I took a shower. So much so that I started playing with my pussy. See, I knew that American bitch could never fuck my husband like I could. Those bitches were known to be scared of Jamaican men and their big wood, but we Jamaican bitches knew how to ride on the big wood, and we knew how to please our men. I inserted my index finger all the way inside me.

"Aargh," I groaned as I slow wined on my finger. I swung my head back as I entered a world of pure ecstasy. Within minutes, I exploded on my finger. I slid it out and licked off my sweet juice. Now that I had let off some of the pressure, I was ready to take on the world. I washed off and got out of the shower. I was on a mission today.

I set the home alarm and locked up the house. I'd never been to St. James, but that didn't deter me from going. I decided to use my GPS so that I wouldn't get lost in the country. I was a city girl and didn't know my way around the rural parts of Jamaica.

The entire ride, my mind was all over the place. I remembered the first time my husband fucked me. I also recalled all the times that I thought he was cheating. Then I thought about how I had to beat that one bitch's ass and ended up getting locked up. The memories of the hurt he had put me through quickly turned my heart ice cold.

The GPS alerted me that I'd reached my destination. I quickly wiped my tears away. There was no room for emotions right now. I took a quick glance at my surrounding, and all I saw was old, broken-down huts. Nothing like the big house that I was used to in Kingston. I turned the car off, grabbed my purse, and got out.

"Mawning, pretty lady."

I clutched my purse closer to my chest and turned around to face this dirty-looking dude with missing teeth. He was smiling at me.

"Good morning. I'm looking for . . ." I dug into my purse and grabbed the piece of paper on which Mama had jotted down the obeah man's name, number, and address. "Elder Randy," I said.

"Well, you're in the right place, pretty lady. 'Im my uncle. Me will take you to 'im."

I shot him a dirty look and was about to turn him down, but I quickly reminded myself why I was there in the first place.

"Sure." I squeezed out a smile.

I followed closely behind him as we walked up a rocky dirt road. After passing a few houses, I followed him into the yard in front of a modest house. I saw two big-ass dogs run from around the back of the house.

"Get back, Caine and Abel," he yelled out to them. "Unc, I got a pretty lady here to see yuh!" he called.

Within seconds, I saw a tall, bearded man dressed in a dress, with a head wrap on his head. "May I help you!" he yelled over the sound of the barking dogs.

"Yes. I want to talk to you in private!" I yelled back.

"I got her, nephew. Make sure Caine and Abel get their lunch. Come on, miss."

I stepped up the stairs and walked into the modest dwelling.

"Si dung, what bring yuh to my neck of the woods?"

"Well, I need your help. I have a serious matter that I need you to deal with for me. . . ."

Two and half hours later, with twenty-five thousand Jamaican dollars spent, I got into my car and pulled off. I was very happy with Elder Randy and the help he was providing. Now it was time to sit back and see how long that bitch was going to be in my man's life. I had also paid the obeah man to tie Omari to me, which meant my husband would be back with me and would never leave me, or his children, ever again.

Chapter 15

Kadijah

Me, Nicole, and Tamia were watching *Love & Hip Hop: Atlanta* at my crib while sipping on some strong-ass margaritas. I'd whipped them up with plenty of 1800. That heifer Joseline was getting on my last damn nerve, and so was Stevie J., with that damn Puerto Rican Princess bullshit.

"I'm so sick of that broad, with her horse-lookin' ass. She makes women think sex and the physical aspect are the only things there are to offer in a relationship. Like pussy is the only way to keep a man. That's why these dumb bitches out here dyin' for a fat ass. Fuck that shit. Mine is all natural, and I can out-twerk all those stiff-ass, fake-booty hoes." With that said, I stood up and started twerking.

My girls got up to join in, and we all burst into a fit of laughter.

A minute later, a commercial came on, and so we all sat back down on the sofa.

"So, how's the job hunt going?" Tamia asked as she sipped her drink.

"It's going good. I have two interviews this week. One on Wednesday and one on Thursday," I replied, filling them in. It was a good thing I was on vacation from both of my jobs until next week.

"That's good, boo. Where?" Nicole questioned me as she picked up her vibrating phone. She took a look at the screen, frowned, and put the phone back down.

"One is at Pappadeaux, and the other is at the Ritz-Carlton downtown. Honestly, I think I'd rather work at the Ritz-Carlton. I'm trying to quit Wet Willie's and the firm soon."

"Both of those are good prospects, though, boo, so just pray that you get one of them. It's not like you have to stay at your first gig forever," Tamia said, offering her advice.

"That's true. You're right. I just want to cook great food for a living. That's all. It's time for me to get my shit on track, so I'm ready for the next chapter."

"So, what's up with Daryn and Omari?" Nicole asked.

I knew that was coming.

Giving Nicole the side eye, I changed the awkward subject. "Why ain't you answerin' your phone?" I said. I glanced down at her phone, which was still vibrating.

Daryn and Omari were both blowing my phone up, but I didn't want to talk to either of them. Well, I did want to talk to Omari, but my pride wouldn't let me. He was a married man who lived in a foreign country, so that made that shit complicated. Daryn was just a pain in my ass that I couldn't seem to get rid of.

"Because I don't want to talk to the nigga that's callin' me," Nicole spat.

"Must be Champ," Tamia said, referring to Nicole's ex-boyfriend. She laughed.

Nicole nodded. "You already know. He's trying so hard, but I don't go backward. Only forward. My pussy's too good for his non-fucking ass, anyway."

I couldn't help but laugh at that. Champ owned a sports bar in downtown Atlanta but had played for the Hawks for two years. After a knee injury fucked up his second year, he was off the team. Nicole was only after his pockets, anyway, so once his contract was done, she was too. She had always said that the sex was awful, but like most women, we'd overlook that for financial stability. The thing was, how long could a bitch go without some good dick?

"To be honest with you, Nicole, I think me and you both have had bad luck in relationships because we're going after the wrong thing," I said. "Not that I'm looking for it or even want it, but what happened to being with someone because of genuine love? Not because of what they can buy or how many cars they have or . . ."

"What is wrong with you, woman?" Nicole asked me. "Did you bump your head when you got into it with that Jamaican bitch?"

"No. I just know that there's more to life than who can fuck the best or how much money a man makes."

"And when did you come to that conclusion?" Nicole asked.

Shaking my head, I said, "I don't know. It just makes sense to me. All this time, I've been the side chick, without even wanting to be. That has to be because I'm giving off the wrong vibe. Maybe men see me only as some bitch to just have sex with. What if I'm makin' men think that I'm only good for one thing? If I gave off the wife vibe, shit would be different."

Tamia shook her head. "It's not about that. I'm sayin' that because I know. I'm the one who is in a relationship. Sometimes I wonder if he is with me only because I'm so laid back and shit. It makes me wonder if he wants to marry me only because I have his child. Men marry women like me, but they cheat on women like me with women like you two."

I sighed. "No, he's marrying you because he loves you and that's what he wants to do. I'm offended by your last statement, though. I mean, what the fuck are you tryin'a say? It's not like we're some hoes who're down for whatever and shit."

Nicole spoke up. "Right. Shit. You act like we only side chick material. We both do have some type of self-respect."

"I'm not sayin' that you don't, but you both are more . . . free spirited and sexually open than me. Not only that, but you're both more . . . outgoing. I've always been the quiet one and—"

"Okay. Whatever," Nicole spat as her phone vibrated again.

"Damn, you need to talk to him." I gave her a sympathetic look.

"Fuck him." Nicole stood her ground.

"I'm just sayin'," I threw in before my own phone started ringing.

"Hello," I answered when I saw my mother's number flash across my phone's screen.

"Baby girl, you need to come to DeKalb Medical now."

"Why, Mommy? What's wrong?" I asked.

"Look, baby, just come. It's the one in Lithonia."

"I know which one you're talkin' about. Just tell me what's goin' on," I said.

"When you get here, I will."

Tears burned my eyes. "'Kay, ma. I'll be there in a minute."

"What's going on?" Tamia asked me with wide eyes.

I filled her in, and she and Nicole were ready to get me to the hospital.

"C'mon. Let's go." Nicole grabbed her purse, and we filed out of my place, leaving the TV on.

When we were in Nicole's whip, I could no longer hold back my emotions. "What if it's my brother? You know he's still involved in that street shit." I began to sob uncontrollably.

"Don't panic, DiDi," Tamia said as she flashed a compassionate look my way. "You don't know what's going on yet."

"But I could tell from my mom's voice that it's bad. She didn't have to tell me what it was for me to know that. I know her." My sobs became even more uncontrollable as Nicole sped up.

"Don't get pulled over for speeding, bitch. We gotta get her to the hospital. Slow down," Tamia told her.

"Shut up and let me drive, ho. If we get stopped, I'll just flash these big old boobs. It works every time."

"But what if a female cop stops us?" Tamia countered.

"Shit, we're in Atlanta. She might like boobs too," Nicole answered.

I couldn't help but laugh, despite what was possibly going on. "I love y'all bitches. For real," I told them as I laughed and cried at the same time.

When we made it to the hospital, I rushed inside and saw my mother and my brother standing there, with worried looks on their faces. So, it wasn't him. That made me feel relieved, but then it dawned on me that *somebody* was in the hospital. *But who?* Then I saw Imani, but I didn't see Cam. What was really going on?

When Jameel and my mom spotted me, they both hurried in my direction.

"Where's Cam?" I asked, going into an instant panic.

"Sis, it was crazy, yo," Jameel began. "Them niggas came to the spot and shit. They started shootin' and—"

"What the fuck happened!" I screamed, ready for him to get to the point. "Where's my nephew?"

"He . . . he's in surgery. He got shot in the stomach," my mother said, finishing the story for him.

My legs gave out on me, and next thing I knew, I was on the floor. The tears wouldn't stop, and I didn't want anybody to touch me. My friends tried to console me, with the help of my mom, but I pushed them all away. I looked at Jameel, and suddenly my heart was filled with hate for him. Anger took over the love I had for my brother.

"This is all your fault!" I yelled, lashing out at him. "You and that bitch!"

Imani looked at me as she wiped her eyes. "What the fuck did you say?"

"You heard me, bitch! If you and my brother wasn't involved in the bullshit that y'all do, this wouldn't have happened. The both of you need to grow the fuck up. If Cam doesn't make it out of this, you're gonna pay for it. I promise you that shit."

"Whoa! Calm down, DiDi. They're going through enough," my mother said, defending Jameel and Imani.

All I could do was shake my head at her. My mother was always taking Jameel's side because he threw her money here and there from his hustle. She had talked all that shit about dirty money at first, but when it started paying her bills, she'd changed her tune.

Although I'd always helped my mother when I could, it meant so damn much more to her when Jameel did. She'd retired from her job, and both of us made sure that she was good. However, being that Jameel spent money like water, he would give her more than I did. That was because even with two jobs, I couldn't afford what he could. Obviously, it wasn't worth it, because my nephew was in the hospital, fighting for his life.

"I'm going to shut up about it, but you both know that you're to blame. You also know that the police will be here soon to question you. What you gonna tell them? Huh?" I said, with fresh tears in my eyes.

"It ain't what you think, sis." Jameel's eyes pleaded for me to understand. "That shit wasn't even about what I do or don't do. Those fools were there to rob me. That shit could've been random as hell."

I shook my head. "We both know that shit wasn't random, Meel. Don't fool yourself, bruh. Your son's life is hangin' by a thread because of the lifestyle you live. It's that simple. I've been tellin' you that for years. Then the triflin' bitch you're with ain't no better. That's right, ho. I'm talkin' about you! You're probably the reason some niggas were there to rob him. We all know how you are! You the type of bitch who only cares about yourself. You set my brother up, didn't you? You could've at least made sure that my nephew wasn't there, you money-hungry bitch!"

I ran toward Imani, ready to clock that ho upside her head. It didn't matter to me that she was supposed to be feeling some type of way about Cam getting shot. She wasn't a good mother, and she had never been. If it weren't for me and my mom, Cam wouldn't have a mother figure in his life. My brother was the best parent between the two of them, but the street shit he continued to do put my nephew at risk.

The reason I didn't like Imani was that she was ratchet as hell. Not only did she not give a damn about my nephew, but she also didn't give a damn about my brother. She was a nasty-ass broad who'd always been known to fuck any nigga who had a little paper. It just so happened that she got knocked up by my brother, but the motherly instinct had never kicked in. Not only that, but she was known for setting niggas up to get robbed.

She was with my brother and all, but that didn't mean that she hadn't got one of her side niggas to try to rob him. Maybe the plan was for her to get some money that Jameel didn't want to give her. He'd told me that lately, he'd been cutting her off money-wise, because she always had her hand out.

"Chill out, DiDi. Damn." Jameel held on to me.

Imani looked at me like I was crazy. "You've lost it, bitch! For real! You need to be upstairs, on the mental ward!"

"Fuck you! You don't even deserve to procreate, bitch! If it wasn't for my brother and my nephew, you would've got your ass whupped!" I snarled.

"They're gonna kick you out of here," my mother said to me in a hushed tone as security made their way over.

"Ma'am, you're going to have to calm down or leave," a tall man said to me in a calm voice. He had a medium build and dark brown skin.

Thinking of my nephew, I put my hands up in surrender and cooperated. "Okay. I'm good."

Taking a deep breath, I calmed down and headed toward the exit. Tamia and Nicole followed me.

"Look, we know you're mad, but you have to think of Cam," Tamia said.

I sighed. "That's why I'm mad. My brother's stupid as hell over that broad. I ain't never liked her, and although I blame my brother too, I know this shit is her fault."

My phone rang inside my purse just then, and I fished it out. Damn. I didn't recognize the number. It was a 404 number, so I answered in case it was a job I'd applied for.

After taking a deep, calming breath, I said, "Hello."

"DiDi, mi so glad you answered." Omari's deep voice filled my ears.

What the fuck? How the hell is he calling me from an Atlanta number?

"This is not a good time." I sighed. "And how are you callin' me from a four-oh-four number?"

He cleared his throat. "I got a Google Voice account since you wouldn't answer my calls. Something told mi

that you'd answer a four-oh-four number. The Internet's
Jah blessing."

"Well, I have a lot going on, and I really don't have time
to talk to you right now. I hope you're workin' shit out
with your wife, because what we had is over. It was just
sex, so I don't know why—"

"It wasn't just sex, and you know it. Stop fooling yourself," he said, cutting me off.

I was taken aback, but I shook it off. He was right. It
was way more than sex, because I found myself thinking
about him all the time. Shit, I could even remember the
smell of his cologne.

"Even if it was more than sex, you're married. That
means you need to leave me alone."

"No, that means nothing. I'm leaving her."

I rolled my eyes. "And? Why do I care?"

"Because mi was g'wan leave her, anyway. It's just
that . . . meetin' you made mi brave enough to do it. I
love mi yute and all, but mi gotta do mi. Mi not happy
wit' her and . . ."

"Look, like I said, it's not a good time, Omari." I watched
as two men in suits entered the hospital.

They had to be detectives. Nicole and Tamia were both
looking at me like they were anxious to ask me a million
questions. The thing was, I didn't have time to talk about
my conversation with Omari. My nephew was a more
pressing issue at the moment, and I was more concerned
about him.

"Oh, mi sorry. Is every ting okay?"

"No. My three-year old nephew was shot, and he's in
surgery."

"Damn," he said under his breath. "Mi sorry ta hear dat.
For real. Mi send prayers to you and ya family. Jah bless."

"Thank you," I managed to say.

"Promise ya keep mi posted. No matter what happened between us . . . mi care, ya know."

Letting out a sigh, I knew that it was time to end the call. "Yeah, okay. I appreciate that, but I'll have to talk to you later."

"Okay. Mi understand. Call mi later."

I pressed the END button on my phone without saying anything else and rushed inside the hospital before my besties could start with the questions. My phone rang again, but that time I sent whoever it was straight to voice mail and headed over to my brother, who was talking to the men in suits that I'd just seen. All I cared about was my nephew. I sent up a prayer for him. If he didn't make it, I didn't know what I would do.

Chapter 16

Omari

I didn't feel like going all the way back to Ochi, so I decided to crash at my man's house. See, Garey was my nigga from another mother. We'd been friends since we both attended Ardenne High School. If a nigga fucked with him, best believe they had to fuck with me too.

I knew that he always had my back, so when I grabbed my stuff and walked out of the house, I already knew where I was heading.

"Yo, boss man, I'm at the door," I said as I stood outside with the bag of clothes that I'd grabbed.

"A'ight, brethren."

He opened the door, and I walked in.

"Yo, I need to crash for a few days, until I find a place." I threw the bag on the floor and gave him dap.

"Damn, mi genna, wha happen between yuh and Angela?"

"Man, the B trippin'. Some shit popped off in Ochi the other day, and she wildin' out."

"Damn, you kno' you my dawg, but Angela is a good woman, so mi nuh 'ave nuh idea why yuh treat har like dat."

I quickly turned around to face that nigga. I was shocked that he would even say some shit like that to me without even hearing the full story.

"Wha the fuck you mean, dawg? Wha mek yuh jump to dis conclusion without even knowin' the situation?" I yelped in a high-pitched tone.

"Calm down, bro. I mean no harm. I was just saying dat Angela seems like a good woman. We a' man, and sometimes we can treat dem a certain way. Yuh my family, so yuh know we riding, no matter what. Come on. Put yo' tings in di room."

I was irritated as fuck by his statement, but I needed somewhere to crash. *Come tomorrow, I'm goin' find me somewhere else to live. 'Cause something about this nigga ain't right*, I told myself.

That wasn't the first time he'd said some off-the-wall shit. In my opinion, he was always defending Angela. If I didn't know better, I would think they were fooling around, but I quickly dismissed that idea, because that nigga might still be a virgin. Don't get me wrong. He kept a gang of bitches around him, but he wasn't fucking nothing. Definitely not my wife. He already knew how we rolled. I quickly dismissed that idea and put my bag in the room.

We chatted it up for a little while, and then I bounced. The minute I got in my car, my mind quickly jumped to DiDi. I'd been trying to call her, but she wasn't answering. That was when it hit me that I could get a Google Voice account with a Georgia number. I knew that was taking things to the extreme, but shit, I was a desperate man, and if I had to take desperate measures, then so be it. I wasn't going to give up that easily on Miss DiDi. I knew if I ever wanted a chance with her, I would have to leave Angela completely and show that I was serious about her. I had no problem doing that. My only thing was my kids. I didn't feel good leaving them behind. Especially not with their mama screaming about not letting me see them. Angela was only making empty threats, because she knew that I would hunt her down and kill her. I didn't play games when it involved my seeds.

***

It didn't take me long to find a two-bedroom in Greater Portmore. It wasn't the big house that I was used to living in, but it was nice. My kids' bedroom was huge, so they would be comfortable whenever they came to visit their daddy. I smiled as I took a quick glance around the room. The thought of my kids coming to stay with me without their mama made me happy.

I paid the landlord and got the keys. I was too happy to move out of that nigga's house also. After that day, I just couldn't rock with that nigga no more. Then again, he might've been avoiding me, because he barely came home the entire time that I was there. Either that or he had found him a bitch.

I wasted no time hiring someone to come in and clean up the new place. After that I bought furniture and furnished the place. It was my first time having my own place since I'd moved in Angela, and I had to say that it was peaceful. I didn't have to hear her constant nagging and fussing at a nigga just because she had a mouth.

As soon as the phone was installed, I grabbed it. I had got the magicJack installed instead, because I had a Georgia number and I could call wherever I wanted in the United States for a flat fee that I paid monthly. Also, if DiDi ever decided to call me, she wouldn't have to get a phone card. She could just call me directly, without accruing any extra charges.

I quickly dialed her phone number, because I was eager to hear her sexy Yankee accent. When she answered the phone, she sounded a bit annoyed. I instantly felt like shit when I realized that she wasn't happy to hear from me. I still stayed on the phone and quizzed her about what was going on. She quickly told me that her nephew was hurt and she was at the hospital. Here I was, being selfish, and she was going through a family crisis. The phone call lasted less than five minutes, but it made my day. I knew we hadn't spent that much time together, but my feelings for her were very strong.

Angela

I was feeling more relaxed after visiting the obeah man. I had faith that he would bring my husband back to me. I hoped Omari didn't think I was just going to walk away from what we'd built. I remembered when I picked up his broke ass. Shit, all the bwoy had was a pair of drawers with holes in them and a pair of old, beat-up Clarks that were leaning to the side. I didn't trip, though. I still fucked him and upgraded his ass. So there it was, that bwoy owed me his fucking life.

I had been getting up early for the past few days. I had been vomiting and hadn't been able to keep anything down. I thought I'd caught a stomach virus, but I quickly dismissed that idea. After the kids left for school, I decided to drop in on my doctor. Maybe he had a better idea of what was going on with me. On my way to the doctor, all sorts of thoughts ran through my head. I hoped I wasn't pregnant, because it had been years since Omari had come inside me, but that fool Garey had busted in me the last time we fucked. God knows I didn't need those problems.

I parked my car and walked in the building.

"Good morning. I want to do a walk-in for a pregnancy test," I told the receptionist.

"Okay. Give me your name. And that will be two thousand dollars to see the doctor."

I gave her my info, paid her, and sat nervously in one of the seats. I glanced over at the two little children sitting in the seat beside me. I swear, I didn't want any more children, but if it would help me keep my husband, then so be it.

After a while, they put me in a private room to wait for the doctor. The doctor came, and I told him about what was going on. He ordered a urine test. I sat there waiting until my results came back, and it was confirmed that I was about four weeks pregnant. I thanked them and left the office. Well, my greatest fear was confirmed, but I wasn't sad or anything like that. Matter of fact, my future couldn't have looked brighter, and my mood had changed dramatically. Life had a way of throwing lemons my way, but I planned on using those lemons to make lemonade.

I got back in my car, pulled out of the parking lot, and turned my music up. I rubbed my stomach. I was eager to tell my husband that we were having a baby. I grabbed my cell and called his phone, but it went straight to voice mail. My mood quickly changed again. Why the fuck that bwoy had his phone off in the daytime? Shit. Anything could've been wrong with me or his damn kids. That bwoy was really living foul. I threw the phone on the seat and turned the music up louder. Lady Saw's "Wife a Wife" lyrics were pounding through my speakers. I rocked to the beat and let the lyrics serenade my brain.

When I got back home, I decided to clean up and wash some clothes. Lately, I hadn't been doing much of anything. I wanted the place to be clean when my husband decided to come home. I opened up the grill and turned the music up loud.

Jah Cure's voice blasted through the surround-sound system.

What will take my love to show you
Am still in love with u
What will take my love to show you
How much my love is true

I was feeling that song so much, so I rewinded it and replayed it a few times. Maybe that wasn't a good idea, because I couldn't stop the tears from falling like Dunn's River Falls.

I was so caught up in my feelings that I was startled when he walked through the door. I quickly dried my tears and smiled. Damn. I guess the obeah had started to take effect and my man was home for good.

"Yo, Angela, you a'ight?"

"Yes, I'm fine, now that you're here." I walked toward him to give him a "welcome home" hug.

"Man, what you doing?" He grabbed my hands and shoved me away.

My first instinct was to slap his ass, but I knew that wouldn't help the situation right now. I had to humble myself until I got that nigga right where I wanted him to be.

"What's wrong, baby?" I asked in a soft tone.

"Angela, please. We need to talk. I am moving out, and I want shared custody of the kids."

I blinked twice and searched my mind. I wondered if I had heard that nigga right. I looked at him, trying to get confirmation. When I got none, I spoke.

"What did you just say?"

"Listen, B, I know it's hard for you, but I'm tired of living like this. It's been years that I haven't been happy. I try to stay around for the kids because I didn't have no father around when I was growing up. But I can't do it anymore."

"Yuh piece of ungrateful bitch! I picked yuh up when yuh nuh 'ave nothin'. I helped yuh to be weh yuh deh today, and here yuh are, tellin' me yuh want a divorce? How can yuh do this? Our vows said, 'Fa betta or worse,'" I cried out. My chest tightened as I gripped it. I was hurting inside and had no idea how to stop the pain.

"I'm sorry, B. I never thought we would end up like dis, but we can't go on living in this unhappiness. I just know it's best for us to get a divorce and still raise the children."

"I love yuh. Please don't do this. I swear, I'll give you anything yuh want. Please don't leave us. I know that Yankee gyal got into yuh head. But, baby, dat bitch can't love yuh like mi." I dropped to my knees and grabbed his leg.

"Angela, get up and stop behaving like dat. Dis has nothin' to do with no other woman. All we do is argue and fight. Yuh kno' dis been goin' on for years now. I will never stop loving yuh, but I'm not in love with yuh."

I used all my might to stand up. I wanted to face this old, wicked-ass bwoy, with his old, ungrateful ass.

"What di fuck yuh saying to me? You owe mi. Matter of fact, yuh owe mi yuh fucking life. I took yuh up, dutty bwoy, and mad yuh into somebody. I did, Omari. Not dat dutty gyal a foreign," I spat.

"Yo, B, I'ma mek all dis slide, 'cause yuh hurting. And again, I'm sorry it turn out like dis."

"Omari, yuh can't go. I found out earlier I'm pregnant. I'm having your child." I was desperate.

"Wha the bumbuclaat you just sey?" He looked at me with a serious expression.

"Yuh hear mi right. Mi go a di doctor today and find out sey mi a breed. Si di paper ya." I walked into my room, grabbed the paper with my test results, and threw it at him.

He grabbed the paper and stared at it. I wished I had my phone so I could take a picture of him. His facial expression was priceless.

"Dis can't be. . . ." He paused. "Ain't no way. It's been years that I don't cum inside of yuh. So how yuh a tell me yuh pregnant?"

"Wha di pussyclaat you saying? Yuh is di only man mi fucking, suh mi know if mi a breed. It's your pickney!" I shouted at him.

"Angela, calm down. Mi nah sey a nuh my pickney. I just don't know how it's possible."

"Yuh is di only man I sleep wit' since we got together," I insisted.

"Angela, mi nuh really wah nuh more pickney. So find out how much for yuh to get an abortion, and I'll pay for it, B."

Shocked would be an understatement! Did my husband just tell his wife to kill his unborn child? This wasn't the Omari that I was used to. I couldn't believe that bitch's pussy had him like that, or was it the fact that she sucked his wood? My chest was burning, and I stood there with my mouth open.

"Omar . . ." I said, trying to speak, but I couldn't get any more words out. Instead, the tears rolled down my cheeks. I tried to search his eyes for a little bit of warmness, but I saw none. He seemed distant, like his body was there, but his mind was not present.

"Yuh know what, Omari? Fuck yuh and dat dutty gyal. Mi nuh need yuh at all. And when dat bitch leave yuh, nuh pussyclaat look my way. Get outta mi house," I screamed from the bottom of my soul.

"Mi need fi get mi clothes, B."

"What clothes? The ones wey mi buy? Even the drawers on yo' ass a mi buy it. You don't 'ave shit in here. Get outta mi pussyclaat house, dutty bwoy!" I leapt toward him.

He grabbed me, shoved me to the side, and ran out the door. I ran to the door, but I was too late. He jumped in his car and took off.

"Nooo!" I fell to my knees, crying, as a sharp pain ripped through my chest. I grabbed my stomach. How could he just walk away from me and his child like that? I cried out more, thinking there had to be a way to pay my husband back for all the pain he had put me through.

Chapter 17

Kadijah

Two days had passed since my little man Cam got shot because of his parents' reckless-ass lifestyle. I swear, I thought about seeking full custody of him if he survived. Of course, I didn't want to put my own brother out there, because he was already in a lot of heat. However, he wasn't the priority at the moment.

Cam had been stabilized, but his condition was still considered critical. At that point, it was touch and go, and we didn't even know if he would survive. He was only three years old, and his delicate little body couldn't take that bullet wound. It had split his small intestines and damaged his spleen. The surgery had taken hours, but, thank God, he was still breathing and his teeny heart was still beating.

"How's Cam?" Tamia asked over the phone.

I was at home, and she was getting ready for a date night with her fiancé. I guessed she was just calling to check up on me, and I appreciated it. The thing was, I didn't really feel like talking. I had had my interview at Pappadeaux and didn't really feel good about it. It was like I was letting everything that was going on affect me.

"It's still critical, but he's stable right now. At this point, we don't know what's going to happen. Like Ma said, we gotta have faith that God will pull him through this. I just hope my brother learns his lesson. Shit, and that bitch

Imani is the worst." If only they had let me put my hands on her ass.

"I don't know why he don't see her for what she is," Tamia said and then sighed. "Should I wear pumps or sandals?"

"Sandals, bitch. Men love feet." I laughed. "Well, that is, if your toes are done."

"Bih, you already know how I do. Ain't no scalawag over here. I keep it tight and right," she told me with a giggle.

"I wouldn't have it any other way. Your fly matches my fly."

We shared a moment of comradery, and then reality set in again. What if my nephew didn't make it? I'd kill that bitch Imani. Something told me that shit was all her fault. Nothing had ever gone down like that before, and it was mighty funny that it happened when she wasn't there. *How convenient.*

"Well, boo, let me go hop in the shower. Hit me up tomorrow. 'Kay?"

"Of course. Oh, hold up. You talked to Cole?" I hadn't talked to her all day.

"Yeah. She said she had a migraine and she was going to bed. She said she called you, but it went straight to voice mail. I think you were at the hospital then."

"Oh, okay. I was." I rubbed my temples, because it felt like I was getting a headache my damn self. "I'll leave her alone, then."

"Girl, you know I gotta ask before I go, 'cause you keep on avoiding the subject."

I rolled my eyes because I knew that the questions were coming about Omari or maybe Daryn. I hadn't talked to Omari since the last time he called, and I damn sure wasn't trying to talk to Daryn. He was blocked, and he wasn't crazy enough to pop up at my crib again after I threatened to get my brother to fuck him up.

Even though I didn't want to talk about either man, I gave Tamia the go-ahead, anyway. "What?"

"What's going on with you and Omari?"

"Nothing. He's all the way in Jamaica, and I'm here. Oh, and must I remind you that he is married?" I was so annoyed, but I was trying my best not to show it.

"What about Daryn?"

"Girl, you know ain't shit goin' on with that. Look, get ready for your dinner date with your man. I'm good. There's a bottle of cabernet sauvignon in the fridge with my name on it. I'm gonna get my sip on and then get some sleep."

"Okay," she said in a skeptical voice. "I'm sorry if I'm meddling, but you're my friend and I care about you. Because of that, I'm going to give you a little advice."

Oh, boy. It was time to pour that glass of wine, so I headed to the kitchen.

"Go ahead with your advice, Mia."

I opened the refrigerator, took out the wine, pulled the cork out of the wine bottle, and filled up a wineglass. Before even walking away from the counter, I took a huge sip. *Mmm.* That shit was good. As Tamia talked, I put the bottle away and then sipped as I stood there in the kitchen.

"Please, try to get some peace of mind. I know there's a lot going on, but it's all a test. Don't bum your interview on Friday. You really want the position at the Ritz-Carlton, so don't let your personal life interfere with the professional goals that you've set for yourself. As far as Omari is concerned, I know that he's married, and I understand the issue you have with him not telling you. Still, something deep inside tells me that there's something there. I could literally see the sparks flying between you two."

"Are you finished?" I was trying to sound polite, but my question may have come off a little harsh.

"Well, damn . . . yeah."

"I'm sorry, boo. I didn't mean it like that. I just didn't want to cut you off."

"Apology accepted. Continue."

"Well, honestly, even if I wanted to go there with him, it's complicated. He said he's leaving his wife, but damn. That means he's fresh out of a relationship. And he has kids. Am I ready to deal with that? Clearly, his wife is cray cray as hell," I explained. "Then add the fact that he lives all the way in Jamaica, which is too damn far to pursue a relationship. I can't do a long-distance relationship with a man who can't be trusted. He cheated on his wife, for God's sake. Why would he be faithful to me, thousands of miles away? Not only that, but I just got out of a bullshit-ass relationship myself. I'm obviously not ready for any of that."

"I get it. I get it. You have to take the time out to get your head straight, boo. I'm going to go get ready. You take care, and call me if you need me. I don't give a fuck if it is my date night. You're my A number one, and I'm always here for you."

"Aw, that's so sweet and one hundred of you, love. Don't worry about me. I'll be fine. Love you."

"Love you too."

When I ended the call, the lonely sound of silence seemed to be suffocating. My mother was at church, and I wasn't surprised at all. I wanted to call her, but she'd texted me to tell me that she'd gone to the seven o' clock service. She'd found God and got saved when I was about fifteen years old. At that point she became a different person. She went from clubbing every weekend to spending three or more days a week in church. With what Cam was going through, it was no shock that church would be where she'd be spending her time when she wasn't at the hospital with him.

There was a knock at the door, and it kind of scared me, since I wasn't expecting anyone. Damn, I hoped it wasn't Daryn's stalker ass. When I peeked through the peephole and saw my brother standing there, I opened the door.

"I thought you were at the hospital. Who's with Cam?" I said to him immediately.

"Imani's there with him. I'm on the way back, but I had to make a run. I just decided to stop by on the way," he said as he stepped inside and closed the door behind him.

"Okay. So what's up? There's a reason you stopped by." I led him to the sofa, and we both sat down.

"I wanted to tell you to back off of Mani, yo. She's goin' through enough right now, and she don't need you comin' at her."

I just stared at my brother like he'd lost his damn mind. What had that ho done to him? Sucked his dick from the back while she played with his balls? What the fuck?

"Look, bro, I don't wanna come off wrong, but fuck that bitch. *She's* goin' through enough? What about *us*? Me and Ma spend more time with Cam than she does. Just because she pushed him out of her pussy doesn't make her a mother. I don't know what she did to you, and it's none of my business, but you need to open your eyes. She had something to do with that shit. I feel it."

He shook his head and stared back at me with the same intensity. "No she didn't. I know who did it, and I'm gon' get them mufuckas tonight. I just wanted to go check on my boy first, you know. I didn't just stop by to get on your case 'bout Imani. Shit, y'all been beefin'. That ain't nothing new. I just want you to consider what she's goin' through. She loves Cam, sis."

Tears stung my eyes as I grabbed my brother's hand. "I know you feel like you gotta get even, but please, don't do this right now. Ma would lose it if something happens to you. Please, just let Cam come through first. If we lost the both of you—"

"Don't say that. You ain't gon' lose me or Cam. I got this, and like I said, Imani had nothing to do with it, so leave her alone 'bout that shit."

His tone was very abrasive, and it made me feel some type of way.

"Why you coming at me 'bout that thot-ass bitch, though? She ain't shit, Meel, and you know it," I said. "The trick fucked your boy when you was locked up. Then she sold all your shit and stole your stash. When you gon' wake the fuck up and stop lettin' some good pussy and head blind you? You swear you hard, but when the fuck you gon' really man up?"

His eyes showed me that he was offended by what I had just said, but I didn't care. It was what the hell it was, and he needed to know how I felt about it. If my nephew lost his life, it was going to change everything. After losing my own child, I didn't know how my brother would be able to deal with that loss. No matter what he knew, I still felt in my heart that Imani was at the root of it all.

"Man up? What you think I been doin'? How you gon' even disrespect me like that? Huh? My son's laid up in a hospital, fightin' for his life, and this the shit you gon' throw at me? Your fuckin' brother?" He shook his head and let out a sarcastic chuckle. "I see where your head at, yo. It sho' ain't wit' your nephew. You hell-bent on gettin' at my baby mama, although you ain't got no proof of what you claimin'. Yeah, she ain't no angel, but that's her son lyin' in that hospital bed too. She got her shit wit' her, but she'd never do nothing to hurt our son. I don't believe that."

"Okay, I'm done. You got my word that I won't try to beat the bitch's skull in again. However, if I find out that bitch was involved, that's her ass. Straight the fuck like that." And I meant it. I'd lose all my sense and become the most uncivilized bitch Imani's ratchet ass had ever seen.

"I know she wasn't." He leaned over and kissed my cheek. "I gotta go, sis."

"Just promise me that you'll be careful . . . tonight."

"I'll be careful, sis, and please . . . don't tell Ma 'bout what's goin' on. I don't wanna stress her out more than she already is."

When he stood, I got up to walk him to the door. He put his hand on the doorknob and then turned to face me.

"Oh, my bad. How was your interview today?" he suddenly asked.

"It was okay, but I know I wasn't really into it, with what's goin' on and all."

He nodded. "You've always dreamed of bein' a chef, sis. Cam's gonna pull through, and I don't need you throwin' your dream away by worryin' 'bout him. He wouldn't want that for his favorite auntie."

I laughed. "I'm his only auntie."

Jameel grabbed me and pulled me into a hug. "I know you feel how you feel 'bout Mani, but she's misunderstood. Maybe you should just try to get to know her. You've always been too overprotective of me, and I don't think you ever gave any chick I was into a chance."

Maybe he was right, but getting chummy with that bitch wasn't on my list of plans. If he wanted me to keep the peace, I'd do that, but getting to know that ho was not an option.

"I said I'll be cordial, nigga. Don't push it."

He laughed and opened the door. "A'ight, sis. Love you."

"Love you too."

I watched as he walked to the car, and then I closed the door after he drove off. Just at that moment, my phone buzzed, letting me know that I'd received a text.

Omari: It's been days since we talked, and I'm really worried about you. Please let me know that you okay.

At that point, I needed somebody to talk to. All my friends weren't available, and my mother was worshipping the Lord. Jameel was on his way back to the hospital, and with all that he was handling, it wasn't like I could really confide in him. He had enough on his plate, and I was stressed out about the thought of him seeking revenge in a few hours.

So . . . I decided to text Omari back.

Me: I'm okay. My nephew is stable, and we're hoping for the best.

Omari: I really wanna hear your voice right now. I miss you.

My breath caught. Shit. Did I miss him too? My heart melted, and butterflies fluttered in my stomach. Why the hell did he make me feel like that?

Me: I don't know what to do when it comes to you. I tell myself to leave you alone, and here I am, going against what I know is right.

Omari: It feels right to me. Please . . . call me.

After letting out a sigh, I returned to the kitchen and thought about calling him as I finished off my glass of wine. Then I refilled my glass and thought about it some more. It wouldn't hurt to talk to him. I mean, at least he was trying to stay in touch. His interest had to surpass the pussy, because the pussy wasn't available to him. It was clear to me that our connection was more than that. Besides, I was bored and restless, and I had nobody else to talk to.

After I went into the living room and sat back down on the sofa, I sipped my drink and continued to contemplate whether I should call him or not. Then I made up my mind. Letting out a deep breath, I dialed the number that he had called me from days ago.

"Hello." His voice immediately stirred a longing deep inside of me.

Damn, I missed him too.

"Hey, Omari. Now you hear my voice, so I guess I can go."

He laughed good-naturedly. "It's not that easy to get rid of me, DiDi."

"I see," I said sarcastically.

"Yuh don't really want to get rid of me, though. Mi can feel it. Shit, mi felt it when we were together. Not only when we . . . had sex . . . but before that. The connection was dere from di moment we locked eyes. You know dat, star. Don't deny it."

"Okay, you're right, Omari. Okay. Fuck it. I admit it. We have a chemistry, but so what? You lied to me about bein' married. I'm not going to keep repeating myself about it. I don't like to be disrespected like that. I deserve more. If it's not you, it's Daryn."

"Who the fuck is Daryn?"

Oh, shit.

"My ex. We broke up right before I went to Jamaica." I filled him in on what had happened. "Now I feel like all y'all niggas ain't shit. All y'all good for is a good nut."

"And mi gave yuh a lotta good nuts, right? The wood was good as hell. Yuh know it. Yuh di one who told mi it was di best yuh ever had. Mi no make dat shit up."

I shook my head and blushed like he could see my reaction. He was right, though. The dick was hella good, but that was beside the point.

"Look, Omari, I entertained the thought of us at first, but it was the fantasy of it all. I was on a beautiful island, and I think it took over my common sense. I've heard about you Jamaican rude boys, and I should've known better. It's just . . ." I shrugged my shoulders. "I thought you were different."

He sighed. "Look, meetin' you and fallin' for you wasn't my plan. Okay? It just happened, and now we gotta do some ting 'bout it."

"No we don't. You're a million miles away, and honestly, I could never trust you."

"Come back to di island, star. I'll pay for it." He said it as if I hadn't just told him that I didn't trust him.

"You cheated on your wife with me. Why the fuck would I waste another minute with you?"

"Because yuh want to. Deep down in yuh heart, yuh know this, what's between us, is nothin' like what either of us is used to. It's irie. Mi like dis feelin'." I could hear the smile in his voice.

"Look, my nephew's in the hospital. There's a lot goin' on, and I can't leave right now, even if I wanted to. I'm not sayin' I want to."

"Right," he said thoughtfully. "A'ight. Just don't be no stranger, okay? Stay in touch wit' mi. Let's start ova and be friends."

Damn it. He was very persistent, but I kind of liked it. "Okay, I will, and bein' friends is cool."

"For now," he added.

Omari's sexy accent was really getting to me, but my thoughts drifted off to my brother. All I could do was pray that he didn't get killed.

Chapter 18

Angela

So, a bitch might fall a few times, but staying down had never been my thing. After lying down on the cold floor and crying my heart out for hours, I realized that Omari was really gone. That cold-blooded bwoy had never even turned around to check and see if I needed a glass of cold water.

I stumbled into the bathroom and decided to take a hot shower. It might help a little. But there was something about the sound of the water that triggered my tears again. I started bawling really hard, to the point where I was gasping for air. I felt my chest tighten and my airways become blocked. I held on to the side of the tub, cut the water off, and cautiously stepped out. This shit was real. I had been through breakups before, had done broken a couple of hearts my damn self, but this pain was different. I was in a daze. All of it seemed like a damn dream, and I was certain I would be waking up soon. I lay down on the bed and tried to catch my breath. At some point, I dozed off.

The nap I took earlier was everything. I woke up energized, and even though I was still heartbroken, I was no longer crying. I think that was all the crying that I was going to do over that bitch-ass nigga.

I cooked dinner for the children and got them into bed before 9:00 p.m. While I was cooking dinner, a plan popped up in my head. I knew that in order to execute it properly, I had to think clearly, without a drop of emotion.

After I made sure the children were sound asleep, I dialed my side nigga's number. It had been days since we spoke, because that nigga was very irritating to my soul. It was bad enough that I had to consider that he was possibly my baby daddy. Ugh, just the thought of that made me upset.

"Hey, babes," he answered cheerfully.

I let out a long sigh, rolled my eyes, and then answered him. "Hey, love. Wha gwaan?"

"Just deh yah, a build a vibe."

"Mi want to see yuh."

"Then nuh dat yuh fi sey mon."

"I just did. I'm here waiting on yuh," I said, and then I quickly hung up the phone.

I swear, I loved his dick and him eating my pussy, but his attitude really turned me off. Nonetheless, I would have to tolerate him for now.

About an hour later, I heard someone knocking on the back door. I knew it was him, so I got up and went to open the door. He walked in, and I wasted no time. I started kissing him passionately while unbuttoning his pants. I was getting ready to give him something that I'd never given him before. His pants dropped to his ankles, and I got down on my knees. I took his limp dick in my hand and started licking it. I tried my best to remember everything that I had seen in movies. I then took his dick in my mouth.

"Lawd have mercy, what is yuh doing, woman?" he asked as he pushed my head down on his wood. I almost choked, but I held my composure and continued sucking. "Aargh, baby. Yes, mi love it, mon," he groaned.

"Be quiet. The kids in dere, yuh know," I said, a little irritated.

I clamped down on it and sucked harder until I felt his wood harden. I knew he was about to cum, so I massaged his wood up and down real fast. I wanted him to hurry up so I could be done with that shit. Sperm shot out and into my mouth. I didn't want to swallow it, so I got up and ran into the bathroom. I quickly washed my mouth out and gargled with mouthwash. I heard the bathroom door open, and he was standing in front of me, with his wood still rock hard.

"Woman, yuh 'ave no idea what yuh just did to me," he said and chuckled.

"Don't worry, babes. I 'ave plenty more of did fa yuh."

By the time I could get those words out, he got behind me and leaned me over the sink. He entered me forcibly, and I cringed as his big wood slid in my wet pussy. He grabbed my hips and pulled me toward him as he slid in and out. I used all my energy and squeezed my muscles together. I worked that pussy on his nine inches of wood, giving him the best backers he had ever had in his life. He gripped me tighter as he thrust harder.

"Aweee, fuck mi, Daddy," I whispered, mindful that my children were asleep. The sound of my voice excited him, and he applied pressure like he was vexed with the pussy. I was a champion gyal, so I bumbled on the wood, letting that nigga know I was a bad bitch.

"Aargh," I growled as he shot his cum up inside of me. Any other time I would've been mad, but not tonight.

We ended up taking a shower and then got into bed. Obviously, he wasn't finished, because he turned my ass around on my stomach, spread my legs, and buried his face in my pussy. He didn't stop there. He inserted his tongue deep in the crack of my ass, then licked every ounce of my hole.

"Aw, aw, please don't stop," I said as my body trembled and I busted. He licked up every drop of my juice, wiping my pussy clean with his tongue.

I was mentally and physically tired and happy from getting that good fuck. However, my happiness didn't last. I wished it was Omari who had done all this goodness to me. I laid my head on Garey's arm and thought about a plan that I needed to execute. I also thought about how Omari had hurt me and my kids. I wondered why the obeah hadn't started working yet. Why hadn't my husband come back home to us? Instead, it was the complete opposite. He didn't want nothing to do with me or his kids.

I looked over at Garey. That fool really thought we were going to be together. Just because he had good dick and ate pussy and ass good didn't mean I wanted him. His name didn't carry weight in the streets like Omari's did.

"Hey, babes." He opened his eyes and smiled at me.

"Hey, you." I smiled back.

I quickly sat up in the bed. I knew this was the time for me to lay my plan out on the table.

"Mi need to talk to yuh," I said in a serious tone.

"Wha a gwaan? You good?"

"I'm pregnant with yuh child," I declared, cutting straight to the chase.

"Yuh serious? Mi about fi 'ave a yute. . . . But wait. How yuh know it's mine and not Omari's?"

"Because I told yuh we barely fucked, and the times we did, him used a condom. Yuh is the only one dat fuck mi raw. And member tha day yuh bust inna mi?"

He sat there quietly, like he was thinking. "A true to boodclaat," he finally said. He rubbed his head. "Yo, so what yuh goin' do? Mi nah wan' Omari find out and sey mi and yuh did a fuck enuh," this scared-ass bastard said.

It would have been hilarious if I didn't know that he was as serious as a heart attack.

I took his hand and mustered up some tears. "Babes, mi really in love wit' yuh. Mi nuh want Omari, but if 'im find out, 'im gonna kill us all, even yuh baby. Unless we get to 'im first."

"Wha yuh saying to me? Yuh want we fi kill Omari? Mi is no killa enuh, babes."

"If we don't tek care of 'im, we all gonna be dead. So please tink 'bout it, 'cause di baby is growing in my stomach. Si di paper yah." I reached over and grabbed the paper with my pregnancy test results and handed it to him.

I watched as he examined the paper, and I knew then that I had him right where I needed him.

Omari

Jah know, I was missing my yute them bad. I had never intended for things to work out like they had. When I married Angela, it was for better or worse, or so I thought. Almost a week had passed, and I hadn't talked to them. So I called Angela's phone, trying to talk to the kids, but being the ignorant gyal she was, she told me they didn't want to talk to me. I knew that bitch was lying. Yes, I tried not to call my yutes' mother out of her name, but I was pissed. She knew that was the only way that she could hurt me.

Instead of arguing with her, I hung up on her and decided to roll me a blunt and drink a Guinness. I was trying to calm myself down, because I felt like I was about to explode. After I took the first two drags, I just sat there, staring off into space. That was when I decided to check on my mother. See, Mom Dukes always had that soothing touch and those encouraging words whenever I felt like

I was sinking. I jumped on my bike, which I had loaned to one of my brethren and had just got back last night. I pulled out of the driveway and sped off down the road.

Mom Dukes was living on Hill View Terrace, in a house that I had bought her two years ago. I made sure she didn't have to struggle anymore. Thinking back, I should've known that Angela wasn't worth shit, because of the way she had carried on when I told her I was buying my mother a house. I had had to check that ass real fast, because no one but me and my siblings knew the stress Mama had gone through to raise us by herself. There was no way that I was going to let a woman dictate what I did or did not do for my queen.

I pulled into Mama's yard and parked my bike. Then I knocked on the grill and waited.

"Who da hell bangin' on my grill like dat?" yelled the most beautiful heavyset woman that I knew.

"It's me, di man of di yaad," I joked.

"Oh, my baby. Let me get the keys."

She opened the grill, and I walked in and grabbed Mama up in a bear-type hug.

"Wha gwaan, Mama?"

"You tell me, nuh? About tweeks ago, yuh call and sey yuh a come check mi, and yuh just now a show yuh face." She gave me that "Boy, I'll fuck you up" look.

"Just a gwaan chill."

"How the kids doing? I call Angela a few days ago, but she didn't pick up di phone."

"Mama, si down. Mi need fi talk to yuh."

"What is going on? Yuh sick?" she quizzed as she took a seat on the sofa.

"Nah. Angie and I are getting a divorce."

Mama looked at me, then stood up and walked toward me. "Is about time you wake up and see dat gyal didn't mean yuh no good. From di day yuh bring dat gyal around, I knew she wasn't no good. Mi keep mi mout' shut because mi love yuh."

"Mi nah lie. Mi used to love har, but it's been years since mi a live in misery. I try to hang on fi di yute dem, but Jah know mi can't do it nuh more."

"Well, do what yuh need fi do for your pickney them. And be careful of dat wicked gyal and har mumma."

I knew exactly what she was talking about. For years I'd heard from Angie and other people how heavily her mom was involved in working obeah. However, I'd never known Angie to be mixed up in that sort of thing.

"Mama, a Jah alone mi fear. No obeah or obeah man can touch mi."

"Son, a scorned woman is dangerous. Don't trust her. You'd be shocked the things some women do when they're angry," Mama said in perfect English. Mama wasn't too fond of speaking patois and had taught us to always speak the proper way.

We ended up talking for a little while longer. If no one understood me, I knew that Mama would. I could always talk to her about any and everything without her judging me.

"A'ight, Mama. Mi about fi bounce. Here go a few dollars. You can go market."

"Lawd Jesus, tank yuh, baby."

We hugged tightly, and then I started to walk away. She grabbed my hand.

"Baby, please be careful out in those streets. I don't want my belly bottom to burn at all for my firstborn," she told me.

"I'm good, Mama," I said and then I walked out the door.

I jumped on my bike. I knew Mama worried about her children, but I was good. Only man I feared was Jah.

Chapter 19

Kadijah

"Wow. She won't let you see your kids? That's fucked up," I told Omari over the phone. "I don't mean no harm, but your wife is cray cray as hell. I mean, I'm crazy to a certain extent, but she tops the cake. If I had walked up in a spot and caught my husband with some chick, I would've jumped on his ass. You owed her, not me. Anyway, that's over and done with now, but it's fucked up."

Me and Omari had been talking more, and I had come to look forward to our phone calls. It was like we were really getting to know each other, now that the physical was out of the way and we were focusing on a friendship.

"You are right. It wasn't your fault at all. I was to blame. I will forever try to make it up to yuh. You know, for puttin' you in dat position. To be completely honest wit' you, star, the feelings been changed for Angie. I stuck it out for my children. Don't think I'm just some foul-ass nigga who runs out on my family. That's not how I really am. I won't stick around to be miserable. You know?"

I nodded, as if he could see me. "Yeah, I know. It's just complicated as hell. I won't lie to myself or to you anymore. If it wasn't for the fact that you're married, I would probably still be there," I admitted.

"Mi got my own spot now, so you can come. Di offer still stands." He had gone back to his patois, which was sexy to me. I didn't mind.

"Nah. Like I said before, I don't have time to go all the way back to Jamaica just to fight. No thank you."

"It'll be different this time. I'm gon' file for divorce and work on gettin' custody of my kids. If she won't let me see them, I will get the government involved. Most men be scared to fuck wit' the system, but I don't care. It's not like I'm in the streets like that no more. I still do street shit if need be, you know, but I'm grown up, wit' kids to think about. Can't keep doin' the same dumb shit."

"Well, it's good to know that you're doing what you have to do for yourself and your children. It's really stand up of you to want to get the courts involved. Like you said, most men bitch about the system and getting the white man involved. The way I see it, if you don't take the steps to fix a fucked-up situation, it'll always stay the same."

"Right. And mi need to be able to get a DNA test for the one she's pregnant wit' now."

"What? She's what?" I was shocked by that news. "Is it yours?"

"It can't be mine, DiDi, and that's my word. Mi ain't nutted in her in forever, but she showed me papers provin' she carryin' somebody's pickney. Not mine, though. Mi tink she cheated on mi, but wan' me to tink it's my seed to keep us together. Mi told her mi know mi neva nut in her, but she insist 'pon mi bein' the father."

Rolling my eyes, I let out a deep sigh. "Do you expect me to believe that you didn't nut in your own wife? Who the fuck do you think I am? Like, really?"

"Mi tellin' di truth, star. Di rassclaat woman been workin' on my nerves for years. It didn't jus' start when mi met you. It's been goin' on. Di naggin' become too much, so mi no wanna have sex most of di time. When mi did, mi used a condom. One last time we did it in di shower, but mi pulled out. She too far along for it to 'ave happened then, though. She had to 'ave already been pregnant."

Even if I did think about going back to Jamaica to see him, now shit was more fucked up than it was before. "Well, what if the baby's yours? You going back?" I didn't think I'd believe him if he said no.

"No, mon, but there's no chance it's mine. Mi know it. Would dat be a deal breaker for us?"

That question caught me off guard. I didn't think there was a chance for us either way. The way I saw it, the fact that he hadn't told me about his marital status was the deal breaker. How could I trust him to be faithful to me? It didn't matter how I felt when I heard his voice. It also didn't matter that I touched myself at night, as I thought about his mouth on me and that huge, powerful dick stretching my walls. Not only was the physical attraction between us a powerful force, but he also seemed to have a genuinely good heart. Despite the fact that he had lied to me, he loved his children and he adored his mother. It seemed to me that he'd just picked the wrong bitch to marry.

"Being married was the deal breaker for me, Omari. I thought we agreed to just be friends? Besides, it's not like I make a trip to Jamaica often, so we'll probably never see each other again." When I said it out loud, it actually made my heart sink.

"Wow. Dat really stung, B. For real. I said we're friends for now." He sighed and then said, "Enough about my problems. How's your nephew? Mi sorry for not askin' 'bout him off top."

"He's alive, but he's still not out of the woods yet. I went to see him earlier, but it's hard to see him like that. The tubes and everything's a bit much, because he's so tiny. Then it's hard as hell to keep my hands off his mama. I was telling you about how we had it out at the hospital. I just feel like she had something to do with my brother getting robbed. I don't really think she wanted Cam to get shot, but her actions may have led to it. My brother was supposed to go after the guys who did it, but he said he changed his mind because of our conversation. He said he's still going to get them, which I'm sure he will, but not right now. I just hope that if Imani was involved, the truth comes out. The thought of her still being with my brother pisses me off, but he always comes to her defense."

"Mi know what ya mean. My mama tried to warm mi 'bout Angie, but mi didn't listen. Yuh just 'ave to let a person see for theyself. Love is blind, and mi know yuh heard dat cliché before."

I chuckled sarcastically. "I've lived it."

He laughed too. "Haven't we all, star."

"Well, thank you for being honest with me this time. At least if I did decide to go back there to see you, which I seriously doubt, there won't be any surprises this time."

"Mi promise yuh there'll be no more surprises, beautiful. Well, not any bad surprises. If you do find yourself in shock, it'll be for a good reason. My word's my bond."

Damn. Tingles were shooting up and down my spine, making me close my eyes and imagine that he was sitting right there beside me. His melodic voice caused me to experience "eargasms," and that was something that I'd never felt before him.

Omari went on to talk about his passion for music.

"I love reggae, but I love all music. A few years back, I clashed with a hot-ass deejay named Rock B. He was the one on top, and after battling him, it was on for me. It was like I became an overnight sensation. Since then, I been spinning and making mixtapes."

"That's how I feel about cooking. It's always been a passion for me. I love all types of food. It's not just about the taste. It's about preparing it. It's like when I cook, I express my soul."

"Oh, my goodness, star, I can relate. When I'm spinnin', it's like I can get all those feelings out and people love it, like I know people love your food. Hmm . . . Food and music just go together, you know."

I was from the South, so I had to agree. Our cultures were different but very similar. We loved to eat and party.

After talking for about an hour, we finally ended the call, because my brother was beeping in. My heart fell to my feet, causing tears to burn my eyes. How could I go from such an ecstatic mood to that? It was so disheartening how quickly life could cause your mood to shift.

"Hey, Meel. Everything okay?"

"Yeah, Cam's still the same. He opened his eyes and squeezed my finger today. That's a good sign. I'm just ready for my li'l man to get better so I can finish them niggas off. They must be all comfortable and shit, thinkin' I ain't comin' for them," he said, sounding like he was drunk as a skunk.

"Are you at the hospital, drunk, Jameel? Where's Imani? Do I need to come there?"

"You were already here all day, sis. Don't worry. The doctors said that his chance of survival at this point is very high. No, I ain't drunk. Just tired as hell, 'cause I can't sleep. Imani is right here beside me."

"Okay," I sighed. "I'm about to cook something real quick, bruh. I'll call you back in a li'l bit, okay?"

My interview at the Ritz-Carlton was the next morning, and I wanted to turn in early so I'd be fresh and ready. That was when I thought about the fact that I hadn't checked the mail in days. Instead of starting dinner first, I decided to check the mail first. Then I noticed that my trash can was literally overflowing. Okay, so a trip to the mailbox and the Dumpster it was.

When I was on my way to the Dumpster, I noticed a familiar-looking car just sitting there, lurking. It wasn't parked in a parking spot. It was just sitting in front of the next building, with the lights on and the motor running. Then it occurred to me. That was Daryn's bitch. I remembered her gold Mercedes.

Instead of even entertaining that ho, I proceeded to the Dumpster and threw the trash bag in it. After I was done, I walked back toward my building. That was when I noticed the car coming toward me out of my peripheral. When I looked, I realized that she was going faster than I thought. Was that psycho bitch trying to hit me? I decided to speed up just in case. Then I had to literally start running, because she was coming toward me quick as hell.

When I was finally standing in the safety of the doorway to my condo, it was clear to me that she had tried to run me over with her car. She had stopped her car in front of my building.

"Why don't you get out and fight me like a real bitch!" I screamed at her.

The only thing the scared heifer did was give me the middle finger. I made my way over to her car, making sure that I stayed on the sidewalk. I had my keys in my hand, so if I couldn't touch her, I had other plans.

She rolled her window down. "You ruined my life, bitch! I should've run you over for real!"

"You stalkin' me, crazy bitch?" I asked her as I used my key to scratch up her car's immaculate paint job. The ho didn't even know what I was doing. "You know that's a crime, right? What would your daddy think of that? You hate me 'cause your man left you to be with me, but I don't want him. You're mad at the wrong one." If only she'd put the window down far enough for me to clock her in her ugly-ass face.

She shook her head, with more anger in her eyes than I'd seen the first time she popped up. "Nah, I'm mad at the right one, bitch! The first time I came over here, I was actually calm about it. I warned you to leave my man alone, but you—"

"I did leave that sorry, lying-ass nigga alone! I didn't do it for you, though. I did it for me. I should pull your scared ass through that damn window. Like you were really brave enough to run me over," I hissed at her.

"Stand in the road and see if I run you over or not, bitch. I can show you better than I can tell you!"

Her eyes told me that she would, which let me know that she really wasn't 'bout that life. If she was, she'd just get out of the car and square up.

"Nah. Get out and fight, bitch! C'mon!" I told her.

"I don't wanna fight you, bitch! I wanna kill your ass! You ruined my fuckin' life!" Tears were falling down her face as she went into a rage and started hitting the steering wheel and screaming, "I hate you! I hate you! I hate you! I hate you!"

My next thought was to go inside and get my gun, because that bitch had lost it. Damn. Was she fucking the same Daryn that I was? The dick damn sure didn't have me acting like that. No dick would ever have me acting like that. Not even Omari's, and it was a hundred times better than Daryn's. I hated to see a woman put a man before herself like that. The shit was sickening as hell.

As I stood there, not knowing what to do next, she suddenly hit the gas and drove off, her tires screeching. Yeah, she was not working with a full deck, and I suddenly knew that it was just the beginning of having to deal with her shenanigans. If she had really wanted to run me over, she could've done it. The bitch had just wanted to fuck with me, and she'd chosen the right one.

Daryn

The knock at my door caught me by surprise as I took the microwavable Salisbury steak dinner out of the freezer. The familiar red box made my taste buds go to sleep instead of dance. Damn, I sure did miss DiDi's cooking. She could burn, and it was one of the things that made her wifey material. Nita couldn't even boil water, so there was no competition.

I walked to the door and looked through the peephole. When I saw DiDi standing there, it made my heartbeat increase with anticipation. Was she ready to finally commit to me again? Had she rethought rejecting my proposal? I really hoped she was there to mend things between us, because I missed her like hell.

After I opened the door, I could tell from the scowl on her face that her visit wasn't even friendly, let alone romantic. Then she went off.

"Nigga, you better get your bitch before I kill her crazy ass!"

I grabbed her hand and pulled her inside before the neighbors heard her yelling.

"What the hell's going on, DiDi?" I looked around before closing the door behind her.

"That bitch just tried to run me over with her fucking car! I kept telling her to get out and fight me, but of course, she wouldn't. You better tell her something, nigga, because she tried it."

DiDi was all out of breath as she stood there in sweats and a T-shirt, with her hair pulled up. Yeah, she looked like she was ready for a fight, but she still looked sexy as hell.

I shook my head, because I hadn't talked to Nita since I left. I'd always had my own crib to go back to when I was with her, so it was all good. Now she knew why I wouldn't move in with her permanently. I had never planned to marry her.

"So, what you want me to do? I can't control what Nita does. It's not like I got a GPS on her ass. You think it matters what I tell her? She hates me for leaving her for you." I was clueless as to what DiDi expected me to do. That bitch Nita would probably try to run me over too.

When she pulled a huge black handgun from her purse, my first instinct was to run, but she wasn't pointing it at me.

"I want you to tell that bitch not to come for me. The next bitch who I ain't sent for who comes for me gon' get a bullet in her fuckin' ass, so you let her know that. I'm sick of bitches thinking I'm the one to be fuckin' toyed with! I'm too fuckin' grown to be fighting over dick!" She cocked the gun. "I ain't scared to use this gun, Daryn, and that's for you and that bitch to know."

She walked toward the door, and I watched her ass jiggle in the loose-fitting pants she was wearing. Damn, I wanted her back so bad, and I wasn't done trying.

"So, can you unblock my number now? I mean, don't you want to talk about us?" I asked her. "I still wanna marry . . ."

Suddenly, she turned on her heels and got all up in my face, like she was about to slob a nigga down. I leaned in, ready to feel her soft lips on mine, but instead I felt her mush me in the face hard as hell. I was about sick of those bitches putting their hands in my face.

"Ain't no us, and ain't no marriage gon' happen, nigga. Get yo' fuckin' life!"

Then she turned and walked to the door. As she walked out, she put the gun back in her purse.

I watched my future wife get in her car and drive off as I pulled my cell phone from my pocket. Handling Nita was the first thing I had to do to get my woman back.

Chapter 20

Angela

The next few days were spent working on Garey. I allowed him to stay at the house with me, and I cooked, bathed him, sucked his wood, and fucked him good. I was a woman who believed if you genuinely wanted something, you had to go after it.

One morning I made him breakfast after the kids left for school. Then we sat at the table and ate like the perfect couple, but we were far from it. I didn't want this bwoy, and after he helped me out, I was gonna definitely get rid of his ass.

"Angie, I been tinking 'bout what you ask mi to do, but I swear mi a have second thoughts. . . ."

"What yuh mean, second thoughts? We have to do dis. If not, I'm gonna have tell Omari that mi and yuh was fucking and that dis is yo' baby. Yuh already know how 'im ignorant. Is dat what yuh want to deal wit'?" I looked at him and folded my arms.

This bwoy was behaving like a purebred bitch! Whining and shit. If he loved me, as he claimed, he would happily do what the fuck I asked him. He was the weakest link, and I couldn't wait for this shit to be over with so I could get the fuck away from this weak-ass bwoy.

"Baby, listen to mi," I said. "I want us fi get 'im out of the way, so mi and yuh need to get it done. Better sooner than lata." I grabbed his arm and looked into his eyes so he saw that I was serious.

I went on. "Listen, if yuh scared to get di gun, mi wi get it. All youh affi duh is pull do trigger and leave. Stop acting like yuh 'ave pussy in yuh heart. Mi tink yuh is a bad man." I knew I would hit a nerve when I said that.

"Of course mam a bad man."

"Of course yuh are. So let's get di son of a bitch out of the way."

I reached over and started kissing him. I knew how weak this bwoy was, and sex would always get him to do what I wanted.

Omari

I was busy the entire weekend. I had shows in St. Elizabeth, Clarendon, and Portmore. As for how I felt afterward, tired would be an understatement, but shit, it was well worth it. My bank account was fat, and now that Angela was out of my hair, I could finally save some money. Speaking of her, I had received a call from her earlier, but I'd been on the phone with DiDi, and there was no way I was going to cut that call to hear Angela bitch at me again.

I grabbed the phone, and Angela's number came up. I wasn't in a rush to get on the phone with her, but I was desperate to get a chance to talk to my yute them.

"Hello," Angela answered cheerfully, which kind of threw me off, because the last time we spoke, she was cussing and yelling.

"Yo, wha a gwaan? Mi miss a call from yuh?"

"Oh, I was calling to see if yuh want to see di kids dem. They been asking for their daddy, so I tink yuh need to see them."

"Angie, cut out di bullshit, B. Yuh know I've been trying to see dem, B."

"Calm down, Omari. I'm not fighing wit' yuh anymore. Come see yuh pickney dem."

"A'ight, B."

I didn't waste no time. I jumped up out of the bed, but my phone started ringing. I looked at the caller ID; it was Garey.

"Yo, boss, wha a gwaan?" I said when I answered.

"Mi deh yah, mi genna. Yo, mi a call yuh fi see if mi can borrow yo' blower. Mi wha do some yaad work inna di day yah."

"Yo a leave mi a leave out enuh. But mi can leave it 'pon di back fi yuh. See the address yah. . . ."

I took the blower and put it out back for him, then locked my door. I was eager to get out of here before Angela had a change of heart. I jumped on my bike and sped off. It took me no time to get to Angela's house. I parked and used my keys to knock on the grill.

My kids rushed out, screaming. "Mommy, it's Daddy. Daddy is here, Mommy," they yelled in unison.

I ain't goin' lie. This was everything that I needed. Just to see the smile on their faces lifted my spirits. Angela opened the grill, and I walked in. The kids jumped in my arms, and I grabbed up both of them. Tears filled my eyes, and I blinked a few times, trying my best not to show any emotions.

We sat on the verandah and start chopping it up. I looked up and noticed Angela standing there. She was no longer smiling, and she had a look of jealousy written on her face. I brushed it off and returned my focus to my two yutes.

I ended up spending the rest of the day with them. When it was their bedtime, I didn't want to leave them, but I wouldn't dare spend a night in that house. Angela and I were finished, and I was careful not to send the wrong message.

After we hugged and kissed, I walked out of the house. Angela made her way toward me.

"Yuh know, yuh can always come home, right?" she said.

"Come on, Angie. Let's no go deh. All mi want is to see mi yute dem. Listen, here go some money for dem." I handed her an envelope with fifty grand in it.

She snatched the money out of my hand. "Money don't fix broken hearts," she said before she walked inside and locked the grill.

I put my helmet on, jumped on my bike, and pulled off. This was one of few times when I actually felt bad about breaking up with Angela. All my life I had wanted the perfect family, the wife, and the kids. And I had that, but it was far from perfect. I hate the fact that my yutes were the ones who were gonna suffer the most, and Jah knows that wasn't my intention.

I was going to hang out at the spot where the fellas were meeting up tonight, but after the visit I had just had, I decided not to. I was calling it a night. I was gonna go home and smoke, drink, and maybe get a chance to kick it on the phone with DiDi.

I glanced in my mirror as I drove, and I thought I saw a dark-colored vehicle following me. I sped up, and I noticed the SUV speed up also. I took a quick left turn and rode around Greater Portmore for a while. Maybe I was paranoid, but I wanted to be sure no one was on my tail. This was one of the few times I didn't have my gun on me, because I was visiting the kids. I didn't see the SUV any longer, so I figured my brain had been playing tricks on me. I decided to head home.

I pulled up to my gate and opened it. I then rode inside and locked it. Shit. I forgot to cut the lights on before I left, I thought as I fumbled to open the lock on the grill.

"Pussy, put yo' bloodclaat hands up," a voice whispered.

I felt the barrel of a gun pressed into my back. I knew then that it wasn't a game. I had done fucked up.

Pop! Pop! Pop!

I felt a hot sensation rip through my body as I fell to the ground. I lifted my head and saw a shadow take off running. I reached in my pocket and grabbed my cell phone and dialed 119.

Jah know, star, the man dem try fi kill me, I thought as I lay there in excruciating pain. I tried to get up, but my knees were weak. I heard my neighbor yelling as he ran over to me. Blood spilled out of the side of my mouth, and I knew then that I wasn't gonna make it.

Chapter 21

Kadijah

"You what?" Nicole shrieked through the phone after I revealed the rash decision I'd made and explained why. "You can't be goin' all the way to Jamaica by yourself! That psycho bitch will probably get you shot up next. Are you crazy?"

Crazy in love, I thought to myself.

"No, I'm not crazy, Cole. I can't explain it, but from the moment I first locked eyes with that man, it was over for me." Wiping the tears away for the millionth time, I added, "And it's too late to reconsider. I'm already in Jamaica. My flight just landed."

Don had called me right away because before Omari lost consciousness, he told him to call me. I caught the first flight smoking, despite my anger at Omari for not telling me that he was married. Honestly, it hadn't even mattered to me at first. I hadn't asked if he was married. I was just a tourist having fun, and shit happened. Neither of us knew our feelings would be so deep in such a small amount of time. Yeah, I was a headstrong woman, but there was just something about my connection to Omari. Most would wonder why I felt that way, but I just did.

I felt strongly that although Daryn had played me, he was malicious, whereas Omari wasn't. He had intent. Omari didn't. Omari had been with the wrong woman all along and hadn't used anybody in the process. He had stuck around only for his children, which was understandable. Daryn, on the other hand, stuck around with that chick for a financial come up. My lack of a father figure made me understand a man risking it all for his children. Not one would risk it all just for his own selfish ass. As far as using a woman for a come up, I wasn't feeling that.

Also, after Don called to tell me about Omari being shot, I blamed myself. I just had to get back there to check up on him and let the police know that I was sure his crazy wife did it. He didn't tell me the truth about his marriage, and I was upset about that, but we'd had so many deep personal conversations since I left the island. Some nights we'd stay on the phone for hours, until the sun came up. We had both grown over the years and knew what we wanted from the opposite sex. We both had expressed those wants, and our desires were similar. Omari had asked me if I'd ever be able to trust him, and I'd told him I didn't know. He had promised that if given the chance, he'd prove himself to me.

"I'm not a gallist anymore. I love and respect women. I know I can love the right woman the right way," he had explained. "I let the physical take over with Angie, and although you and I have been physical, you stimulate me on a mental level like no other woman ever has."

Not only was there a physical connection between us, but we had an emotional connection too. I felt like it was worth it for me to lie to my mother and brother about my reason for traveling to Jamaica. They thought I had an interview for a chef position at a restaurant in a resort on the island. I'd lied and said I applied for the position when I was there. My brother had even paid for my flight.

"You bitch!" Nicole yelled in my ear. "You did that shit on purpose. You didn't call me until you got there, 'cause you knew I'd talk some fuckin' sense into your ass! Does Tamia know you're there?"

I cleared my throat. "No. I called you first. . . ."

"Because you knew she would've definitely been the voice of reason. So, did you tell anybody in your life on this side of the world that you were going back to Jamaica to see some man who's married? Did you mention that he got shot? Oh, and did you add the fact that you think his wife did it? Oh my God. You're officially crazy. I'm so glad I didn't get no dick while I was there. I'd hate to be doing stupid-ass shit like you. That nigga's dick must be platinum coated or something. What the fuck, DiDi?"

As I rolled my eyes in frustration, I spotted my Louis Vuitton luggage set rolling my way. "Ma and Meel know that I'm here, but they think I'm here for a job interview. Don't you spill the beans. Don't tell Mia, either."

"Oh my God. It's even worse that you lied to your mama." She let out a sharp breath.

"It's not about his dick, either. We have a strong connection, and it goes deeper than the physical. I realized that when I got home. We've talked about everything, from how he was raised to his philandering past with women. He was always the one feeling like he needed a lot of women, looking for something to fill a void. It's like we have that in common. Looking for the wrong thing in the wrong people. Doesn't mean we're bad people at all. Just lost. I feel that connection to him."

I sighed. "I can't control how I feel, and I didn't plan it. I was pissed at him for lying to me, but that didn't stop him from pursuing me even after I left. I know that he feels just as strongly for me as I do for him. If it was me, I know he'd be there if he could be. He needs me, Cole. Try to understand that."

Nicole was silent as I wrestled with my bags. Damn. I really didn't know why life was throwing me all types of curveballs in such a small amount of time. So much had happened in the past weeks, but I was a strong woman, and I refused to crumble.

Nicole finally spoke. "Bitch, I need you to understand that you're asking for trouble with that ho he's married to. I mean, at first, I actually thought it was cute that you were feeling old boy. He *is* sexy, and he seemed to be a sweet guy, but I thought once you got home, you'd get over it. There's no way it's a coincidence that he's in the hospital, with bullet wounds, after his wife caught him with you. You don't know who that bitch is affiliated with. Jamaica got some of the most ruthless gangstas in the world. You heard Omari talking about shottas and shit. Now you're over there, possibly in danger, and your mom and brother have no clue. Don't make me have to take a damn flight. . . ."

"No, Cole. You can't do that—"

"Damn if I can't!" she snapped, suddenly making me have second thoughts about what I was doing. I couldn't back down, though. Shit, I was already here.

"Let me do what I have to do. I ain't scared of that bitch. If she succeeds in getting me killed, she'll be the first suspect, because of my connection to Omari. Then she'll be a suspect in Omari's shooting. I doubt she'll be that damn dumb."

"Hmm. You never know. So, since you're there, and I can't stop you, I'll just say this. If that bitch gets out of pocket in any way, you better let me know. I'll be on the first fuckin' thing smoking to personally come shank her ass. You hear me?"

I couldn't help but let out a chuckle. "Yes, I hear you."

"I'm serious."

I pulled my luggage on wheels, with my phone cradled between my ear and shoulder. When I finally spotted Don, I let out a sigh of relief.

"I know you are. I'll call you back, Cole. I just spotted Don, so . . ."

"I hope he's not setting you up, Di. What if that bitch Paula got him to call you so she and that bitch can get at you? Did you think about that shit at all?"

Not really. I hadn't had time to think about it. And in my opinion, there was nothing to ponder. I just had to come back and make sure that Omari was okay. The need to be by his side was overwhelming, and there was no explanation for how I felt other than love.

"Like I said, I'll call you back, Cole."

"Okay. Damn. Bye."

She hung up in haste, and I knew why she had. Nicole played hard, but deep down inside, she was really a very mushy, emotional person. She was worried about me. While I understood why, I didn't want her to carry that burden. Angela wasn't a threat to me, and I wasn't the least bit worried about that bitch. If anything, I was going to expose her for the trifling, vindictive person she was and prove that she was the reason Omari was fighting for his life in the first place.

My whole vibe in Jamaica was different the second time around. First of all, I wasn't drunk, since I had no reason to celebrate. Damn, it was funny how the tables could suddenly turn. The mood inside Don's car was somber, and after our initial hellos, there wasn't much conversation.

I decided to speak up. "So, how is he?"

"Better than when I talked to you, because they stabilized him. He's still unconscious, though," he answered.

I nodded as I looked straight ahead. He was taking me to my hotel, and then we'd be going to the hospital from there.

"So, you really called me simply because that was what Omari wanted?" I had been curious about that, but what Nicole had said really had me thinking.

"Yeah. What do you think I called you for? How else would I have your number?" He glanced over at me, with a confused expression on his face.

"I'on know. Shit, your girl is Angela's best friend. What if I'm next and you're in on it?"

"Paula's not my girl, and even if she was, why would I do that? What would I gain? If anything, I'd have too much to lose." He shook his head as he reached in the ashtray for a blunt.

As he lit it and took a pull, the smell ignited my senses and made my mouth water. Taking a few pulls of that shit would be right on time.

"Okay. I guess you're right. So, do you think Angela had something to do with Omari getting shot, or do you think it was random? Was he robbed or . . . ?"

"He definitely wasn't robbed. His wallet was full of cash, and his cell was on him. His bike and car were safe in the driveway, and his place was untouched. That shit was personal as fuck. As far as me thinkin' Angie was in on it . . ." He shrugged his shoulders. "I can't say for sure, 'cause I wasn't there, but I do suspect she may have had somebody do it. Omari been tellin' me he thought she was cheatin'. Maybe her new nigga's some type of lame who is all whipped and shit, but if I find out, he's gettin' popped ASAP."

"I have not one doubt in my mind that bitch's behind that shit. You just have to help me prove it."

"How will I do that?" he asked.

"You're fuckin' her friend good, right? Shit, have a nice romantic evening with her. Cook. Fuck her good. Shit, eat the pussy if you have to."

There was a frown on his face, which almost made me laugh. I didn't, though.

"I'm just sayin', Don. Do and say whatever you have to, to get some info out of Paula. That bitch that Omari is married to is her bestie. I'm sure she knows something."

Don nodded in agreement. "I'll do whatever to help my brethren, star."

"Good. Because if he doesn't make it, she'll get away with murdering him. Then, if he does survive, who's to say she won't try to finish the job? Either way, the bitch needs to go to fucking prison. I just hope he makes it." The tears were burning my eyes again, and I willed them away.

"Here. Hit this. It'll help." I looked, and he was passing the spliff to me.

"Shit, thanks." I took a few pulls and immediately started to relax.

As silence surrounded me, all I could do was think. Neither all the ganja in the world nor the sights and sounds of such a beautiful island could help my fucked-up mood. The possibility of Omari losing his life before ours even started together had me all in my feelings.

Don called Paula to ask about Angela's whereabouts in a slick way.

"Sup, love? Mi on di way t' see mi brethren dem, but mi no wanna pop up on Angela and shit. Where ya gyal?"

"She waitin' at home fi her mom to come watch di yute," Paula said, confirming that Angela wasn't at the hospital.

After that, it was finally time for me to see Omari. I could only hope to get to him before that heifer got there. The thing was, I was trying to avoid conflict. Fighting that bitch in a hospital would not be a good look.

We got to the hospital, and I rushed to Omari's side. As I stood over him, my eyes started burning yet again and I broke down. His beautiful eyes were closed. Tubes were coming from everywhere, an IV with clear liquid was feeding his veins, and machines were beeping. It was an all too-familiar scene, as I had just witnessed this with my nephew.

Don had let me go in Omari's room alone, while he stood outside in the hallway. All I could do was cry as I grabbed Omari's stiff hand and laid my head on his chest.

"I'm so sorry," I sobbed. "I didn't know she would do this to you. You have to make it, Omari. You have to." I willed myself to move so that I could whisper in his ear. "Because I love you. Please fight. I love you, and I want to be with you. Okay. When you get out of here and get your divorce finalized, it's going to be you and me, baby."

I closed my eyes and let the hot tears fall down my face. The agony was too much. If only he'd just wake up and talk to me. If only I could just hear his voice.

Angela's voice filled my ears instead. "Wha di fuck, Don! Mi know yuh didn't bring dis bomboclaat whore 'pon my husband's bedside!"

When I turned around, she was standing there, staring at me with eyes like daggers. I knew she wanted to put her hands on me, but not as much as I wanted to put my hands on her. Don stood between us.

"Mi no tryin'a disrespect yuh, Angie, but Omari would wan' DiDi here. . . ."

"Fuck DiDi! Mi no give no fucks 'bout da whore my husband fucked!"

"Bitch, fuck you! I really wanna lay your ass out right now, but I won't do it, because of Omari! Unlike your trifling ass, I won't be wasting my time with unnecessary drama while he fights for his life," I growled.

"Wha'? Yuh neva left di island? Yuh must've tought mi husband would leave mi fi yuh. When yuh find out he wasn't, yuh got angry, huh?" she asked with an evil grin.

I shook my head when I realized what she was trying to say. "You sound stupid as hell, bitch. I been left. I came back today, after Don called to let me know that Omari had been shot."

"Mi 'bout to call security!" She stepped out into the hallway. "Security! Get dis bitch out of mi husband's room. Dis bitch tried to kill mi husband! Security! Security!" That bitch was screaming at the top of her lungs.

Don gave me a sympathetic look. "C'mon." He grabbed my arm. "Let's get you out of here."

As we walked past Angela, she flashed a satisfied grin my way. Security was heading in our direction.

"Yeah, Yankee whore! Mi will make sure yuh neva see him again! Security, take a good look at dis woman! She tried to kill mi husband! She not allowed to step foot in dis hospital again! Si mi?"

The two men dressed in uniforms nodded and walked toward us.

"Angie, yuh 'ave no proof fi wha yuh claimin'!" Don snapped at her. "We're leaving," he told the security guards.

As we walked toward the elevator, I thought about going back to choke that bitch. How dare she say that shit out loud, knowing damn well that she was the one who was responsible? Once we were inside the elevator and the doors had closed, I looked up at Don.

"We gotta bring that ho down asap," I said.

He nodded but looked skeptical. "Yeah, but I'm sure Paula is gonna tell her that I brought you here. She won't trust me now."

"Looks like you got your work cut out for you." I leaned against the wall of the elevator, with a heavy head and heart. What the hell had I gotten myself into?

Chapter 22

Kadijah

The bullshit that had gone down at the hospital with Angela had me heated, but I had to call my mother when I got back to the hotel.

"How was your flight?" She sounded all giddy.

Trying to match her ecstatic tone was hard. I knew that she was proud of me, but would she be if she knew what was really going on?

"It was fine. How's Cam?" My nephew was on my mind, and I needed to know that he was okay. It would be just my luck that his condition would change for the worse while I was gone.

When I went to pick up money from Jameel's, I was hoping to catch Imani doing something that made it clear that she was up to no good. She wasn't even there when I got there, but was en route to the hospital with her mom, like she'd said. Just like with that bitch Angela, I was going to stop at nothing to expose Imani. Just because I didn't have anything on her yet didn't mean that there wasn't any proof out there. When I got back home, I'd just have to get it. At the moment, my priority was to handle Omari's crazy bitch of a wife.

"He's still improving. Are you all right?"

Of course, she could sense that something was wrong. Mothers always knew. Her intuition was on point, but I worked on throwing her off.

"I'm good, Ma. Just tired. I'm about to get me some rest."

"Okay. What time is your interview?" she asked.

Damn. Why was she making me continue the lies? "It's at nine a.m., and it's an hour earlier here, so I have plenty of time to get some rest."

"Well, good night, honey. I'm going to pray that you get whatever God has planned for you."

"Good night, Ma, and thank you so much. Love you." Her statement kind of scared me in a way, though. No good could come from the lies and the fact that I was in love with a married man.

"Love you more."

When I hung up, I felt the opposite of tired. As a matter of fact, I was restless. Being alone in Jamaica was different than having my girls with me. If they were here, chilling in the room would be cool. At least then I'd have someone to talk to. I decided to take a shower and head down to the bar for a drink. Shit, that was exactly what I needed.

"A very strong Long Island iced tea please. Top shelf," I said to the bartender.

She nodded and scurried off to fix my drink. Before I could even get comfortable on my seat, I heard a man's voice behind me.

"Bonjour, beautiful," he said with a French accent.

When I turned around, I was face-to-face with a handsome, blond-haired, blue-eyed white dude. He looked like he was in his late thirties or early forties. His smile was contagious, so I found myself smiling back.

I knew that *bonjour* meant "hello," so I was cordial. "Hi," was all I offered as the bartender brought my drink to me.

"Her drink's on me," he told her.

The last thing I needed was some man hounding me over some drink. My experience with white men was minimal, so I hoped he would just buy my drink and leave me the hell alone.

After he paid, he decided to sit down on the bar stool beside me. *Well, damn.* My hopes were crushed. All I wanted was to get a little tipsy and forget about the fact that Angela was trying to make it look like I was the one involved in Omari's shooting. There I was, all the way in Jamaica, and I wasn't even allowed to see Omari. It was all because of her. I wanted to kill that bitch.

"I'm Caesar. And you are?" He stuck his hand out for me to shake.

As rude as my true nature was, I didn't want to piss him off. Instead of being a bitch, I shook his hand and thanked him for the drink. "Thank you for the drink, Caesar. I'm DiDi."

"Nice to meet you, DiDi." His smile was all bright and wide.

"You too," I added for good measure.

"So, what brings you to Jamaica? Vacation?"

I wished, but he didn't have to know what I was there for. "Yeah, you can say that."

"Me too." That smile was still plastered on his face. "I thought you were a native woman, but your accent is American."

"Yes. I'm from Atlanta, Georgia. Have you heard of it?" I sipped my drink, and his eyes were glued to mine.

"I've been there . . . on business a few times."

I nodded. Well, since he was there and I had nobody else to talk to, why not talk to him? What harm could it do? We were in a crowded hotel. "Oh, okay. What kind of business are you in?"

"Sales," he answered vaguely.

Shit. I was bored with the conversation already. The sound of an acoustic guitar playing over the sound system wasn't helping my mood. If only I was there to enjoy myself, I wouldn't have to settle for the monotony of the moment.

"So, what are your plans for the night?" he suddenly asked.

I glanced at him and shook my head. "After this drink, I'm going to my room and getting in bed."

"Alone?" He was clearly flirting.

Oh, hell nah. I was not interested at all. "Yes. Alone," I confirmed.

He sipped his drink. "Doesn't sound like much of a vacation to me, madame."

That motherfucker was starting to annoy me, and just when I was about to stand up and politely leave him sitting there, I felt unusually dizzy. I had asked for a strong drink, but what the fuck had that ho given me? When I looked up, I noticed that she wasn't there anymore. Instead some tall, dark-skinned dude was working the bar. Where had she gone? Had a shift change happened that fast?

"Oh, shit." I sat back down, and he leaned in close to me. His breath reeked of garlic and liquor. *Eww.*

"Are you okay?"

I wasn't okay. The room felt like it was spinning, and my eyelids were getting heavy. *What the fuck?* Had he slipped something in my drink, and if so, when? How? I had been watching him the whole time.

"I guess *we* got plans tonight . . . beautiful," he whispered.

I felt him put his arm around my waist and lift me up from my seat. With little effort, he walked with me in tow. My legs were literally dragging behind me, and nobody seemed to notice.

"No," I heard myself mumble. "Please, let me go." My voice was low and incoherent over the buzz of the music and the chatter.

"Damn it. I didn't give her enough. She shouldn't still be talking." His voice was a low murmur, as if it wasn't meant for me to hear.

Who the fuck was he talking to? Was he on the phone? Shit. I could feel myself starting to black out. He had definitely given me enough. It was just working slow. What were his intentions, and where was he taking me? Then I thought about my conversation with Nicole. I shouldn't have ever gone to Jamaica by myself. Although I had thought I'd be safe and sound inside the resort, I'd been dead-ass wrong.

Despite the fact that I was out of it, I could still feel the night's air on my skin. The smell of the ocean in the distance still ignited my senses. However, I just couldn't open my eyes. All I wanted to do was sleep, and as soon as he slid me onto the backseat of a car, I felt myself slipping out of consciousness.

Chapter 23

Angela

I sat nervously waiting to hear something. I kept looking at my phone. It had been a while since Omari left, and he should have met his demise by now. I was eager to call Garey but quickly decided not to, just in case he was in the middle of carrying out the killing. I couldn't take it anymore. I got up and walked out to the gate. Some of my neighbors were out sitting on the wall, playing dominoes. Some girls were sitting farther down, gossiping, like they did on the regular. Any other time, I would cock my ear in their direction so I could hear the latest gossip, but tonight was different. I had my own gossip going on, and, baby, it was nothing nice.

"Cho bomboclaat, why dis nigga don't ring me as yet?" I asked myself out loud. Just as I was about to turn and go back into the house, I heard my cell phone ringing on the chair in the living room. I quickly ran through the grill and snatched the phone up off the chair. Without looking at the caller ID, I answered. My heart was thumping as I awaited the good news that he was gone.

"Hello!" I shouted into the phone.

"I just got a call that my son was shot, and dem bringin' him to University Hospital. Mi is on mi way dere," Omari's mom said in a panic.

"Say what? Is he dead?" *Fuck*. I shouldn't have said that out loud.

"Gyal, did you hear me? Mi pickney just got shot and is on 'im way to hospital."

Before I could respond to that rude-ass bitch, she hung up in my face. Yeah, I had heard that bitch, but I was trying to make sure she meant he was dead. I quickly dialed Garey's phone, but he didn't pick up. My mind started racing now. If Omari was still alive, that meant that Garey had fucked up.

"Oh, Lord Jesus!" I screamed as I put my hand on my head. My phone started ringing in my hand. It was Paula.

"Yeah," I gasped.

"Weh yuh deh? Mi just hear sey Omari got shot!" she screamed into the phone.

"Yeah, his mumma just call."

"Yo, mi and Don's on our way up the hospital. I don't know who would be that crazy to try him like that. My girl, mi wi see yuh up deh."

Soon as she hung the phone up, I walked into my bedroom. I swear, this was some bullshit. That nigga was supposed to be dead. I opened my closet and grabbed a black sundress that I had. I was preparing myself early, so by the time they announced him dead, I'd be already dressed for the part. I was ready to give the performance of a lifetime.

Next, I dialed Mama's number. The kids were already sleeping, and I wasn't going to wake them up for the foolery that was taking place.

"Child, yuh know it's mi bedtime," she answered.

"Ma, Omari got shot, and I need you to watch these kids while I rush to this hospital."

"Oh, Jesus Christ. When did this happen, and who would do such a horrible thing like that?"

"Ma, I don't have all the details yet. I just need you to get over here, so I can go."

"All right, all right. I'm getting up right now."

I hung up the phone and got dressed. I was eager to hear from Garey. His ass had really fucked up by not making sure Omari was dead. Cho, that was what I got for trusting a lame.

After Mama showed up, I jumped in my car and pulled off. My heart was racing, but not because his ass had got shot. More because I knew I was the one behind his shooting. I wasn't sure if he had seen who shot him or if the police were onto Garey. My insides trembled as thoughts of prison hit me. I was a known hot gyal, and there was no way I would look good in no orange jumpsuit. I pondered if it was a great idea for me to go to this hospital. What if Garey started running his mouth and involved me in that bullshit? I thought about turning the car around and heading back home, but it would look suspicious if my husband got shot and I didn't show my face. I cut on the music and let my window down, trying to ease my fear.

I parked and entered the hospital. It was like a mad-house up in there. People were sprawled out on the floor, and I could hear others yelling for help. I walked up to where I saw a security guard and spoke to him. He pointed me toward a room where more people were located. I quickly spotted Paula.

"What are they saying?" I asked when I reached her side.

"They don't know what's going to happen. Right now he's critical."

"Oh, my! No!" Conjuring up tears, I held on to my best friend.

It took everything in me not to show how I truly felt, but I spent the night by my husband's side. In the morning I returned home to take a shower and check on the kids. I'd be sure to check on my husband, who should already be dead, the next day.

When I returned the next day, Paula and Don were outside Omari's hospital room.

"Angie, don't go inside. I got something to tell you. . . ." Paula grabbed my arm.

I was curious as to why she had told me not to go in the room. I pushed her hand off me and jetted toward the room. After I took a few steps, I stopped and blinked twice. I couldn't believe what I was seeing in front of me. This Yankee bitch was hovering over my husband, whispering some shit to him. I looked at her, then back at Don, who was standing in a corner in the hallway. I didn't give a fuck if Omari and that Yankee bitch were fucking around, but for that bold bitch to show her face up in there was definitely unacceptable. I knew that if Omari were in a better state, he would not have a bitch disrespecting his kids' mother like that. I marched up to Don. My words to him were not good, and I spoke with conviction.

"Don, you is a pussy hole, you know that, right?" I poked his ass in the forehead.

I didn't stop there. I marched into that hospital room, and I went off on that foreign bitch the raw Jamaican way.

Security must've heard the commotion, because they showed up. I straightened my clothes and let the officers know that bitch should not be allowed anywhere near my husband again. I even went as far as insinuating that she had had something to do with his shooting. Then that pussy-hole nigga Don had the fucking nerve to defend that bitch. See, Don had no idea that he was playing with fire. He had better be careful; his day was near also.

After the ho and Don left, I closed the door to the hospital room and took several steps closer to Omari as he lay in the bed with an IV and tubes.

"Hmmm, husband, you sure know how to cause drama, even when you on your deathbed. What are you waiting on to take your last breath? Why can't you just die, so your kids and I can live in peace?"

Tears welled up in my eyes as I looked down at his ass. I felt hate and anger filling my veins. He wasn't the man that I had married years ago. He was a cheating-ass nigga who deserved to fucking die. I grabbed a pillow that was tucked under his side. I was about to finish off what Garey had started.

"What the hell yuh doing wit' dat pillow?" His mother's voice startled me.

"Oh . . . uh, I was just about to put it up under his head." I placed the pillow back on the bed and smiled at her.

"Really? What was that I hear you yelling? You seemed to be yelling something about dying."

"Oh, yes. I was telling Omari that me and di kids dem can't lose him."

She shot me a dirty look and walked toward her son. I could tell that she wasn't buying what I had just told her.

"Get away from my son. I don't trust you one bit. My son is fighting for his life right now, but soon as he pull through, I'ma make sure he divorce yo' ass and get custody of my grandbabies."

"Ha-ha. Listen up, yuh silly old bitch. I was trying to be cordial, because yo' son is almost dead, but just in case you ain't get the memo, yuh or yuh pussyclaat son can't come near mi pickney them. Bitch, it's my pussy that brought them in dis world. So while yuh worrying 'bout me and mines, yuh need to be praying to God to let yours live." I gritted on that bitch.

"Hmmm. This ain't the time or place, but I promise yuh, God nah sleep and yuh will get yours one day. Mark mi words."

I wasn't going to stand there and argue with that old, beat-up-ass, wrinkled bitch. I walked out of the room. I spotted one of the security guards from earlier and approached him.

"Aye, I do not want anyone, including that woman that was here earlier, to visit him. Somebody tried to kill my husband, and we still don't know who and if they're going to come back to finish off the job. This is serious, yuh hear me?"

"Me hear you, miss. What about his family?" said the guard.

"Nobody . . . but maybe his mother," I said reluctantly.

"All right, miss. I will make sure the other officer know about it."

I dug into my purse and pulled out a five-thousand-dollar bill and shoved it into his hand. See, in my country, money talked and bullshit walked. I walked off while he was still saying something.

Paula was standing out in the hallway when I got out there. I thought her ass would've left with her man. She was my bitch and all, but ever since she started fucking with Don, she'd been acting funny and shit. I needed to know her position, because I had no problem cutting a bitch off.

"My girl, what happen up in dere?" she asked me.

"Yuh know sey the Yankee gyal was up in dere, and yuh don't say nothing?"

"Jesus Christ, Angie, mi nuh try tell yuh not to go up in deh, eh? Yuh push mi off a yuh and walk up in deh."

"Mi and yuh is friends, and yuh see a gyal up inna di room wit' mi husband, yuh suppose to go up in deh and act bad. If a did mi, a dat mi woulda do."

"Angie, if yuh and the gyal fight, yuh know sey mi would be in it. But di different is Mari's fighting for him life, and dis is not the place to bring no war. You si mi?"

I wasn't trying to hear that shit she was preaching. I knew Paula, and I knew that if it wasn't for Don, her ass would've caused havoc up in that hospital room.

"Angie, yuh need fi chill out. Not everybody is against yuh. Right now, Omari's fighting for his life, and dat's all we should be worried about, right? I know yuh hurting, but trust me, dat shit between him and the Yankee gyal nah go work fi long."

"So did Don call har? How she know what happen to Omari?"

Paula shook her head. "I have no idea. I swear, Don know mi and yuh is friend, so he don't really say too much around me."

"Yo, I'm ready to get the fuck outta here."

"Really? Did yuh talk to the doctors?"

"Dats what 'im 'ave a mumma fa. Mi a go home to my pickney dem. A dem alone mi 'ave."

"Awee, I know yuh hurting, and as mi friend, mi is hurting too. This too shall pass, mi friend. . . ."

I was tired of Paula's holier-than-thou ass, and I didn't want to cuss her out, because she was my ace, and so I just walked away.

"Wey yuh gone!" she yelled as I walked through the hospital door and into the darkness outside.

I was happy to be away from all of them, I swear. I was pissed the fuck off that Don and that bitch would try me like this. I got in my car and started it. I heard my cell phone ringing. I reached over and grabbed my bag, then dug inside for my phone.

"Hello."

"Yo, wey yuh dey?"

I looked down at the caller ID. It was Garey. I looked around to see if anyone was watching me. I didn't see anyone in plain sight.

"Where the hell you been? I been calling yuh all night," I barked.

"Yo, the ting dun. Yuh must get the call already."

"Yuh is a fool. Yuh did a half-assed job." I was kind of careful about the words that I chose *because* I wasn't sure if this nigga was setting me up.

"Half-assed job? Come on, Angela, the man drop out permanently. There is no way 'im mek it."

"Well, I have news fi yuh. I just lef from up a University, and unless fi mi husband 'ave a twin, he is very much alive."

"Yuh bloodclaat serious? Yow eh yuh dey now?"

"I'm just about to pull out of the hospital parking lot. On my way home."

"Yo, mi gonna meet yuh dere in half an hour."

I didn't respond. Instead, I just hung up. That nigga couldn't do one fucking thing that I asked him to do. I knew one thing: my ass wasn't going down with him at all. He better pray to God that bwoy hadn't seen his face when he tried to kill him.

I got home, and Mama left. She had a million and one questions, but I wasn't in the mood. Bottom line was, I didn't know what had happened to Omari. I mean, I hated to lie to my mama like that, but there was no way I could tell her what was going on. My mama might love her obeah man, but killing was not her forte.

I changed into a sexy nightgown. I knew Garey was on his way, and even though he had fucked up, I still needed to hear how everything went down. I also knew that if I wanted to keep his mouth shut, fucking and sucking him good was the way to go.

My phone started ringing, and I snatched it up. "Hello."

"I'm pulling up. Open the back grill for me," Garey said.

"Why? Just come through the front. That nigga don't live here anymore or run any bloodclaat ting up in 'ere."

"All right, Miss Lady. Mi hear you. Mi pulling up now."

I opened the front grill, and he walked in. I locked the door and walked into my bedroom. He followed me and sat down on the bed. I didn't waste any time.

"So, a wha happen? Yo go fi kill do man, but 'im still alive," I said.

"Yo, B, mi a tell yuh sey, mi shot the man more dan one time. Mi nuh know how 'im still breathing."

"Hmmm. Omari is not dead. He is stabilized, and it don't look like he going anywhere no time soon."

"Cho bloodclaat." He stood up, took his Kangol hat off, and rub his head. Garcy looked disheveled, like he had been through hell and back.

"Yo, did he see yo' face?"

"Nah. It was dark, and mi walk up behind him. Man, mi shot the man three times, so how the fuck is it possible?"

"Garey, I don't know. Yuh go fi kill di man. Yuh shoulda mek sure the job complete before yuh left 'im. Yuh betta pray to God sey 'im don't know it's yuh. Mi know one ting. My ass ain't going down for yo' fuckup."

"Angie, cool yuhself. Di man neva si mi. Me and yuh is the only people that know what happen. So if wi kip wi mout' shut, then nobody can't know nuttin'. Don't even trust that gyal Paula, 'cause she deal with Don real hard."

"Trust? Not even my mumma, mi nuh trust. My pussy alone, mi trust." I patted my front.

As we continued to talk, I could tell he was nervous as hell. That wasn't good, because there was an old saying: "Pressure busts pipes." I couldn't risk him getting scared and shit, because he'd start running his mouth.

"Come on. Let me relax you a little bit," I said as I got behind him and started massaging his stiff shoulders.

"I could definitely use some TLC right now," he whispered.

Since I was fucking with Garey, I knew some freaky shit was about to go down. Before I knew it, he had my wrists handcuffed to the bed rails and my ankles tied to the bedposts. My body looked like an *X* as I lay on my stomach, nude, while his tongue worked miracles on my pussy. He was super aggressive tonight, and I was loving it.

"Stick it in," I begged, wanting to feel his rock-hard wood. *Fuck the foreplay*, I thought. Don't get me wrong. A bitch loved to get head, but there was nothing like feeling meat tickling your clit.

"Nuh say nuh more," he replied.

I knew he wanted to fuck too. Well, at least his magic stick wanted to fuck, because I had felt it rubbing on the back of my knees.

I turned my head to the side and glanced at the mirror hanging on the wall. I arched my back just a little, giving Garey easy access to my pussy. I didn't know what turned me on more, looking at my nude body or looking at the face Garey made while we fucked.

"Hmmm," I moaned out as soon as Garey's thick pipe drove into my wetness. "Yes, baby. That's what mi talkin' 'bout."

"Is this what you want?" he asked, inching farther in. "Mi can't hear you." He penetrated even deeper.

"Yes, Daddy, this wha mi want." I let out soft moans, then held my breath as his wood traveled deeper into my slippery pussy. "Fuck me," I begged.

Looking at his facial expressions in the mirror turned me on. His hands were on my lower back and were holding me down, giving my back the perfect arch. My ass was in the perfect position to take in all his wood.

Watching his dick slide in and out my pussy sent chills through my entire body. "Shit, yes," I moaned. My juices were on his dick, giving it a shine. "Oh, yesss, Garey."

"Hmmm, baby, da pussy yah good yuh fuck," he said, not missing a beat.

"Da wood ya good," I countered as his dick continued to penetrate my wetness. "Yo, Garey, fuck mi pussy. A your pussy dis. Oh, shit, yes." I dug my fingers into his back.

Each thrust felt like he was ripping my guts out.

"Fuck me harder. Oweiii, mi pussy a buss out!" My ass was rippling like a tidal wave as it bounced off his dick.

"Fuck yuh harder?" Garey held all his weight on top of me and gave me all ten inches. My moans and groans became unbearable. It felt like he was in my lungs.

"Bumboclaat. Mi sorry," I said, singing a different tune.

"You asked for it," he groaned, pulling his wood out of my pussy and punching it back in repeatedly.

I wanted to run, but my legs were bound and my wrists cuffed, so I had nowhere to go. I had to take all of him.

His thrusts became steady, hard, and long. His sweat dripped on my back. When I felt his body trembling, I couldn't be mad, because my thick cream was gushing out, creaming his wood. He collapsed on top of my back, gasping for air.

I used the little bit of strength that I had left to push him off me. I was tired, and my pussy was hurting from that beating that he'd just bestowed upon me. I'd been fucking Garey for a while, and I'd never seen him perform like that. It seemed like every bit of emotion that he was feeling had been taken out on me tonight. I wasn't going to lie. Although the pain had been unbearable, I had still enjoyed the sex. In my mind, the whole time, I was paying Omari back for the way he did me. I would've loved to see his face if he had walked in and seen his right-hand man beating his wife's pussy up. Hmm, maybe one day I should make that happen. I smiled at that idea as I got up and walked into the bathroom, ass still jiggling. I looked over my shoulder and smiled. Garey was paying full attention. . . .

Chapter 24

Kadijah

The loud popping sound of gunshots jerked me into consciousness. I stirred and opened my eyes. A second later I realized that I was in a car. All I remembered was being at the hotel bar. The car made a sudden stop as it crashed into a parked car with a loud boom.

Then I noticed that the driver was slumped over the steering wheel. Blood was dripping from his head, and there was a bullet hole in his back. He was the white dude who had bought me that drink. I sat up. When I looked back, I realized that we'd barely made it out of the hotel parking lot.

Confusion overtook me. When did I get in that damn car with him? Then fear took over. Who shot him? Was I going to be shot too? Damn, I felt so sluggish. It was like my muscles had been turned into mush. I had no idea what was going on, but suddenly the car door opened.

"You okay, miss?" asked a tall, muscular, caramel-complexioned man with a slight Jamaican accent as he extended his hand for me to get out of the car.

I nodded. "I think he drugged me," I said in a weak voice, my speech slurred. My vision was slightly blurry as he helped me step out of the car.

He nodded and let me put my weight on him. "I called the paramedics, because I know his MO."

I was more confused than ever. My head was all foggy, and it felt like I couldn't think straight. What the hell was he talking about? The thing was, it was also hard for me to speak. It was like my throat was dry as hell and my tongue was glued to the roof of my mouth. So, all I did was nod.

After the mystery man pulled me out of the car, there were lights all around me and the sound of sirens. When two paramedics made their way over to me, I was so out of it that I rested my head on the stranger's shoulder. *Mmm.* He smelled really good, and he was nice looking.

A second later, there was a light in my face. "Ma'am, keep your eyes open," said one of the paramedics. He was a short, dark-skinned dude with pimples all over his face.

"Huh?" I asked, letting the heaviness of my eyelids take over. It felt like I was spinning around and around. There was no way one drink had done that. "He . . . he . . . dwugged me. . . ." My voice trailed off, and it felt like my face was numb.

Then I heard the man who had saved me say, "The culprit's name is Aaron Lomas. You heard of him?"

An officer spoke up. At that point I couldn't see anything from the bright light in my eyes. "Oh, yeah. He's a human trafficker."

"Yeah, well, I've been workin' undercover, and we finally got him. Too bad he's dead," the mystery man said.

Shit. I had to disagree. It was a *good* thing he was dead and I was alive. Or was he really dead? I froze. Did they really know?

"Don't worry. You're safe," the other paramedic assured me.

Before anything else could be said, I was out like a light.

***

"Are you awake?" I heard a voice ask.

When I looked around, it was clear that I was in a hospital room. The bright lights and the sterile white sheet over me told it all. Plus, it was cold as hell, and the smell was distinct. At the moment, I didn't remember anything, but suddenly, a familiar face appeared in front me. He was the one who had rescued me.

"Who are you?" I asked, although my voice was barely audible.

"I'm Officer Terrance Crawley. I was on an assignment to catch—"

Suddenly, I started coughing, and he grabbed a glass filled with water and a straw. My throat was so scratchy.

"Sip this," he said. "They had to pump your stomach."

I did, and it helped. After clearing my throat, I asked, "What the fuck's going on?"

"Well, uh, you were almost kidnapped by a predator. Aaron Lomas is from the UK, but he is known for visiting different countries and targeting female tourists."

"Why?" I was curious, despite everything else.

"So they can become sex slaves."

My heart skipped a beat. Was I that damn stupid? I had let my guard down because of love and had almost become the victim of one of the worst crimes ever. Being sold into the sex trade was just as bad as slavery, if you asked me. Nicole's words meant way more now than they had before.

"Well, I'm so glad you were able to stop him. I mean, I'm not naive. I know that type of shit happens, but . . ."

Officer Crawley glanced at me. "He didn't die."

"What?" I squinted my eyes as I tried to focus.

He nodded. "We may need you to testify against him."

Shaking my head, I said, "Nah, I can't do that. Do you hear my accent? I'm not from here. I live in the United States. I can't afford to go back and forth."

"So, you'd rather he just keep running an organization that kidnaps unsuspecting female tourists and sells them into the sex trade? He has hundreds of people working for him. Human trafficking is a big business, and you can help stop him."

Shaking my head again, I stared at him blankly. "I'd rather he not, but it's not my responsibility. I'm here just . . ." Then it dawned on me. "What hospital is this?" Was it the same one that Omari was in?

"Does that matter?" He stared at me.

As much as I wanted to say something, I couldn't. "Look, you have enough evidence against him. Why do I have to testify? You were after him before I came along."

"True, but . . ."

"Look, if you must use what happened to me, why don't you just get my toxicology report or something? You saw him put me in his car. He clearly drugged me and was ready to pimp me out. Don't get me wrong. I'm glad you intervened, but I have to go home. I can't testify. I'm sure you have enough evidence against him, though."

"Yeah, but . . ."

"Leave please."

Officer Crawley looked down at me as I told him that. "Okay, but . . . I really need to build this case. . . ."

"Not right now."

He passed me his card. "Okay. When you get out of here, call me. I need to get your official statement. It'll help put him behind bars."

Then it hit me. That bitch Angela needed to be behind bars too, and Officer Crawley was going to help do it. Shit. I had another case for him to build.

So, the nurse finally told me what hospital I was in, and it was the same one that Omari was in. All I wanted to do was see him, but I knew that security wasn't going to let me. I was told that I would be discharged soon. They just wanted to be sure that whatever Aaron Lomas had given me was out of my system.

There was no way in hell I'd return to Jamaica to testify against that pervert. I just wanted to get things over with as far as exposing Angela's role in the attempted murder of Omari was concerned, and I wanted to see Omari make it out of this hospital alive. Hopefully, he'd be able to get his kids and raise them himself. His poor excuse for a psychotic wife didn't deserve to be a mother. He definitely didn't want a person who was capable of cold-blooded murder to raise his kids.

It was indeed true that Omari had been wrong for cheating on her and misleading me. However, he had decided to leave her, because he clearly wasn't happy. Why hadn't she just let him be? It wasn't like he wasn't willing to be there for her and their children. Although I didn't think I could ever trust him if we got together, I had my theory about things.

Omari wanted to be the opposite of how his father was. Once Angela was pregnant, he couldn't bear the thought of not being in the household with his children. I believed that at one point, he was actually in love with her. After a while, her crazy ways came out, and they turned him off. Therefore, he looked for peace in other women.

He'd found that in me, and we'd bonded in some way. Despite how we'd met and how things had happened, I had a deep connection with him. It wasn't just physical, though, because our conversations had actually made us close. He had shared his deepest, darkest secrets with me. They were things that Angela didn't even know. He'd told me that when he said deep things to her, they always went over her head. When he told me deep things, I'd have an even deeper response. He was attracted to that.

The urge to get up and find his room took over. I remembered that he was in room 213. I was in room 146, so I had to get on the elevator. It was around three in the morning, and I was hoping that security and the rest of the hospital staff was slim to none at this hour. My clothes were on the chair in the corner, but I didn't want to walk up and down the hallway dressed like I was going out somewhere. Then again, I couldn't walk down the hallway with the hospital gown on, either. My entire ass was out, of course. Then I thought about it. It would be nice if I could get some scrubs. I had a plan. The nurse would probably be coming around to check on me again soon.

Ten minutes later, like clockwork, she walked in.

"Uh, I'm going to be discharged in a few hours, but I don't want to wear that." My eyes drifted to my dress and high heels.

Her eyes were filled with understanding when she looked over at me. "What can I do to help?"

"Well, I'm here on vacation. I don't have any family or friends here to bring me anything. Do you have an extra pair of scrubs I can wear and some shoes? I'll pay you for them," I said, noticing that she was close to my size.

"Oh, no." She shook her head vigorously. "I became a nurse because I like to help people. You don't have to pay me. I know about what happened to you, and that's terrible. Now that I think about it, I have some scrubs and shoes in the car. They may be a little big, but I'm sure you'll be more comfortable leaving in that. Uh, what size shoe do you wear?"

"An eight," I told her.

"Well, that's perfect. I wear an eight and a half. I'll be sure to go get them before you're discharged. You seem more alert, so whatever he gave you must be out of your system."

"Do you know what he gave me yet?" I was just curious to know. Long-term effects had crossed my mind.

"Not yet. It takes a while for the toxicology results to come back."

I nodded. "Well, thank you for everything. I'm going to try to get some sleep."

"No problem. I'll go get the scrubs and bring them now. There's about to be a shift change, and I don't want to interrupt your sleep. Then you'll have the scrubs to put on when you leave."

"Thank you again," I said to her back as she left the room.

She looked back at me and said, "You're welcome," and a smile decorated my face.

Less than thirty minutes later, she was back with light blue scrubs and comfortable nurse's shoes. I pretended to be sleep as I watched her place the neatly folded garments on top of the outfit I'd worn to the hospital. I quickly closed my eyes when she glanced over at me, and I lay still until she left the room. After waiting a few minutes, I jumped up, grabbed the scrubs, and went into the bathroom to change.

The security guard was dozing at his post outside Omari's door. He woke up when I got close to the door, and glanced up at me but didn't flinch, since I was dressed like a nurse. My hair was back in a ponytail, and I didn't have on any makeup. All he did was nod in my direction and started nodding off again.

I walked into the room. Omari's heart monitor beeped as his chest moved up and down. Thank God he was still alive. Some of the tubes that had been connected to him had been removed, but the IV was still in his arm. He looked like he was in a peaceful state. Still, tears welled up in my eyes. I knew better, although I didn't know the extent of his injuries. Don had told me that Omari had been shot in the back multiple times, and though he'd lost a lot of blood, no major organs were damaged. They had given him blood, and he was going to make it. Thankfully, none of the bullets had hit his spine, and he'd be able to walk.

"Baby," I whispered, leaning over to kiss his face.

His skin was warm, and I could tell that he was filled with the vitality of life. If only he'd wake up. His eyes twitched slightly, although they were closed.

"Wake up, baby," I said a little louder, letting my wet tears fall on his skin. My lips were still on his face.

"Mi must be dreamin', star. . . ."

Did he just say something? I was startled as I looked down at him.

"Baby? You're awake?" I said.

"Mi was lost in a dream, but ya voice brought mi back, star." His voice was weak, but he was talking to me. "Ya really here?" His eyes were barely opened, but they were open, nonetheless.

"I'm really here, but I'm not supposed to be. Do you know why you're in here?"

I looked back, making sure that the security guard wasn't watching. Then I wrapped my arms around him.

"Yes, mi was shot in di back."

I nodded, and then I covered his lips with mine. Then I asked, "Did you see who did it?"

"Nah. Mi only felt the shots."

"I think your wife was involved."

He nodded and said in a somber voice, "Mi don't know who was involved."

"I'm going to help you. . . ."

"No, don't get involved. Mi no wan' no harm to come 'pon you. Let mi handle it."

"I can't let you handle it. That bitch you're married to is crazy. She told security not to let me see you 'cause I'm the reason you were shot. I'd never do anything to hurt you. Ever." I rested my head on his chest and listened to his heart for myself. The sound was strong. I knew he was a warrior; it had been obvious when I first laid eyes on him.

"Mi glad ya here, DiDi." He kissed my cheek. "Not under these circumstances. But ya jus' who mi wanted to see, ya know?"

I nodded and let the tears spill.

"Stop cryin', star. Mi gon' make it."

"I know." I sniffed. "I have to go. I don't want to get caught in here, but I had to come see you." My hand was on top of his.

"Mi love you, star."

Staring down at him, I confirmed it. "I love you too . . . star."

"When mi get outta here, it's gon' be mi and yuh. Mi don't know how mi gon' do it, but it's gonna be done."

I squeezed his hand and leaned over to kiss him again. Then I turned to leave and headed back to my room. Once I was there, the tears started again. I was so thankful that I still had my life. Calling my mother crossed my mind. Shit, my whole life would've changed if Officer Crawley hadn't been there to stop that motherfucker from putting me on the ho stroll in some foreign country.

And now Omari was awake. What a miracle. I was going to make sure that he didn't ever have to worry about that ho he'd married again. As I gripped Officer Crawley's card in my hand, I knew what I had to do, and I had to do it fast. Once that bitch realized that Omari was awake, she was going to do everything in her power to make sure the job was finished.

Chapter 25

Angela

I was pissed the fuck off. How the hell had I paid this nigga money to work the obeah against my husband and not a damn thing had happened? This nigga's mother must be working some good-ass roots, because obeah didn't touch him, and he got shot and didn't die.

I got up bright and early. I waited until the kids left for school, and then I took a quick shower and got dressed. I was about to confront this rassclaat obeah man. This was not sitting well with me. He was supposed to be one of the best in the business, so I needed answers.

The entire ride to the country, my mind was occupied. All kinds of thoughts were wreaking havoc on my mind. Omari's condition was getting better, and only God knew what the fuck he knew. Garey was acting like a big fucking baby. I swear, if I thought I could get away with it, I would kill that nigga my damn self.

I looked up and realized that I'd reached my destination. I parked and got out of my car. Just like last time, I bumped into the rotten-toothed homeless-looking dude. He had got up when I got out of my car.

"I see you back, pretty lady." He grinned, showing the horrible state that his mouth was in. He proceeded to walk toward me.

"Please get the hell out my way." I put my hand up as a guard. I then hurriedly walked away from him and up the hill.

I was so eager to get to the house that I forgot about the dogs that were there. I heard barking, and memories of my last visit flooded my mind. I stopped when I reached the gate in front of the house.

"Who you?" asked a tall, albino-looking man who had suddenly appeared on the other side of the gate.

"I'm here to see—"

"What is your name, and do you have an appointment?"

"Listen, mi name Angie, and no, mi nuh have no appointment."

"Well, I don't know. He sees people only on Thursday, by appointment only."

The sun was beaming down on my head, and I was getting irritated with this yard boy. I hadn't driven this far to hear any bullshit about an appointment.

"Listen, go tell yuh sey that a lady name Angie that was here before is here to see him."

He looked me up and down, then stormed off into the house. The old, mongrel-looking dogs were posted up like they were ready to attack.

I guessed he got the okay, because he came back out and opened the gate.

"Get back! Get back!" he yelled to the dogs.

Soon as we got on the verandah, I heard the obeah man's voice. "Come on in, Miss Lady. I didn't expect to see you this soon."

I entered the room where he'd been the first time I was here. He was sitting in the same chair. This time his face wasn't as friendly.

"Sit down," he said.

I sat. "Listen, no disrespect, but I pay you thousand to work obeah against my husband. But yuh know what? Nothin' happened. Not a damn thing!" I said, unleashing my anger.

"Calm down, ma'am. Did you follow my instructions?"

I stood up and leaned toward him. "I did everything you asked mi fi duh, but nuttin' happened. The Yankee gyal still around and in our lives."

"Hmmm . . . That is strange." He took his glasses off and shook his head. "I need to look into this more. I've been in business more than twenty-five years, and I've never had one unsatisfied customer. God knows I done work wonders—"

"Listen, mi nuh care how long yuh a do business. All mi know sey mi gi yuh mi fucking money and the bwoy and him gyal still deh."

"Calm down. I'm gonna try something else, but it's goin' to cost you. I'm telling you, you should be prepared to deal wit' the consequence. Death might also be involved. Do you understand?"

"I'm ready for whaeva. At this time, I don't give a fuck who dead. How much money we talkin' 'bout?" I was ready to spend all his money. There was no way I could put a price on my happiness.

"To do what I'm going to do, it's gonna cost you about fifty grand."

"Listen to mi. I don't 'ave a problem shelling out mi money, but you better mek sure it works dis time. If not, I promise I will be back here, and it's not gonna be nice." I stared in his dark, cold eyes.

He didn't say a word. He got up and walked into the back room. I took that to mean our meeting was over. I didn't have that much cash on me, but I knew the town was close and I could get cash from an ATM. So I headed back to my car and drove into town.

I got the cash and went back to give it to him. He handed me a bag with new mixtures. I thanked him and left. I hoped that motherfucker came through this time, because God knows I was sick of all this pussy-claat drama.

Omari

Three days later I was released from the hospital. I was kind of disappointed that DiDi had not returned to visit me after the day I woke up. Angie picked me up from the hospital. She had volunteered, and I didn't want to fight, so I had agreed.

"You want to come to the house until yuh feel better? Mi mean, you will 'ave mi and di kids to help yuh out," she said as we got in her car.

"Nah, B. I'm good. Mama gonna stay wit' mi until mi feel better."

"A wha the bloodclaat? Yuh act like sey yuh betta than mi and my pickney dem. Omari, wey yuh feel like? Don't you dare forget weh yuh come from!" she yelled.

I couldn't believe that bitch saw that I was still in pain and she wanted to try to start drama.

"Listen, B. Just drop mi off at mi place."

I gave her my address. Leaned my seat back and zoned out. She was still running her mouth about how ungrateful I was. I couldn't help but wonder why the fuck, if I was that ungrateful, she was still trying to get me back.

When she pulled up to my address, I saw Mama standing outside. She had told me earlier that she would be waiting on me. Soon as Mama saw Angie's car pull up, she dashed to the gate. I caught the dirty look that Angie shot my mother's way. I was so over that bitch, you had no idea.

"Come on, baby," Mama said as she helped me out of the car. I wasn't two steps out of the car when Angela pulled away, burning tires.

"You should've let me get you. The last thing yuh need is dis dutty gyal knowing weh yuh lay yuh head." Her voice trembled as she spoke.

"I know yuh nuh like Angie enuh, but, Mama, she is still the yute dem mudda. Mi just can't stop dealing wit' har, 'cause mi nuh want lose mi yute dem."

She helped me to my bedroom, and I sat on the bed. Damn, it felt good to be home. Ever since I was young, I had never liked anything that had to do with doctors or medicine.

"Yuh talking foolishness. Tek the gyal to court. Let the judge know sey yuh inna yuh pickney dem life. Yuh can get shared custody. Dat gyal is wicked, and the sooner yuh get har outta yuh life, the better it is fi yuh. Omari, please don't take dis lightly. Dat gyal is evil."

I knew she was serious and meant every word she was saying. It made me think about what DiDi had said about Angela being involved in the shooting.

"Anyway, son, how yuh feeling?"

"Ma, I ain't goin' lie. Pain is there, but the medicine can help that. Mama, these niggas violated me. . . ."

"I know, baby, but God say, 'Let vengeance be mine.' Him is not sleeping, and trust mi, yuh is God bless, and no weapon form against yuh will prosper."

"I hear you, Ma, but I ain't gon' sit back and wait—"

"Bwoy, hush yuh mout'. Don't you do anything foolish."

We continued talking for a little while longer. Then she brought me some chicken foot soup that she'd made. When I tell you I ate that soup fast as hell, believe me. A nigga was famished, and that soup definitely took care of that itch.

After I finished the soup, I took a shower and got into bed. My body was still sore, and I wasn't in any shape to be ripping and running. I grabbed my phone. I was eager to read my messages and see what calls I'd missed.

Tears welled up in my eyes when I saw my kids' picture on my home screen. Man, they were my life, and I was happy that God had given me a second chance with them.

Neither Angie nor anyone else could stand in my fucking way. See, they had no idea how deep my love for my seeds really was.

Memories of the night I woke up in the hospital entered my mind. I had heard a voice. I knew that voice from somewhere, and I searched my brain. That was DiDi's voice, but it couldn't be. I knew then that I was dreaming. The soft, sexy voice lingered in my head, and I felt a hand touch mine. I slowly opened my eyes, but I quickly closed them. The bright light had hit me as soon as I opened them.

I was eager to find out who it was that had just touched my hand. I used everything in me to open up my eyes again. In real life, DiDi was standing in front of me, in what appeared to be a nurse's uniform. I was really confused. How did she get here?

That was when it hit me that I was not at home. Instead, I was in the hospital. The last thing I remembered was trying to open up the grill to my crib. Before I could, I heard a gun being cocked, and then it was pressed against my back. I remembered when I felt the burning sensation and my body got warm. I just knew then that I was about to meet my Maker.

My attention quickly focused on DiDi. I wasn't too worried about how she'd got there. I was just happy that my empress was right here by my side. She started rambling about how she was the reason why I'd been shot. I had no idea what she was talking about, or why she would think such a thing. Whoever did that to me had to have a personal beef with me and not with her.

I wanted my woman by my side, but she said she had to go. I was too weak and in no condition to fight with her. My heart sank as I watched her storm out of the room. My mind was speeding a mile a minute.

"Nice to see that you are awake," a heavyset woman said as she walked in. She had a big smile plastered across her face. "Was that a nurse that just walked out of here? She must be new, because I didn't recognize her."

I looked at her like I was shocked. There was no way I was going to tell her that was DiDi. I had no idea what was going on, but I kept my mouth shut.

"Your pulse is good. Your blood pressure is a little bit low, but considering the way you came in here, I have to say God was definitely on your side."

I didn't respond; instead, I just smiled at her. I couldn't lie. I was a blessed yute, because I could've been dead up in somebody morgue right now.

The nurse chatted for a little while longer, and then she left. If I didn't know any better, I would think that she was flirting with the kid. Any other time, I would've flirted back, but Jah knows I was trying to change. I had one woman on my mind, and that was the one and only DiDi.

I heard the door open. I was hoping it was DiDi coming back in.

"Yo, star, yuh finally wake up." Don stormed in and came over and gave me a big hug.

I cringed when I felt a sharp pain in my chest as he hugged me. "Damn, brethren, you a'ight?" I asked him.

"Yo, mi good. Is you mi worried 'bout, dog. Mi tink mi dida go lose you."

I had never seen Don in this state before. That was a nigga who showed no emotion, not even when he was hurting.

"I feel you, mi genna. Just Jah alone know why 'im see it fit to save mi life." I choked up a little when my kids popped up in my head just then. I realized how close I'd come to losing them.

"Yo, we need to find out who the bumboclaat nigga that did this shit. Tha pussy deh need fi dead," he hissed angrily, though he kept his voice low, as he was trying not to be heard by security.

I knew Don was dead-ass serious, and I agreed with him. I just knew I was in no position to clap back at a nigga at this time. First things first. I needed to get up out of there and get my strength back up. I was a man of action, so talking right now about what I was going to do wasn't going to help a thing.

"Aye, yo, guess who rolled up in ya earlier?" I said.

"Who?"

"DiDi, my nigga. The Yankee chick. Yo, I think it's her voice that helped me to wake up. The nurse said I was in a coma since the day they brought me in."

"Yo, yeah. I hope I didn't overstep no boundaries. I hit har line to tell har wha 'appen to yuh. I didn't know she would fly here so fast. Look like the girl a mad ova yuh, ma nigga."

"Yo, trust mi, I feel like she's di one fa me, dawg," I revealed.

"My yute, how you gonna do dat? Yo, Angie nah go no weh, ennuh."

The mention of Angie's name riled up some anger in me. I remembered the last time I was there visiting the kids. She had thought it was a joke that I was done with her. I swear, I appreciated everything she'd done to look out for me early on in our relationship. But I was not going to become a prisoner in this thing just because of guilt.

To be honest, before I got shot, I had been thinking about going up to the embassy to apply for a visa. I knew a lot of my brethren had flown out early in the year. Seeing DiDi again just confirmed that I needed to get my shit and fly out of this place.

"Yo, mi G. DiDi think dat Angie was behind the shooting," Don informed me. "I mean, it did happen after yuh lef' her."

I took a few minutes to let what he'd just said sink in. I mean, to be honest, I knew that Angie had some fucked-up ways, but I was confident that she wouldn't do anything to hurt me. Right then, however, doubts entered my mind. My mother had always warned me about how wicked Angie was. I hadn't paid it any mind, because I knew that Mom Dukes just didn't care for her too much.

I shook my head. "Yo, dawg . . . that's just DiDi talking out of anger. I hate that ever since we been talkin', it's nothing but drama in our lives. Mi just hope this won't run har off."

"I didn't believe that shit, either, 'cause Paula woulda tell me dat. Yuh know Paula and Angie tight as hell."

"Yo my yute, mi nah pree none a dat. Mi ago talk to the doctor and see when mi can get outta here. By the way, you see the nigga Garey?"

"Bumboclaat! It's funny you bring dis up. A, the other day, mi and the brethren dem a sey, it's a long time since we linked up wit' dat nigga," Don replied.

"That's strange. . . ."

Just then the doctor entered the room.

Don backed away from my bed. "Yo, mi G. Mi a bounce. Be easy, yo. I'll see yuh tomorrow."

"A'ight, yo."

I then turned my attention to the doctor, relieved that I'd be able to see my kids soon.

Chapter 26

Kadijah

A few days had passed by since I left the hospital. So far there didn't seem to be any ill effects from whatever that creep had put in my drink. At this point, I still didn't know what it was. The lab would be notifying me when they got the toxicology results back.

I was in a taxi, on the way to see Officer Crawley, while I talked to my mother on the phone. She was all concerned because I was still here.

"Why ain't you back yet? I don't understand. You had an interview, and now it's time to come home. Do you have enough money? Are you being safe?"

"Mommy, I'm fine, and I have enough money. I'm still here because they said they will be calling me back soon for a second interview. There's no point in me going all the way home to just come back." The lie easily rolled off my tongue without me even having to think about it. "How's Cam?" I asked, changing the subject.

The mention of her grandson seemed to lift her spirits, and her voice sounded happier. "He's such a fighter. He's sitting up and talking now. He misses his auntie. You're the first person he asked for."

My heart fell. Of course I was. His mother wasn't shit. And I still planned to get to the bottom of that shit that had happened to my nephew.

"Give him some kisses and tell him I'll be home soon."

"I will, sweetie. The doctors said he'll be released next week sometime. They're concerned because of the nature of what happened. The cops have been here a lot, and somebody from DFCS came here today. I'm worried. . . ."

"Don't worry, Ma. If we have to, one of us will get him. He won't be in the system. Not if I can help it." I sighed heavily. "How's my hardheaded-ass brother?" He just wasn't trying to hear shit I had to say about the bitch he'd procreated with. Cam was a blessing, but his mother wasn't worth a damn.

Then I thought about Daryn's ex-fiancée, who was stalking me. I couldn't wait to get back home to handle that bitch too. That nigga had been texting me, but I had nothing to say to him. He was out of my life, and I had to get his bitch out of my life too. I didn't give a fuck if her father was a lawyer. I figured I'd lure her into my house and shoot that crazy heifer in the damn head. If she was willing to run me over with a car, she was a threat to my life. It would be self-defense.

"He's right here. You wanna speak?" she said.

"Yeah, let me talk to him." I needed to know if he'd done anything to retaliate for Cam's shooting.

"Sup, sis? You good, baby? You got enough money?"

"Hey, and yes, I'm good. I have enough money too," I assured him. "But I really wanna know if you did anything yet."

He immediately knew what I was referring to. "Nah, but I'm goin' to. Just wanna focus on bein' here for my li'l man. Them niggas gettin' all comfy. I'm gon' hit 'em when they least expect that shit."

"You around Ma?" I asked him.

"Nah. I stepped out the room. I knew you was gon' ask me that."

"What about yo' baby mama? Where her triflin' ass at?"

"Don't start, DiDi." He let out a sigh of frustration. "I'm so tired of playin' referee wit' y'all."

"Dump that bitch, then."

He sighed. "It don't matter who I'm wit'. She'll never be good enough for yo' ass."

"Not true. If you actually picked a woman who was worth a damn, she'd be good enough for me. The hoes I've met ain't shit. You just choose the wrong—"

"We're at di police station, miss," the taxi driver said, interrupting my rant.

"Look, tell Ma I'll call her later. Okay?" I hoped he hadn't understood what the driver said. He and Mama had enough to worry about. I didn't want them to worry about me too.

"Yeah, a'ight. Be careful, sis."

"You too. Love y'all."

"Love you too."

I ended the call, paid the taxi driver, jumped out of the taxi, and went inside. My phone vibrated just then, and I looked down to see Tamia's number. I sent her to voice mail, just like I'd been doing to Nicole since our last conversation. Hearing their rationality was only going to make me second-guess my actions, and I didn't have time for that.

Omari hadn't called me, and I'd called Don several times, without getting an answer. So far, all I had to rely on was Officer Crawley to get that bitch Angie away from the man I loved. He thought I was stopping by today to talk about that pervert Aaron Lomas, but I was there to tell him what I believed about who shot Omari.

I stopped at the first desk I saw and told the beautiful young woman with cocoa-brown skin and long, dark brown dreadlocks that I was there to see Officer Crawley.

"What is your name, miss?" She glanced up at me with slanted eyes.

After I told her my name, she picked up the phone and dialed a number. She then informed Officer Crawley that I was there to see him.

After she hung up the phone, she pointed and said, "Go to the left. His office is the first door on the right."

"Thank you." I nodded and walked in the direction she'd pointed me.

I passed by several officers sitting at desks that were positioned around an open space. The chattering and the phones ringing was very distracting. It was like I couldn't think straight with all this noise. Was that because of whatever Lomas had given me?

When I made it to Officer Crawley's office door, I knocked, and he called out for me to come in. Being that he had his own office, I figured he had some kind of clout. That was a good thing, given that I needed him to solve a case. If he didn't have pull, he really wouldn't be of much help to me.

When I walked inside his office, I noticed that he had papers scattered all over his desk, which was a mess. Okay, I was going to need him to get more organized. Without saying a word, I sat down across from him.

"How're yuh feelin'?" he asked as he reached out to shake my hand. "Do you want anything to drink? Coffee, water?"

"No, I'm okay," I told him. "Thank you."

He nodded. "Irie. Well, tell mi. Yuh changed your mind about testifying?"

"No." I shook my head. "I'm here for another reason."

Officer Crawley put his fingers together as he leaned his elbows on the desk. His forehead wrinkled, and a frown came across his lips. "Though I'm disappointed that yuh don't want to testify, I'm interested to know what reason that is."

"Well, someone I know here was shot recently, but he survived. I think I know who did it."

His stare was blank and he didn't blink as he asked, "So, yuh think yuh know who did it? That's not enough."

"Well, I know the victim because . . ." I cleared my throat. "We had a short affair. Not that long ago, my friends brought me here to celebrate my graduation from culinary arts school. I met him, and he didn't tell me that he was married. Eventually, I fell for him, and one thing led to another. His wife found out, and we got into a fight. That is motive. It's not a coincidence that somebody tried to kill him right after he cheated on her," I explained in one breath.

"Uh, okay, but we need more than motive, Kadijah. We need witnesses, opportunity, physical evidence, and a weapon. If yuh don't know for a fact that his wife did it, we have to prove it."

"Okay, well, do what the fuck you have to do to prove it!"

"Yuh have real feelings for this mon, don't yuh? After what yuh just went through, yuh seem more concerned for him."

"I can't let her kill him. You have to do something. At least look into it. Please." My eyes burned with tears as I thought about the possibility of that bitch finishing him off.

Officer Crawley had understanding in his eyes as he said, "Mi know dat island gyals can be . . . um . . . very aggressive about dey men, but dis . . . mi will really 'ave to look into."

"Okay. That's all I ask. Just look into it. I can bet my life that if she didn't pull the trigger, she at least got somebody to do it."

"Mi promise to do di best mi can. Uh, what's di victim's name? Mi need to look into the investigation so far."

"Okay, but I have to tell you this. If you question her, she's going to say that I was the one involved. I assure you that I wasn't."

"Hmm, well, investigating means dat we must look into everybody involved wit' di victim. Even yuh."

"That's understandable, but I wasn't here at the time of the shooting. I was already back in the United States. I can prove it."

"Good," he said, with a thoughtful expression on his face.

I gave him the information he needed and then shook his hand before leaving. When I stepped outside, thankfully, the taxi driver was still parked in the same spot. I walked over to the taxi and opened the back door.

"Oh, wow. I really appreciate you waiting," I told the driver as I climbed in. I had a smile on my face.

He smiled back at me. "Mi needed a nap, anyway. Back to di resort?"

"Yes, please."

I leaned back in the seat and took a deep breath of tropical air. It smelled so fresh and clean, and that was what I wanted with Omari. A fresh, clean slate. Then my phone buzzed again. It was Don.

I answered quickly. "Hello."

"DiDi, mi really need to talk wit' yuh. Yuh at di hotel?"

"Uh, not right now, but I will be soon. Is Omari okay?" The sound of my heart beating erratically against my rib cage had to be loud and clear.

"Di brethren's fine. He's home wit' his mom. Call mi when yuh get to di hotel. Mi come to yuh." After he said that, he hung up.

My breathing was shallow, and it felt like I was about to have a panic attack as tears slid from my eyes. What could he possibly have to talk to me about? It was like it was too much for me to bear. With what was going on at home and what was going on in Jamaica, I needed a moment of peace. I closed my eyes.

"Yuh okay, miss?"

I opened my eyes, wiped the tears away, and nodded as the taxi driver looked at me in the rearview mirror with concern. "Hopefully, I will be soon," I simply said, then leaned back and closed my eyes again.

Sitting across from Don in the hotel bar, I sipped on a nonalcoholic beverage as I waited for him to get to the point. When he still hadn't got to the point after five minutes, I spoke up.

"Okay, let's skip the formalities. What's going on?"

Don took a gulp of his Red Stripe and then looked over at me. "Di brethren don't believe Angie was involved."

"But what do you think?" I knew that he hadn't come here just to tell me that.

"Honestly, at first, mi didn't believe it, either. Mi figured it was some old street shit dat came back to haunt him." He cleared his throat and continued in perfect English, without patois. "Then add the fact that Paula didn't say anything about it. I know how close she and Angie are. They tell each other everything."

"Uh, if you think about it, Don, she may not have told her anything. That's not something you just share with somebody."

"Yeah, but they're so close. Anyway, I overheard a conversation that Paula was having with Angela on the phone." He guzzled the rest of his beer and continued. "She said something about Angela fuckin' our boy Garey."

"Ohhh, so she's fucking his boy." I said it with a satisfied grin on my face. "That self-righteous bitch. You tell Omari?"

He shook his head and then signaled for the bartender. It was the same dude who had been working at the bar when Aaron Lomas put a drug in my drink. For some reason, he avoided making eye contact with me. That stirred something inside of me. What was that all about?

"Another Red Stripe please," Don said when the bar-tender approached.

The bartender nodded and then walked off in a hurry.

Don answered my question again, this time with words. "No. He needs to concentrate on gettin' better so he can take care of his yute dem. I wanna handle this shit for my boy. He ain't in the condition to do it."

"I talked to a detective about it today. I was leaving the police station when you called."

He gave me a questioning look. "Huh?"

After I filled him in on how I'd met Officer Crawley, I noticed there was a frown on his face.

"Damn, yuh really could've been fucked up," he said. "Good thing he was there to save you. Wow."

"Tell me about it," I agreed.

"But I don't know about you talkin' to him, DiDi. It could start some shit."

"I don't care about that. All I care about is making sure Omari gets justice. If it wasn't Angela, oh well. We'll move on. But if it was, she needs to be punished. I think she won't stop until she does the job. We have to protect Omari. Don't you agree?"

"Yeah." The bartender came back with Don's beer, and he immediately took a huge swallow. "I noticed that nigga Garey ain't been around since the shootin'. I'm startin' to think like yuh. The only thing is, I wanna dish out street justice. Now you done put the cops in on the shit."

"Remember that bitch tried to accuse me of killin' him. I have to cover myself. Shit, I ain't trying to be locked up in Jamaica."

"I feel yuh."

My phone began to ring, interrupting our conversation. It was Omari, and I was relieved to see that he was finally able to contact me.

"It's Omari. Don't mention anything to him about what we talked about," I said to Don.

Don shook his head and finished his beer. "No worries. We'll talk later." He threw some bills on the bar and stood up to leave.

I answered Omari's call.

"Please tell mi yuh still here," he said before I could even say hello.

"I'm still here," I confirmed.

He sighed. "Mi need yuh. Can yuh get to me?"

"You sure it's a good idea?"

"Baby, it's di best idea."

That was all he had to say. I ended the call, then ran outside and stopped Don before he got to his car.

"Don, take me to him, please," I called across the parking lot.

He nodded and waited for me to catch up to him.

When I got to Omari's, I told him that I'd taken a taxi. I didn't want to explain to him why Don had been able to drop me off so fast. By the time Omari had made it to the door, Don was long gone.

"Jah know star. Yuh really here. Bless up!" He kissed his fist and held it up to the sky. Then he kissed me deeply while we were still standing there on the porch.

"Can I come in?" I asked with a smile. He smelled so damn good. "Your mom's here, right?" My eyes searched his.

I was nervous about meeting her. What if she thought I was a home wrecker? Lying down with a married man was something that was frowned upon.

"Yeah, but she's anxious to meet you. She hates Angela." He chuckled and then grimaced from the pain.

Holding on to him, I made my way inside the house. I made it a point not to comment on his fucked-up-ass excuse for a wife. "Take it easy, baby."

We walked into the living room, where Omari's mother was sitting on the sofa.

"Ma, dis is DiDi. DiDi, dis is mi beautiful mother." Omari beamed as he introduced us.

There was a radiant smile on his mother's face, which made her high cheekbones seem even higher. She was a very attractive older woman, with perfect ebony skin and pretty light brown eyes. Black definitely did not crack.

She stood up and hugged me instead of shaking my hand. That really surprised me.

"It's nice to meet you, DiDi," she said, seeming way too glad to learn that her son was interested in someone else.

"It's nice to meet you too."

"Hmm, you're beautiful, and your aura's good. Mi already like yuh better than that witch he married."

I almost laughed, but I held it in.

"Ma." Omari frowned disapprovingly. "Let's go in the back so we can talk in private, DiDi."

"Mi 'bout to go take a nap. Don't let mi impose. See yuh later, DiDi," his mother said.

"Okay. Enjoy your nap," I told her.

She winked at me. "Mi plan to. Yuh enjoy your talk." Then she disappeared down the hall.

"I like your mama," I told him as he held on to me and pulled me close.

"Mi so glad yuh here."

Looking up at him, I shook my head. "Even though you're all fucked up?"

"Dem bullets were worth yuh comin' back to mi, sunshine."

My heart skipped a beat as I shook my head again. "You're crazy."

"Yeah, maybe." He nodded and kissed me. Then he sat down on the sofa and leaned back. "Come put dat pussy 'pon mi lips, gorgeous."

I sat next to him, and his eyes blazed as he stared at me. My pussy was wet instantly.

"But your mama's in there," I said.

"So, she know what it is. She won't be comin' out here. Mi word." He licked his lips. "Besides, mi love di way your pussy tastes. Since mi no strength to fuck, I figure I'd taste that pum pum."

"Why is sex even on your mind right now?"

He shook his head. "Mi wanna taste yuh. We not havin' sex. We'll talk when mi done pleasin' yuh. I missed yuh . . . and the way yuh taste. Now, come sit 'pon mi lips."

I removed my shorts and followed his request.

"Ohhh . . . mmm . . ." Trying to muffle my moans as he sucked my clit was difficult, so I resorted to covering my mouth with my hands.

His hands were on my ass as he devoured what he called my "passion fruit." When I came, he held me in place and slurped up every single ounce of juice that escaped my aroused sex.

"Mmm . . . so succulent and sweet," he whispered.

Afterward, we kissed, and then I lay down beside him on the sofa.

"So, mi wan' yuh to know what's been on mi mind," he said as he held on to me.

"Okay." There were butterflies in the pit of my stomach.

"Mi tinkin' 'bout gettin' mi visa and leavin' here to be wit' yuh. What yuh tink 'bout dat?"

I held on to him tighter, but I really didn't know how to answer that. Part of me wanted him more than anything, and part of me wondered if I could trust him.

Chapter 27

Angela

Nothing seemed to be working out lately. To say I was feeling frustrated would be an understatement. Garey's ass had fucked up, and the damn obeah man had taken my money for a second time, but I still hadn't seen anything happen. Omari still hadn't come back home, not even after he survived those gunshots. I hadn't been able to eat or sleep lately, because my damn nerves were so torn up. And because of the baby that was growing inside my belly.

Earlier, I had looked in the mirror and hadn't liked the person that I saw. Under my eyes were black circles, and you could tell by looking at me that I had not been eating.

"Damn you, Omari. How can yuh do dis to mi and yuh pickney dem?" I screamed.

The pain wasn't getting easier to deal with. Instead, I was hurting deep inside. I felt empty and betrayed. All sorts of evil thoughts crept up in my head. I tried to dismiss them, but they would not go anywhere.

I heard someone knocking on the grill. Quickly wiping my tears, I got up to see who it was. I was shocked to see Paula standing there. I wasn't in the mood for any company, but she was already here. I grabbed the key and opened the grill.

"Wha gwann, mumma? Mi a call yuh from when and can hear yuh," Paula said when she stepped inside.

"Mi deh yah. Just goin' through some bullshit and decide fi stay to mi self fi a likkle."

"Angie, yuh look a hot mess. Wha really a gwaan wid yuh?" She put her arms akimbo and stared me down.

I knew I looked like shit, because I hadn't done anything except wash my ass.

"Paula, trust mi, yuh nuh 'ave no idea weh mi a go, true." I walked farther into the house. She followed close behind me.

"Well, mi bring yuh lunch and a big bottle a rum cream," she said.

Even though I didn't feel like eating, I was famished and could really eat something. We went into the kitchen, and I sat down at the table. Paula unpacked the lunch and put a big plate of fried fish and festival in front of me.

"Wey yuh buy dis?" I asked her as she sat down across from me.

"Is over Hellshire Beach, mi go and pick dis up fi we eat fi lunch. Mi figure yuh up yah and need some company."

I smiled at her. That was one of the reasons why I loved that bitch. No matter what we went through in life, we could always depend on one another to be there.

I got up and poured myself a glass of the rum cream, not caring that I was pregnant. That was just what I needed.

"Paula, let me ask yuh a question," I said as I sat back down.

"What's up, babe?"

"Why yuh tink Omari nuh waan mi nuh mo'? I mean, yuh is mi friend, and yuh been dere from day one. Yuh see how mi help di bwoy." I stared at her, waiting for some sort of explanation, because I'd been racking my damn brain for real, trying to come up with answers.

"Angie, yuh don' know sey a so man stay still. To be honest, yuh know Omari was a gallist, but still, him shouldn't duh yuh like dis. It's funny, because mi tink yuh and him was good. Mi try fi find out from Don what the fuck happen, but yuh know him and Omari tight as fuck, so him nah sey nuttin'."

"Don is a pussy hole too. No disrespect, 'cause yuh is mi bitch, but Don a deal wid slackness yo. How 'im ago treat dis Yankee gyal betta dan mi? How I'm gonna find dat bitch inna mi face like that? A shot Don fi get." I took a few big gulps from the glass, emptying it, and then got up and quickly poured myself another glass. The tears started flowing, and anger gathered in my soul.

I sat back down. "Yuh know what? I wish he was dead. 'Im lucky sey him survive, but yuh know, next time, 'im won't be dat bloodclaat lucky," I blurted out, not giving a damn if I was letting the cat out of the bag. I took several gulps of the rum cream and put my glass back down.

"Wait . . .Wha yuh just sey?"

"Yuh heard mi. I wish he was dead, and next time, the dutty bwoy not gonna be so lucky. . . . Him mumma will be right over Dovecot, burying his rassclaat." I picked my glass up and put it to my mouth and drained the last bit of liquor.

"Angie, look 'pon mi. Yuh serious? Is you shot Omari?"

"Bitch, yuh trippin'. I didn't sey I did it." I was thinking maybe I should shut my mouth right about now.

"Angie, so who shot him? Oh my God, him almost dead!" she yelled.

"Paula, shut up already wit' yo' dramatic ass. Omari hurt mi and mi pickney dem, and tink sey him a go run round here, showing off that Yankee bitch. Do you have any idea how embarrassed I am? A bitch come from America and tek mi husband. Not some nigga that mi a fuck around with, but my fucking husband. Yuh have no idea how hurt I am. Yuh know how many nights mi si down inna, contemplating murder? Shit, mi even tink 'bout fi kill mi pickney dem so him can feel the pain that I'm feeling."

"Angie, stop chat foolishness. Yuh betta than that. Mi know yuh love Omari and everything, but nuh man shouldn't mek yuh feel like yuh wan' kill yuhself and yuh pickny dem. Them innocent in all a dis."

"Omari or dat bitch don't deserve to live. Dem pussy deh need fi dead. Dat Yankee bitch need fi realize sey she can't come a my bloodclaat country and just tek my man like that!" I cried out.

Paula got up and walked over to me. She hugged me tight and started rubbing my back. "Babe, mi know yuh a hurt, but risking yuh freedom ova a man is not worth it. Look at yuh. Yuh beautiful. Yuh have yuh own house and money. Trust mi, a good man soon come through and scoop yuh up."

"I don't just want any man. I want my husband. My kids need their daddy. When mi sey I do, I meant dat shit!"

"Angie, calm down—" Before Paula could finish her sentence, her phone started ringing. She read the name on the phone screen and answered the call.

"Yes, babe. Let me call yuh back. Mi ova here wit' Angie," she said into the phone.

I knew she was talking to Don, and that angered me. The hate I had for him was just as intense as the love that I had for Omari and the hate that I had for his whore.

"Well, that was Don. Him want mi to meet him a Half Way Tree Courts. We supposed to be getting a new bedroom set," Paula announced after she'd ended the call.

I shot her a strange look. "Y'all moving in together?"

"Girl, no. Him still have him place. But him ova my place every night, and di other day di bed bruk down."

"Oh, okay."

We talked for a few more minutes, and then she decided to leave. She stood up from the table. As I stood up to see her out, I stumbled.

Damn. That liquor has crept up on me, I thought as I
tried to maintain my balance.

"My girl, just gwaan hold di faith. Trust mi, everything's
gonna work out. Omari goin' wake up soon and realize
that yuh is a good woman. Dat Yankee gyal might just be
using him, and him don't see that." She gave me a hug,
and I hugged her back.

I walked her to the door and watched as she left. I
locked my grill, headed into my bedroom, and lay down
on the bed. I was tipsy and had one thing on my mind
right now to help ease the pain. I wondered what Garcy
was doing. I picked up my phone and dialed his number.
The kids were still in school, and I knew I could get a
good fuck before they got home. I lay on my back while I
listened to the phone ring.

"Hey, B. What's good?" Garey said when he picked up.

"Hey, baby. I was wondering if yuh want to come ova
real quick. Mi pussy is on fire and need yuh bad," I teased.

"Oh, yeah? It's like that? Say no mo'. I'm on the way."

He hung the phone up in a rush. This pussy had that
nigga so fucking gone, it was ridiculous. I decided to take
a quick shower before he got here. At that moment I had
no worries. All I wanted to do was fuck that nigga good.

Thirty minutes later, he was pulling up. I opened the
grill to let him in. When I walked into the bedroom, he
followed closely behind me. I had on a little sundress and
no underwear. I wasted no time and removed my dress,
revealing my neatly shaved pussy. I knew it would catch
his attention and send him into a sexual frenzy.

"Damn, yo. Yuh ready fi Daddy," he said.

He peeled off his clothes and then grabbed me up.
He pinned me against the wall and started kissing me
aggressively. I started kissing him back. He then took
my bread into his mouth and sucked like he was starv-
ing for me. My pussy was on fire, and I wanted him right

that second. He picked me up and threw me on my bed, onto my stomach. He parted my legs and started licking my ass. He dug his tongue inside, sending electric volts through my body. I was used to him eating my pussy, but eating my ass was something new. I really enjoyed it as he pushed his fingers inside my pussy and then played with my clit. He was definitely a freak who knew how to take a woman on an emotional roller-coaster ride.

"Aweee, gi mi di wood now," I begged.

I guessed he was ready to dig into my soul, because he got up and slid all the way inside my wet pussy. I parted my legs more so he could get all the way up inside. Then I threw my ass back at him, and he gripped my waist and pulled me back toward him.

"Angie, a my pussy dis, Jah know," he said as he thrust deeper inside me.

We were both hungry for each other and didn't hold back at all. We tore my entire bedroom up. We went from the bed to the dresser to the floor, savagely in tune with each other's body. Thirty minutes later, his wood got larger and his sperm shot out all up inside me. I was too tired to move. That man had just satisfied my sexual urges, and I wanted to savor the moment.

Chapter 28

Kadijah

Me and Omari talked about everything we could think of until the sun went down. I left out everything about Officer Crawley and my close encounter with being a sex slave, though. He was going through enough already. Then I thought about something. His mother hadn't disturbed us yet.

"You think your mama's okay?" I asked as I played with his dreadlocks.

"Ma's fine. She's just givin' us our privacy."

"You sure? Maybe you should check on her." It had been about four hours, and to me, that was a pretty long nap. Seemed like she would've at least peeked out by now.

Omari reluctantly stood up, with a frown on his face. He was clearly in pain, so I shook my head.

"Sit back down. I'll go check on her." I had seen what room she'd walked into.

As I stood up, my heart started to beat really fast. Some type of foreboding feeling took over me as I knocked on the door to the room she'd gone into. She didn't say anything. I knocked again and waited a few seconds.

"Just checking on you!" I called out before turning the doorknob.

The door was unlocked, so I went in the room, and she was lying there like she was still asleep. Instead of assuming that she was, I walked over to her. The first thing I noticed was how still she seemed to be. I couldn't even see her chest moving up and down to show that she was breathing. My eyes burned with tears of despair, and my pulse quickened. I shook her gently, and she didn't even stir. Her body felt stiff and cold. I instinctively checked her wrist for a pulse. She was gone, and I didn't know how to tell Omari. Tears flowed down my cheeks.

"Omari! Get in here now!" I screamed frantically.

As the paramedics worked to revive his mother, I held Omari in my arms while he cried. The feeling of his hot, wet tears on my neck made me feel so helpless. What could I possibly do to make it better? He'd just been shot, and now his mother was dead.

"Why di fuck is this happenin' to mi, DiDi! Not mi mudda! Nooo!" His scream pierced my soul.

They covered her body with a sheet, and it was confirmed. There was no hope.

"Looks like she had a stroke," one of the paramedics said. "We just called the coroner to come get the body." He was short, stocky, and brown skinned, and he had pop eyes.

"Di body!" Omari screamed with all his might. "She ain't just a fuckin' body! Dat's mi mudda yuh talkin' 'bout!"

"Calm down, baby," I said as I held on to him. "They're just doin' their job. I know how much you love her, but they're working. This isn't personal to them. Please, you have to calm down. You're not one hundred percent yet. Please, baby."

He allowed me to lead him over to his mother, who was still lying on the bed. When he pulled the white sheet away from her face, he broke down like a little boy.

I had to hold him up, because if I didn't, he was going to be on the floor. As he sobbed and kissed her face, I felt like he was going through so much because of me. *Thou shall not commit adultery.* We both knew that, but damn it, I hadn't known he was married, and I couldn't help who I loved. However, the guilt was literally killing me. Although I hadn't shot him or killed his mother, I somehow felt responsible.

The coroner had just taken Omari's mother's body away, and he was silent as he laid his head on my breasts as we sat on the couch. I rubbed his head without saying a word. He wasn't crying anymore, but he wasn't talking, either. I understood why he was so quiet. What was there to say?

After I had filled the paramedics in on his condition, they'd given him something to sedate him. Mixed with his pain meds, it was a cocktail that put him in a catatonic state. When I looked down, I realized that he was knocked out, drooling and all. The sound of my phone vibrating made me slowly position his head on a throw pillow on the sofa. It was Officer Crawley calling. My heart skipped a beat. There was just too much going on, and I wanted to ignore him, but I couldn't.

Instead, I slowly stood and moved away from Omari. There was really no point in me being so careful. He was knocked out, and I was sure that a nuclear bomb wouldn't wake him up. So, I quickly made my way to the guest bathroom before answering the call.

"Hello?"

"Hi, Kadijah. It's Officer Crawley."

"Uh, I know," I said, with annoyance in my voice.

"Uh, yuh okay?" he asked, sensing my mood.

Rolling my eyes, I sighed. "Officer Crawley, it's been a long, fucked-up day. Just get to the point."

"Okay. Mi checked into the leads you gave mi and visited the victim's wife's home. Well, let's say, mi watched her home. She'd previously been questioned and claimed no involvement. First, a female showed up at her home, and after she left, a man soon come. Dey kissed before she closed the grill. Yuh might be right. Mi see motive."

"That must be his friend Garey," I said, filling Officer Crawley in, glad that he had been watching that vindictive bitch.

Killing Angela had crossed my mind, but that evil, sadistic ho wasn't worth me throwing my life away. There was no way I was going to rot in prison or hell for her. *Fuck that*. I was determined to have a good career, make a lot of money, and eventually have a family. Would I have that with Omari? Who knew? Only time would tell. I still hadn't really said anything about what he said earlier about going to America. Now that his mother was dead, that would have to wait.

Officer Crawley's voice cut into my thoughts like a knife. "His friend? Whose? The victim's?"

"Yes. I just found out earlier that she's sleepin' with his friend."

"Oh, shit, rassclaat. Excuse mi language. Mi will work on gettin' search warrants for his residence and hers. We have to find the gun dat he was shot wit' and connect it to either the wife or his friend before we can pursue charges. Yuh understand?"

"Absolutely. Uh, Omari's . . . the victim's mother died today. She had a stroke, and I really don't want him to know about what's going on with his wife and his friend right now. Can you avoid bothering him? I know that eventually, cops will be here to continue the investigation of his shooting, but . . ."

"Enough said. Mi will make sure nobody bothers 'im right now. Okay?"

I nodded, as if he could see me. "Thank you so much, especially for looking into things, like I asked. They have children, and they're all he has now. I'd hate for her to be raising them after trying to get their father killed."

"So, yuh tink she didn't pull the trigger herself?"

"No, I think her li'l side nigga did it. His coward ass shot Omari in the back. He could've at least been a man and let Omari see his face."

"Let mi work on gettin' di warrants. Mi will be in touch."

"Okay," I said and then hung up.

Before I walked out of the bathroom, I flushed the toilet and then washed my hands, just in case, by some miracle, Omari had woken up and noticed that I was gone. But when I got back to the living room, he was still knocked out like a light. I was tired too, but before I could even get comfy beside him, there was a knock at the door. My instincts told me to ignore it, but they kept on knocking, and I didn't want the noise to wake Omari up. I snatched the door open, and Don was standing there.

After stepping out on the porch, I asked, "What's goin' on?"

"Brethren called me earlier. Every ting's okay?"

"Oh." I took a deep breath. "His mom died."

Tears shined in Don's eyes. "Wha yuh sey?"

"His mother died," I repeated. "She had a stroke. He's asleep now. The pain meds and something they gave him knocked him out, for now. What about when he wakes up? Then what?"

Don leaned against the door and wiped his eyes. "Damn! Fuck! This is all gettin' outta hand."

"What do you mean?" I was curious.

"Mi was wit' Paula earlier. She sey Angie was talkin' craziness."

"Like what?"

"She sey she worry 'bout Angie, 'cuz she mention killin' di yute to get back at Omari."

My blood ran cold. "What the fuck! He needs to know that."

Don shook his head. "No, don't. . . . Angie's jus' talkin' on instinct. She not tinkin' rationally. Paula also said she said somethin' 'bout him really dyin' the next time. As much as Paula loves her friend, she's afraid she'll do something to hurt somebody or herself." He cast his eyes down, like he was trying to hide his own grief. "Yo, Mari's mother was like my own. Dat's fucked up."

"Yes, it is. I don't know what to do or say. . . ."

"Just be there for him. Di reason he and Angie didn't work was that she wasn't di one, anyway. Mi told 'im dat. He was more concerned about bein' there for di yute she breed wit'. Mi know dat a man and woman can breed but not be in love. Maybe mi made different. Mi got two yute. I tek care of dem, but mi no marry dey mom, 'cause mi wasn't in love."

He went on. "Paula fuss at mi. She sey mi a traitor to Angie. Mi neva liked dat gyal. Mi felt like she used what she had to lure di brethren in. Mi told him to strap up wit' har, 'cause mi know how he felt 'bout givin' his yute whut he neva had. Now dat shit done bit him in di ass. She don't love him. Neva did. She just don't want nobody else to have 'im. 'Specially not some Yankee gyal. True, brethren went 'bout it di wrong way. He should've ended tings wit' Angie first, but that's how shit is when the unexpected happens. He's only human. He really loves you, DiDi. Dat's why mi fucks wit' yuh like I do."

Wiping my tears away, I said, "I don't give a damn about how me and Omari met, or about the circumstances, at this point. He was wrong as fuck, I agree, but she's takin' shit too damn far. How can a real woman be okay with taking the father of her kids away? Then, when he survives, she thinks she's going to still have him. Not only that, but she threatened to kill their babies too?"

I shook my head as I quivered with anger. I really wanted to get my hands on that ho again.

It was like she was more concerned about the fact that I was American than about the fact that her own husband didn't love her. She couldn't see the error of her own ways. At the end of the day, that bullshit didn't matter one bit. How could she not care more for the beautiful children he'd blessed her with? The fact was, she'd given him babies, she had his last name, and he still wanted me. Ha! That was why she was mad. *Fuck that bitch.* My nationality or hers had nothing to do with the fact of the matter. She thought bearing his kids and fucking him was going to keep him. *Not!*

What most women didn't understand was that the physical could spark a man's interest, but it never kept it. Omari had told me that he and Angela had never once had a deep conversation, but he and I had had several in a short amount of time. She had thrown money at him when they first met, had sucked his dick, and had fucked him good. As if that was enough. Obviously, it wasn't.

In her eyes, that was how you kept a man. What she wasn't aware of was what my mother had always told me. You could fuck a man into oblivion, but only for a while, since a nut lasted just so long. But if you stimulated his mind, you had him for life. Well, though I had no doubt that my pussy could maintain a man's interest, it would only be for so long. If I wanted him forever, I had to show him that I was not only his fuck buddy but also his friend and confidant, one who'd always be loyal to him. If only he could do the same, though. Shit. One day we'd be old and gray, and we'd have to have something else to fall back on.

Looking at a nigga's saggy balls and hating him was not what I was looking forward to. I wanted to be able to laugh and cry with my old, wrinkled husband. Love went beyond anything that you could touch. It was something that you felt beneath your skin and cherished for an eternity. When I thought about it, I wanted Omari forever. Could I trust him, though? That was still the question. What if he met somebody who intrigued him more than I did, and he did the same shit to me that he had done to Angie? It didn't matter to me if she was American, Jamaican, Chinese, Arab, Dominican, or from fucking Timbuktu. I wanted to know that the man I loved would be dedicated to me and only me. For once, I felt Angela's pain.

The morning sun filtered through the blinds, and I squinted my eyes, trying to focus. Then it occurred to me that I was still in Jamaica and that Omari had lost his mother. The somber feeling came over me again. Then I felt his lips on my cheek.

"Tank yuh fi bein' mi rock, sugar dumpling," he whispered in my ear. "Mi know yuh 'ave your doubts 'bout mi. Mi understand why. Mi cheated on mi wife wit' yuh, but mi neva connected wit' Angie, to be honest. Not on a mental. Not like wit' yuh. Sometimes yuh can marry di wrong person."

Looking at him, I wondered why that was the first thing on his mind early in the morning. He had just lost his mother, and he was concerned about putting me at ease.

"None of that matters right now," I told him. "Are you hungry?" I touched his face, wanting to make it right in some way. But how? I couldn't imagine losing my mother.

"Nah, mi not hungry."

Giving him a stern look, I said, "But you have to eat, baby."

"Mi just lost my mudda!" His eyes were filled with anger, and I was clueless as to what to do.

"Yes you did, but I'm here! I can't replace her, but you have me!" My eyes filled with tears. "Now, though I'm not her, I can be here for you as best I can. Let me. Okay?"

He shook his head and held on to me tightly. "Okay." Then he looked at me. "Can mi be honest?"

"I wouldn't want it any other way," I told him.

"Mi tink she let go 'cause she met yuh. Mi tink she actually loved yuh so much instantly dat she could finally let go. She knows her son's in good hands now."

With a gulp, I grabbed his hand. "In that case, let me feed you. She would want me to do that. Please."

We stood and walked into the kitchen. I had looked up a few traditional Jamaican recipes, and now I whipped him up a few Jamaican things for breakfast. Don't forget that I was a certified chef who could cook just about anything. I made him sit at the table, and then I fixed his plate and placed it before him.

"Dumplings, ackee and saltfish, plaintains . . . ? Okay, Yankee gyal. Yuh must want mi last name. Yuh tryin'a impress me? If so, it's no need. Mi already gon' over yuh."

"Nope, not tryin'a do shit but take care of you as best I can." I didn't want to bring his mother up again. "Just try to eat as much as you can."

He grinned up at me and tasted his food. "Mi mudda must've jumped into your body, 'cause dis tastes as good as wha she'd cook."

Satisfied that he liked the food, I took a seat across from him. Glancing over at him, I asked, "Are you okay, baby, considering that—"

He cut me off. "Yuh here, so of course mi okay. Yuh love mi for mi. Not my dick, not my pockets, but mi. Dat's all mi need."

More doubts started to settle in. Did I love him too fast? Would he be mad when he found out that I was involved in trying to get the mother of his kids and his friend locked up? Of course, I hadn't mentioned to him the fact that Don showed up just hours ago to tell me about how Angie had lost what was left of her mind. It was killing me to know that she'd threatened to kill their kids. *Shit.* I had to tell him what was going on.

"Don't be mad at me," I suddenly said.

"For what?" His face was contemplative as he ate his food.

After clearing my throat, I said, "Well, I, uhhh . . ." Then I filled him in on what had happened with Aaron at the hotel and how I'd met Officer Crawley. "Considering what you've been through, I wasn't going to tell you, but—"

He cut me off. "Baby, really, yuh went through dat? Mi so sorry." He abandoned his food, came over to me, and comforted me with his embrace. "Why would mi be mad?"

"I didn't finish." He went back to his seat and started eating again. Then I told him about my meeting with Officer Crawley and the fact that I'd pointed his wife out as a suspect in the attempted murder.

Dropping his fork, he scowled at me. "Wha did mi tell yuh!" His voice was way louder than I thought he had the strength for. "Stay outta dis!"

"She did this to you! Don't you see that shit!" I screamed.

"Mi mudda's gone. . . . Yuh tink mi wanna lose mi yute too!" He threw his plate of food against the wall.

"Calm down, Omari. I—"

"Don't tell me to calm down, DiDi! Mi 'ave lost everything that means anything to me, 'cause . . ."

"Of me?" I asked. With fresh tears in my eyes, I stood up and went to get my purse.

"No. Mi didn't mean it like dat . . . ," he said as he followed me, but I was already on my phone, calling a taxi.

When I ended the call, he just stared at me. "DiDi, listen."

"Fuck you! You keep defendin' that bitch you married because she pushed your babies out of her rachet-ass pussy! Just know this! She loves your ass more than them, because she threatened to kill them, just like she tried to kill you! You're so fuckin' blind, though, 'cause that ho gave birth to your yute!" I said, mocking him. Then I opened the front door and walked out.

"Who told you dat!" he yelled, but he couldn't follow me. "DiDi, who di fuck told you dat!"

I didn't even bother to respond. Damn, I didn't want to turn my back on Omari, but shit, I needed my space. Like he'd said, he'd lost everything he loved because of me. It was best for me to go home and handle what really meant something to me. I'd made a man a priority, when it should've been all about me.

Chapter 29

Omari

Jah know star, I couldn't believe mi mudda was gone. I'd experienced hurt and pain all my life, but nothing compared to losing my queen, the woman who raised me. She'd never turned her back on me, no matter what I went through in life. DiDi walking out on me didn't even bother me at the moment, because I missed my queen so much.

I lay on my verandah, just thinking. I was on my second cup of Hennessy White. It didn't matter that I was mixing alcohol with pain medication. I had Jah Vinci's "Mama Love" on repeat. The part that kept getting to me was when he said, "All when mi fadda gone leff I, Mama cry." I clutched my chest as pain ripped through it.

"Father God, what have I done to deserve this?" I asked, and then I looked up for answers. It pissed me off that I couldn't get any. I picked up an empty bottle that was nearby and threw it up against the grill, shattering the bottle into small pieces. I was devastated, and there was nothing to undo or ease the pain.

Not only was I mourning Mama's death, but I was also trying to figure out who the fuck had shot me. I knew the streets talked, but for some reason, the streets were hushed about my shooting. I was no fool. I knew that somewhere out there, somebody knew who had done it. Funny thing was, at the time I hadn't had beef with no niggas.

I heard a car pull up, so I picked my head up to see who it was. I saw my kids running toward the grill. I stumbled as I went to grab my keys.

"Daddy, Daddy, Daddy!" My youngest daughter ran to me and hugged me.

I stumbled again but quickly caught my balance. "What's up, guys?" I asked as I hugged both of them. I swear, I didn't want to let go. But those seconds of happiness that I felt were quickly interrupted by the sound of Angela's voice.

"Look at y'all, happy to see y'all Daddy," she said.

"Hey, Angie," I said in a cold tone.

"Hey, Omari. How you holding up?"

I looked at her and remembered how much she despised my mother, but there she was, pretending like she gave a fuck.

"Omar, mi know mi and yuh mudda never see eye to eye, but I had respect for her. I know you hurting, because di two of yuh was close."

I didn't feel the need to respond, because I wasn't sure if she was being genuine or just being fake. With Angie, you could never tell.

I sat there kicking it with the kids. It was crazy that no matter how hurt I was, my kids always managed to put a smile on my face. I noticed that Angie was cleaning up. I hadn't asked her to, but she had taken it upon herself. I wasn't going to argue with her, because honestly, I was really enjoying my time with the kids, and if that meant dealing with her ass for a few, I was fine with it.

"Daddy, can we spend the night over here?" my princess asked.

I rubbed her long braided hair. "Babe, yuh got see wha Mommy sey."

"Mommy, please, please, can I spend the night wit' Daddy?" she pleaded while batting her big brown eyes.

Angie looked at me, and I shrugged my shoulders. There was no way I was going to be the one that disappointed my princess.

"Well, mi ago run to di house and grab y'all some clothes," Angie said.

"Mommy, and some Burger King too, please."

I was starting to sober up and wasn't feeling it. The pain of losing Mama was still tugging at my broken heart. The kids had been tired from playing all day, so their mother had bathed them, and now they were out like a light. After I kissed both of them good night, I decided to go back to smoking and drinking. It had been two days that my mama had been on that ice, and it was killing me. I rolled me a big head, grab a bottle of Hennessy White, and walked out on the verandah. I sat down on a chair and wasted no time getting started with my indulging. The tears started rolling down my face as thoughts of my mama not coming back popped into my head.

Propping my head back on the chair, I closed my eyes and thought about my childhood. Just then I felt someone touch me. I popped my eyes open. I noticed it was Angie. She was massaging my shoulders. I inhaled deeply. My mind was telling me to get her off me, but the flesh was weak. The effects from the alcohol and the weed didn't make it any easier. I was feeling good as fuck. I grabbed her hand and pulled her in front of me.

"Yo suck mi wood fi mi," I said as I tried to undo my zipper.

She didn't protest. Instead, she released my rock-hard wood from my boxers and dropped to her knees. Took my full manhood into her wet, warm mouth.

"Damn, Angie!" I yelled out in ecstasy as I pulled her head down closer.

"Just relax and enjoy it, baby," she said in a very calm, sexy voice.

I closed my eyes as Angie took me on a blissful ride of sexual ecstasy.

"Aargh, mi about fi buss." I grabbed her head and applied pressure. My sperm squirted into her mouth as she opened up wider. "Aarghh!" I yelled as I tried to squeeze out every drop into her mouth.

I still wasn't satisfied. I wanted more. I wanted to fuck her! Even in my drunken state, a voice in my head was telling me no, but I ignored it. *Shit*. After all, nobody was there but us.

Angela

I was shocked when I got the news that Omari's mother was dead. I didn't feel any kind of emotion, because I didn't like the bitch, and I knew the bitch hadn't really cared for me. If you asked me, the bitch hadn't had a man and had wanted her damn son for herself. Maybe the obeah was starting to work, after all.

I knew how close Omari and his mother were and how vulnerable he was right about now. I got the kids dressed and brought them over to his house. I didn't call or anything. Shit, I was hoping his bitch was over there, so I could really show that American bitch how we Jamaican bitches got down. But I was disappointed when I got there, as he was there by himself, drinking, and I could tell he'd been smoking too. The smell of weed wafted through the air. I'd seen him high before, but he wasn't really a drinker, and I could tell he was toasted. However, he was doing his best to hide it from the children, but I knew better.

I started straightening up his place. I was just showing that bwoy that he might've dissed me, but I didn't see
that Yankee gyal anywhere around here. All I saw was the
same bitch Angie, whom he had dissed. I was sweeping
the floor when a thought popped into my head. I waited
until my daughter came into the kitchen to get juice. I
grabbed her by the arm.

"Hey, baby. Yuh know yuh daddy is feeling sad, right?"
I said.

She looked at me and nodded yes.

"Well, you can cheer him up by asking him fi spend di
night. Him would love that."

"But mi have church tomorrow with Grandma."

"Don't worry 'bout that. Mommy will mek sure you get
dere." I smiled at her.

"Okay, Mommy. Mi gonna ask Daddy if mi and my
brotha can spend di night."

"All right, sweetie." I went back to sweeping.

I walked on the verandah just in time to hear baby
girl doing just what I had told her to do. I continued
sweeping, minding my business.

I knew that he wouldn't be able to say no to her, and
when he looked at me, I shrugged, because to be honest,
if he told her no, that would be on his conscience. It
wasn't like he'd been seeing his kids on the regular. He
had gone from being a full-time daddy to a part-time one,
all in the name of chasing new pussy.

The kids had been bathed and had gone to bed. They
had had a long day kicking it with their daddy. It had
been hard for me to sit back and watch that phony
shit, him behaving like he missed them so damn much.
Bullshit. If he missed them that much, he wouldn't
have left.

I had to put on my fake face just so I didn't reveal how I really felt about this old, fake-ass nigga. I lingered, folding clothes, until he started back drinking and smoking out on the verandah. I looked at him through the window and determined that he was drunk just by his gestures. I knew this was the right time to make my move. I just hoped it didn't backfire on me. I opened the door and walked over to him and start massaging his shoulders. After years of being with him, I knew what his weakness was. I had prepared myself, nonetheless, because I didn't know if he would push me away. He hadn't, so that gave me the green light to go ahead and massage him.

I was shocked when he pulled me in front of him and demanded that I suck his wood. I gladly got on my knees and pulled his wood out of his underwear. I wasted no time, quickly devouring it with my mouth, sucking it like a woman who was about to lose her life. I'd always enjoyed making love to Omari's wood. I was a desperate woman who was on a mission to get her husband back.

I started sucking his wood hard, seeing that he was under pressure, and he grabbed my head and pulled it down closer to him. I didn't ease up any. Finally, his veins got larger, and sperm oozed out of his wood. I set my mouth in a position to catch every last drop. I used my tongue and cleaned up every last drop. I was hoping for some dick, but I didn't know what he had in mind.

Without warning, he strained to pick me up and carried me into the house. I hung on for dear life when he bumped into a wall a few times as he staggered inside. He laid me in his big bed and got on top of me.

I couldn't resist his strong fragrance, which I could detect underneath that weed smell. It made my pussy wet. I had to take charge; there were no ifs, ands, or buts about it. I knew what I wanted, how I wanted it, and when I wanted it. I pushed him off me and got up.

"Omari," I called out and got his undivided attention. I bent over, acting like I was picking up something.

"Yo, Angie," he replied, turning around and getting a good glimpse of my fat, round, soft ass.

I smiled my evil she-devil smile, wanting to get my fuck on.

He walked up to me, licking his lips. "Damn, boo. Mi want you bad," Omari whispered in my ear. He followed that with a kiss that made my body shiver. I was silent, knowing that too much talking was a turnoff. I let his lips and hands do the talking. But his mouth kept talking too.

"Tek what's yours and stop yapping at the mouth," I finally said. I wanted to feel his greatness ripping out my soul. His body united with mine, as one.

Omari didn't say another word. He slid my panties down and pressed me against the wall. His dick was poking my ass as he tried to find the right hole. It didn't take long before his copperhead snake–like dick found its way into my wetness.

"Oh, yes," I moaned as he penetrated, taking slow strokes into my womanhood. "Hmmm." I could feel his wood touching my cervix. My breathing became heavy and louder as his wood researched my insides.

I stood on my tiptoes, because that nigga was literary running me up the wall with thrust after thrust digging deep into my pussy. He must've really built his strength up in the past couple of days. My moaning became unbearable. He put his fingers in my mouth, and I started sucking them as if I had a wood in my mouth.

He continued taking slow strokes, and that shit drove me crazy. Watching his shadow slide out of my pussy had my insides on fire. My blood was flowing through my body, my heart was racing, and my mouth was twerking his fingers.

"Yes, Omari. Yes," I mumbled, feeling my insides about to erupt like a volcano over his dick. I bite down on his fingers as my body trembled and my juices flowed down between my legs.

"Omari, this your pussy!" I screamed as my insides shivered, my walls got tighter, and I exploded all over his wood.

"Aargh! Mi 'bout to bust. Aargh, Angie."

I held him tight, digging my fingers into his back. He exploded inside of me without a care in this world. I smiled as he managed to catch his breath.

He backed away from me a few minutes later. I thought he was about to put me out. But no, that nigga just lay down and went to sleep. I was tired too, so I decided to take a quick shower. I was happy to lie beside my husband after that powerful lovemaking. I couldn't help but wonder where the fuck that Yankee bitch was while Omari was fucking my pussy good.

Anyway, she'd be just fine, I thought as I dozed off.

Chapter 30

Kadijah

I had been home for about two days, just reflecting on the things I'd been through lately. Avoiding my best friends was starting to get to me. They both had their choice words for me, and I was ignoring their voice mails and texts, because I didn't want to hear it.

After I arrived home, going to the hospital to see Cam had been the first thing on my list to do. When I'd got there, Imani's trifling ass was there too, but I'd just ignored her. Shit, I'd had enough drama.

"So glad you're home, baby girl. How was your second interview?" my mother had said after she hugged me so tight that I couldn't breathe.

"I decided to come on home. They hadn't called me yet, and I was homesick." I hoped it would be the last lie I had to tell my mother.

"Yeah, glad to have you back here, sis," my brother chimed in and hugged me next.

Once I was done greeting my mom and my brother, I pretended not to see Imani and went over to my nephew's bedside. His eyes shot open, as if he knew I was there.

"Aunt DiDi . . ." He sat up and wrapped his little arms around my neck. "I missed you."

"Aw, I missed you too, baby boy."

That hospital visit had taken place right after I got off the plane two days ago, and now I was sitting in front of the television at home, on my third glass of merlot.

A bitch was tipsy as fuck as I thought about what had gone down in Jamaica. As happy as I was to be home, I still felt like there was so much unfinished business there. I hadn't even heard from Omari since I left. Which was probably for the best. Feeling for him, due his mother's death, I wanted to call and check on him, but I couldn't.

After I left Omari, I'd made my way back to the resort. When I arrived there, I'd seen a swarm of police cars in the parking lot. Once I made it to the door, I spotted Officer Crawley and another cop escorting a male bartender out, the same bartender that I'd noticed the night that Aaron tried to kidnap me. When Officer Crawley saw me, he stopped and allowed another officer to take his place.

"What's goin' on?" I asked him.

"Turns out di bartender was in on it. Yuh didn't see Lomas drug you, because he didn't. The bartender did."

I nodded. I now knew why that bartender had looked all suspect when I was at the bar with Don. "Well, good thing you got him, but I'm leaving in a few hours."

Officer Crawley nodded. "Okay. Well, I'll be in touch."

Rolling my eyes, I told him as a reminder, "I'm not coming back to testify. Like I said—"

He cut me off. "With the bartender's testimony, we won't need yours. He agreed to take a plea and testify against Lomas Mi doubt he'll even go to trial, with so much evidence against him. Mi just need yuh fi the other case we were talking about. We'll have those warrants in a few days. Mi will need yuh to make an official statement."

Shaking my head, I declined. "I'd rather remain anonymous. Look, I have a life in the United States. I don't live here, and I can't involve myself any further. You know everything that I know, and I don't have anything else to say. Find the damn weapon and arrest them."

I said good-bye and then walked away, knowing in my heart that I should've told him about the threat that Angela had made about killing her kids. As much as I wanted to continue fighting for Omari, I couldn't. He clearly didn't appreciate what I was trying to do, and he was convinced that Angela was not involved in his attempted murder. Not only that, but he felt I was the reason he'd lost so much. True, he hadn't said it, but he'd been on the verge of saying it and caught himself.

As far as I was concerned, Angela was delusional. How could you fuck your husband's homeboy, get him to shoot your husband, and then act like nothing ever fucking happened? It was like she still wanted to be with him. What was wrong with that bitch? Omari was just as crazy as she was, if you asked me, because he was so blind to who she really was.

The way I saw it, fuck him. Maybe what I had felt for him the entire time wasn't love, after all. I had probably been just deeply in lust, because our one sexual encounter had been the bomb, and we'd had an explosive chemistry and great conversations. It was best for me to just leave it alone.

If Angela finished him off, that was on him. I had tried to help and could only hope the police stopped her in time. I'd hate for anybody else to get hurt, especially their kids, but I had to wash my hands of the situation and focus on me and my own family. I'd already risked enough, including my life. I was done.

As I stared at the television and got intoxicated all alone, there was a knock at the door. As I got up to answer it, I figured it was Nicole or Tamia. When I peeked and saw Daryn standing there, I opened the door, feeling a rage take over me.

"What the fuck do you want? I said all I had to say to you! Why don't you just give the fuck up!" I hissed, letting my pent-up anger spew out.

Daryn shook his head, with a regretful look on his face. "I confronted old girl, and she was just in her feelings. She said she really wasn't going to do shit and she ain't no threat to you. She promised to back off, since I told her that you got a gun and you'll use it if you have to."

"So, why are you really here, Daryn?"

"I love you, DiDi. I really want you to consider marrying me. I know I fucked up bad, but . . . I'm willing to . . ."

My laugh came out hysterical as I doubled over and slapped my thigh. "What the fuck? Are you kidding me? Next time you or your bitch pop up over here, I'm going to put that mufuckin' gun to use. Now, get the fuck away from my door, before I use it!"

He backed up and shook his head at me. "You've really lost it."

I nodded and flashed him a crazy look. "Hell yeah, nigga. I've lost it. Thanks to you and every sorry-ass nigga like you! I hate your fuckin' guts. I'll never fuckin' marry you. Honestly, I'd much rather bury your tired ass! Now, fuck off, before I go get that damn gun you were just talking about!"

That nigga literally ran off like his drawers were on fire or something. I laughed out loud again and locked the door before heading back to my spot on the sofa. For some reason, yelling at that fool had made me feel a little bit better. I decided to finally face my girls, so I picked up the phone and called Nicole first.

My girls and I decided to meet at a spot downtown. Nicole ended up coming over to scoop up my almost drunk ass, because I didn't trust that I could drive. Tamia ended up meeting us at the spot. The dress code was casual, but I had on a pair of flats, because I'd started the party at home. My short, tight black dress was popping, though.

Tamia was waiting for us at the bar. It felt good to be around my girls again. They both hugged me, and there was none of that judgmental shit when I filled them in on my time in Jamaica without them.

"Damn, bitch. I would say, 'I told you so,' but I won't rub it in," Nicole told me sympathetically.

"Right. You really could've been in a fucked-up-ass situation, but thank God you weren't," Tamia added.

"Yeah, it could've been worse," I agreed.

"Can't believe Omari's mother died like that, though. Shit. That heifer he's married to probably put a root on his ass and you. That might be why so much shit's goin' on," Nicole pointed out.

I shook my head and laughed it off as I sipped my drink. "Bitch, you need to be in somebody's nuthouse. Roots are not real."

"Shit. Maybe not to you, but they might be real to her," Tamia noted, agreeing with Nicole.

Rolling my eyes, I said, "Both you hoes are nuts."

That shit was only folklore. There was no way to put spells, or roots, on people. It was all just a waste of time and money to hire a person to do something like that. I believed in actually doing what I wanted to do up close and personal. It was too bad I hadn't had the chance to pimp slap that ho Angela a few times before I left Jamaica, but hopefully, Officer Crawley would take care of her ass.

A fine, tall, dark-skinned man who was at the bar turned to look at me. He had an athletic build and close-cut waves. His eyes lit up with recognition, and so did mine.

"Sean," I gasped, surprised.

"DiDi!" He jumped off his bar stool and wrapped me up in a tight bear hug. "Oh my God. It's so good to see you."

"You too. I can't believe it. What? It's been, like, two years?"

"Yup. Ever since you cut me off, talking 'bout you were seeing somebody and we couldn't do our thang no more. That shit tore my heart up." He smiled and looked over at Nicole and Tamia. "Hey, Nicole and Tamia. It's nice to see you ladies too." He hugged them as they exchanged pleasantries.

We had gone to high school with Sean, and although he'd liked me since middle school, I was all into the dude I had got pregnant by. Of course, that guy had cheated on me, and Sean and I had ended up seeing one another for about a year after I had the miscarriage. The relationship had never got serious, because he'd ended up transferring to a university in Texas to play basketball. We'd drifted apart, but whenever he came home, we would end up in bed together. Of course, when I met Daryn, I had put a stop to our casual romps.

Suddenly, for some reason, my body was on fire. Shit. Honestly, Sean was good as hell in bed, and it had been hard to leave him alone. The thing was, I had wanted to be faithful to Daryn. I had actually really cared for him at one point and had seen a future together for us. If only I had known then what I knew now.

"So, you still with . . . him?" Sean asked, putting his focus back on me as my girls chatted with each other.

"No. We broke up. Long story. Don't ask."

He grinned. "Don't worry. I won't. I also won't rub in how glad I am."

I laughed. "Why are you glad? You live all the way in Texas. Well, are you still in Texas?"

He nodded and sipped his Corona. "Not for long, hopefully. I'm actually here because I had an interview this morning. I'm going back tomorrow. Hopefully, I'll be moving back soon. My mother's getting older, and my pops died last year. She needs someone here with her."

Sean was a high school math teacher and basketball coach. He'd just started teaching when I called off our little "affair."

"I'm so sorry to hear that."

"Thanks," he said, with a nod.

Peeking at his left hand, I had to ask. "So, no lucky woman has snatched you up yet?"

"Nah. I was engaged to somebody, but she wasn't the one. Broke it off about six months ago." He glanced over at me. "Long story. Don't ask."

"I won't."

We continued to chat it up, and he bought me and my girls a couple of rounds of drinks. As I stared at Sean's handsome features, I was glad I'd decided to step out of the crib for a minute. Moping around and feeling sorry for myself weren't going to help. Honestly, despite everything going on, I was having a good time. I had to get back on it as far as finding a job, though. My focus had been on the wrong shit, and I had to prioritize again. When I was in Jamaica, I had got a call back from Pappadeaux for a second interview. That would be in the next couple of days. I would've been so upset if I'd lost out on an opportunity while chasing Omari's ass.

"So, Sean, you still diggin' my girl, huh?" Nicole's tipsy ass asked, putting me and him on the spot.

He chuckled. "I've always been diggin' your girl. She only wanted me for one thing, though."

Laughing, I hit him playfully on his muscular bicep. "I did not!" I had started to feel the alcohol really taking effect. Shit, I was drunk as hell, as my voice was slurred.

"Then she cut me off for some sorry-ass dude she ain't even with now." Sean shook his head and pretended to be hurt.

"I personally told her that you were a better catch than Daryn, but she didn't listen to me," Tamia said, chiming in.

"Oh, wow. Did you just turn on me?" I asked my friend as I giggled drunkenly.

"Nah. I'm just calling it like I see it," Tamia said nonchalantly. "I mean, you didn't even know Daryn like that, and I never trusted his ass."

Shrugging my shoulders, I attempted to explain myself. "If we must bring that up, I didn't want to be in a long-distance relationship. I wanted my man here with me, although I obviously made the wrong choice. Please, don't rub it in my face."

Tamia nodded and drained her glass of Bahama Mama. "Okay, boo. I feel you. We all make mistakes."

Nicole winked at me and nodded in Sean's direction. "You definitely made a mistake, baby girl."

I gave my friends a look and then flashed one at Sean. "Y'all will not be gangin' up on me tonight."

"I can think of some things I'd love to do to you tonight," Sean said, flirting.

"Oh, yeah, it's time to go. I think my friend could use some good dick right now," Nicole teased.

We all laughed, but damn, my drunk ass *could* use a good nut. Just a few days ago, I'd been in Jamaica, thinking I was all in love, and now there my drunk ass was, contemplating giving my old flame some pussy.

Tamia shook her head in agreement. "I'm usually the one telling you not to do something, but I gotta agree with Nicole. Shit, you're single. Get your fuckin' slut on, bitch!"

Shaking my head at them, I couldn't believe they were telling me to go ahead and fuck Sean. As I looked over at Sean, he had this sensual-ass look on his face, like he wanted to kiss me or something. As much as I wanted to fuck him, I didn't want to open up my heart and make shit complicated. It wasn't like he was some dude I had never had love for. And my feelings for Omari still hadn't been sorted out yet. Then I thought about it. There was no need to overthink it. It wasn't like Sean was asking me to be his woman.

"Let's go," I told Sean, with a sultry look on my own face.

My girls started going off, squealing and shit like schoolgirls. They were such a bad influence. We all laughed on the way out of the bar. After I hugged Nicole and Tamia, they went off to their cars, leaving me in Sean's care. I hoped he hadn't changed into a serial killer over the years. Shit, if I could trust Omari, I could trust him. Sean and I walked to his rental car.

"Oh, shit." Sean patted his pockets. "I think I left my wallet at the bar. The car key is in there. I'll be right back, beautiful." He kissed my cheek and walked back inside.

Less than ten seconds later, I saw somebody headed in my direction out of the corner of my eye. At first, I thought nothing of it and began checking my Facebook timeline. Maybe I could find a video to entertain myself as I stood beside Sean's rental car, waiting for him. It was a red Prius. I wondered what kind of car he drove for real, because that shit didn't fit him to me.

When I felt somebody grab my hair, I dropped my phone and went into fighting mode. My fists met the person's face, but I still couldn't see who it was as the person swung at me. Then I realized it was a woman. Damn, did Sean have some bitch he was fucking with in Atlanta who had run up on me? What the fuck was really going on? As I threw my hands, holding my own, drunk or not, I felt somebody lift me up. That was when I got a good look at that bitch. I kicked her in the face, and she huddled on the ground, protecting her face with her arms.

"What the hell's goin' on here?" Sean asked, sounding just as confused as I was at first. He was the one who had lifted me up.

"That bitch's fuckin' my man!" spat Nita, Daryn's desperate-ass ex, as she got up. "I followed you here, whore!"

Sean had to pull me back, because I wanted to kick her in the damn face again. Damn. I wished I had my gun on me.

"And you waited till I was by myself to run up on me. You scared ass! I ain't fuckin' him no more, bitch! I was, but I gave him back to you! Get the fuck over it!"

"I saw him at your place today. I followed him. I don't understand why he can't just get over you and be with me!" she screamed.

Shaking my head at her, I actually felt sorry for the ho. "Do I have to spell it out for you, crazy bitch! I don't want him. Did you see how fast he left? Well, I'll tell you what I told him. The next time either of you come near me, I will fuckin' kill you. Do you understand, bitch!"

Sean spoke up. "I think you need to get up outta here, yo. She's with me. We're together. She's moved on from him, and from what I know, you should too. He doesn't seem to be worth it."

That bitch had the nerve to burst into tears. "You don't know him!" she screamed as she walked away. "I'll leave you alone," she added over her shoulder.

"Yeah, bitch. That's what you better do if you want your life!" I yelled.

Sean picked up my phone, then tugged on my arm. "C'mon, before security rolls up."

Sean passed me my phone and then opened the door for me so that I could get in the car. Looking down at the screen, I was glad the phone hadn't broken. Damn. I couldn't believe the shit I'd been through these past few weeks. Damn. Some good head and dick would be right on time.

***

"Ohhh, fuck! Shit . . . ," I moaned. Sean was putting it down on my ass.

"Uhhh . . . damn . . . I missed this pussy . . . mmm . . ." He continued to stroke me deep, and I was preparing for orgasm number three.

After he ate me out, like I knew he would, I'd been ready to feel him inside me. I'd made sure to remind him that it was just a sexual thing. I didn't want him to have any expectations afterward, although I had promised him that I would keep in touch.

"Mmm, I almost forgot how good this dick is. . . ." My fingernails raked across his back as he put my legs on his shoulders.

His lips were on my neck as he took me there again. He was so deep, and I could feel my juices sliding down into the crack of my ass.

"Come on. This good dick," he coaxed in my ear.

"Mmm . . . yesss . . . I'm cumin'. . . ."

He slapped me on the ass, and I was feeling so damn good. The alcohol and his expert grind had me in a zone. At that moment, Omari and his psychotic bitch were the furthest thing from my mind.

Sean couldn't keep his hands off me as we walked down the hall of the Hyatt located in downtown Atlanta. He was going to drop me off at home before he headed to the airport to go back to Texas. Suddenly, what I saw in front of me made me do a double take.

"Shit," I hissed and pushed Sean back so that we would be out of sight.

When I leaned against the wall, he gave me a questioning look.

"Shhh." I put my finger to my lips and then peeked around the corner.

They were still standing there, waiting for the elevator, and I quickly pulled out my cell phone. After pulling up the camera, I turned the flash off, zoomed in, and snuck a couple of photos to prove what I'd just seen. When the elevator doors opened, they stepped in. I told Sean the coast was clear.

"What's up, DiDi? What? You saw your nigga or something?" Sean quizzed, his tone jealous. "Didn't that chick jump on you over him?"

I rolled my eyes at him. "No. I just saw my brother's baby mama all hugged up, kissing another nigga."

I sent the photos to my brother, feeling satisfied that I had a clear view of their faces in one of the pictures. Although I didn't know who the dude was, I knew that was Imani's scandalous ass.

Chapter 31

Omari

I rolled over and jumped up in the bed. What the fuck was Angie doing in my bed, buck-ass naked? I rubbed my hands over my face and took another glimpse to make sure I wasn't dreaming. Sure enough, Angie was in my bed.

Oh my God! What have I done? I thought.

"Good morning, babe," she said as she reached over and rubbed my arm.

"Angie, what happened, man? This was a mistake."

"Ha-ha. Mistake? Yuh saying making love to me was a mistake? I didn't force anything on yuh. If yuh ask mi, it seemed like yuh was enjoyin' yuhself."

I looked at her face and realized that she was enjoying herself now. The smile revealed her evil intentions. I'd been fucked up last night, and she'd taken advantage of that. Jah know, DiDi's face flashed in my head.

"Angie, mi sorry if mi lead you to tink there is something between us. Jah know, I'm sorry."

"Sorry? We are still married, and I'm carrying your child." She pointed to her stomach.

Fuck. I thought she had got rid of the baby. Man, my life was fucked. There I was, chasing DiDi, but Angie claimed that she was carrying my seed. I had never denied my seeds before, and since I didn't have any proof Angie had ever cheated, I couldn't accuse her of anything.

"So, Angie, yuh plan on carrying the yute? I mean, things kind of slow right now far as money, and I have no idea when I'ma be able to go back 'pon di road. . . ."

"Omari, cool yuhself. Mi have my own money, so all dat shit yuh talkin' is bullshit."

"Angie, bottom line is mi nuh want no more yute. Mi 'ave two, and mi satisfied wid dat. Plus, we are no longer together."

"So, what the fuck yuh saying? Yuh can fuck mi, but mi is not good enough to be with? Omari, wat's wrong wid yuh head? Wey dat gyal do to yuh? Why yuh acting like dis?"

"Angie, stop! This has nothing to do wid DiDi. This is about us. Dis marriage is ova. Jah know, mi know yuh hurting, and mi wish dat we didn't have to guh through dis, but I'm tired of us breaking up and making up. I'm sick of being unhappy, yo."

"Come on, Omari. I been dere through everything. Is me who love yuh, not dat gyal. We can have dis baby and move on wit' our lives," she pleaded. She placed her hand on my arm.

Shoving her hand off me, I stood up and looked around for my boxers but didn't see them. I grabbed a pair from my drawer and slipped them on. It was too early to be dealing with that bullshit, but there was no other way to deal with it.

"Angela, yo, dis is over and done wit'. I love yuh 'cause you the mudda of my yute dem, but mi not in love wit' yuh. I will be filing fa divorce after I bury mi mudda. Please don't mek dis hard fi mi."

"Fuck yuh and yuh dead mumma, Omari. Yuh is one ungrateful bitch-ass nigga. All the shit I did fa yuh, and dis is how yuh repay me?" She stood up and got in my face.

I grabbed both of her hands and pushed her back on the bed. Angie had no idea how I was feeling, and she shouldn't push me right now. I was trying hard not to disrespect her, but she was making it hard.

"Yo, get out of mi place," I told her.

"*Your* place? Old, broke-ass nigga talking 'bout *his* place. You mooched off mi, and now yuh telling me to get out of yuh shit. Boy, you suck mi pussy while mi a bleed." The evil side of her had emerged. Angie was very bitter and could be dangerous.

"Calm yo' voice. The yute dem still sleeping, yo."

"Shut yo' bloodclaat mout' up, acting like yuh give a fuck 'bout mi pickney dem," she yelled.

"That's it. Get dressed and get out of mi place."

"Go suck yuh bloodclaat mumma, Omari."

I lunged toward her, but I caught myself and backed away. I looked at her, smiled, and shook my head. That bitch had no idea that I had been about to kill her ass with my bare hands. I walked out of the room, leaving her behind, cussing and yelling. That fuck last night wasn't worth what I was dealing with right now.

I rolled myself a blunt and checked my phone. There was no call, not even from the one person whom I had expected to call. What was really going on with DiDi? The last time we were together, she had behaved a little hostile toward me. I knew that one of the issues she had with me was that I didn't believe the shit that she was saying about Angie. I mean, Angie was a lot of things, but she wouldn't get me hurt. I wouldn't believe that shit.

I was sitting on the verandah when she walked out of the house with the kids. I was pissed because I had told *her* to get out, not my kids.

"Daddy, Mommy say we have to go," my daughter whined.

I was going to respond, but I just looked at Angela and shook my head.

I hugged and kissed my kids good-bye before taking a few more pulls from my blunt. I had to meet up with my brothers and sisters to see how we were going to do this burial. Mama had always told us that if she died, she wanted to be buried in Meadowrest Memorial Gardens. Being the oldest, I figured I was going to make most of the decisions that needed to be made.

Today was the hardest day of my life. It was the day that my heartbeat, aka my mama, was being laid to rest. My sister had stepped in and handled all the funeral home arrangements and had made sure that Mama would be buried in a nice dress. Even though Mama had struggled to raise us, I could say that we had all come out good. My youngest brother was the closest to her and wasn't taking her death too good. I just hoped he didn't go out there and do anything stupid, because that would definitely break her heart.

Mama was a good woman who had helped many, even though she hadn't had much to offer. But she had helped everyone in our community. The attendance at the church showed just how many lives she had touched, because Gregory Park Baptist Church was packed. She'd been going to that church for over ten years, and the attendance showed how much they cared for their members. I was a broken but proud son today.

After the church service, everyone made their way to the cemetery for the burial. The preacher spoke for a while over the casket, and then Mama was lowered into her final resting place.

"Ashes to ashes . . . dust to dust," the preacher said.

My chest tightened. I was trying to keep all my emotions in, but I was slowly breaking apart. I couldn't take it anymore. I stormed off to my car. I climbed behind the wheel. I had a bottle of Cîroc in my glove compartment. I took it out and took it straight to the head.

"Mama, Mama, I need you," I cried out.

I knew I was a grown man, but I was hurting and didn't give a damn who the fuck heard me.

I heard a knock on my window. I looked up and saw that it was Angie. *Damn.* I wished that bitch would disappear, already. I slid the window down.

"Yo," I said.

"I saw yuh storm off, so mi come check on yuh."

I looked at that fake-ass bitch and considered spitting in her fucking face. But I noticed some of the church people were standing close by. I put the alcohol bottle down, got out of the car, and squeezed up close to where she was standing. "Listen to mi, yuh bloodclaat gyal. Get di fuck outta mi life, and don't come back."

I then walked away from that bitch and headed back over to the burial. It was my mama's day, and I planned to keep it like that.

After the funeral, we all got together at Mama's house. I was proud to step over the threshold, knowing that I had been able to buy her, her first house. Everyone sat around eating, drinking, and sharing the memories they had of Mama.

At one point, I felt like I couldn't breathe. I loosened my tie and walked outside. There was no breeze blowing, and the air smelled stale. I sat down in a chair and just tried to get my mind settled. I wished this was a terrible nightmare that I would wake up from.

Three days after Mama's funeral, I was still in a funk. I'd been drinking and smoking nonstop. Trying my hardest to block out the pain that I was feeling. I heard my cell phone ringing.

"Yo, my G," I said when I answered.

"On my way to you."

"A'ight. I'm here."

I really missed hanging out with the fellas. I really hadn't been out since I got shot and then Mama died. I was feeling a lot better, although whenever it was about to rain, the pain from those bullets would be killing me. I hadn't been sleeping at night, because I had really been racking my brain. I needed to know who the fuck had tried to kill me. I had even started looking at other suspects. With fame came jealousy, and I knew some of these niggas didn't really fuck with me. But I couldn't seem to come up with a nigga who had beef with me, unless it was some shit that I didn't know about. . . .

My thoughts were interrupted when I heard Don's bike pull up. Shit. I sure missed riding. I hadn't been out riding since I got shot.

I opened the grill. "Whaddup, mi genna? How yuh feeling, yo?"

"Living. Yuh feel me?"

"Fo' sure."

I walked in the house, and Don followed me. Then I grabbed a six-pack of Guinness and rolled a few blunts, and we started smoking and talking about business. I'd been out of the loop lately, so Don filled me in on what had been going on in the music world and also who had some hot songs out. I heard my nigga Vybz Kartel had just dropped a hot new album. This nigga was definitely a genius, and he was the baddest deejay right about now.

"Yooo, my G . . . I need to holla at yuh about some shit," Don said at some point in our conversation.

"What's good, fam?"

"You my nigga, and mi love you like mi brother. Yuh know I try to stay out dat shit wit' yuh and Angie, but this, mi can't stay outta."

"Wha yuh talking 'bout, bro?" I asked.

"Word in the street is dat Angie and Garey been sleeping around fa a minute now."

"What Garey yuh talking 'bout?"

"Yo, our nigga Garey."

I felt my blood start boiling. My hands started trembling. I put the Guinness bottle down on the table and searched Don's eyes to see if I could catch a glimpse of deception. I pounded the table a few times.

"Yo, wha tha pussyclaat yuh just said to me? My nigga fucking my wife?"

"Sorry, dawg. I hate to be di one that bring dis to yuh. But yuh need fi know, 'cause Angie act like she a angel."

"Jah know, star, this bitch need to get killed. Fuck dat. Both of them motherfuckers need to get killed." My lips trembled as anger traveled through my body. "Yo, my yute. I couldn't believe when mi hear dat shit. Now it mek perfect sense to mi. The bwoy stop coming round like he used to, and I call him phone di otha day and no answer. . . . That pussy hole done violated for real. 'Im could have any other bitch, but my yutes' mudda. That's a fucking violation!" I yelled with conviction.

"Yo, a dead da bwoy deh fi dead," Don said, lashing out.

I rolled another blunt and drank another Guinness. I tried to remain calm in front of Don, but that shit was weighing down on me. That bitch! She had given me a hard time about DiDi, but all along she had been fucking my "partna."

We kicked it for a little while longer, and then he left. Alone again, I took a moment to gather my thoughts. I had a plan, though, and being angry wasn't helping. I calmed myself down just enough to talk on the phone, and then I placed a call.

"Hello," she said in a low voice.

"Yo, yuh home?"

"Yeah. Why?"

"I'm coming through to see yuh," I said.

"Why, after the way yuh deal wid mi tha other day?"

"Cool nuh, mon. I just need to see yuh and di yute dem."

I wasn't trying to stay on the phone so she could start a fight, so I ended the call. I stormed into my bedroom and grabbed my gun out of the drawer. I hadn't used it in a while, but the way I was feeling, I could kill that bitch today. I decided to ride my bike there, even though I had some pain in my upper body. *Shit.* I couldn't sit around moping and waiting for those wounds to heal.

I tucked my gun in my waist, put my helmet on, and pulled off. As I drove, I tried to think back to see if there were any signs that Angela was fucking with that nigga. I knew that nigga would always be defending her and shit, but I hadn't thought anything of it. He was not a gallist, and taking my bitch was the last thing I would've thought he'd do. Garey knew how I rolled, and he also knew I wasn't some pussy nigga. Why the fuck would he try me like that over some pussy?

I pulled up to the gate and opened it. I left the bike outside the gate and walked toward the grill. Angie walked out of her house, smiling. I guess she thought that it would be a happy visit or that I had come to dick her ass down.

"Hey, boo," she greeted.

"Whaddup?" I said as I walked inside the house. Angie followed me. I looked around, making sure that no one else was there.

"What's going on, Mari?"

I turned around to face that old, dirty, two-faced-ass bitch. "Yo, who yuh really pregnant fa?" I pushed her against the wall.

"Wha the bumboclaat yuh talkin'about?"

"Aye, gyal, answer the bloodclaat question." I slapped her across the face.

"Omar, it's your baby. I swear, mi neva cheat on yuh before!" she screamed.

I pulled out my gun and pointed it at her head. "Angie, mi only asking one more time. Is yuh and Garey fucking?"

She picked her head up and looked at me, shocked.

"Answer me, bitch," I spat.

"It was Garey, Omari. He forced mi fi 'ave sex wit' 'im. I swear, mi neva wanted to," she cried.

"Bitch, I'ma kill yuh ass." I cocked the gun back and pressed it against her head.

"Wait! Stop! Mi 'ave something fi tell yuh."

I eased the gun away. "Talk up, bitch."

"I know who shot yuh."

"Talk then, bitch." I put the gun back to her head.

"It was Garey! Garey shot yuh. Him wanted mi for himself, so 'im try fi kill yuh."

I didn't believe her. I thought she was trying to put everything on him. "Bitch, stop fucking lying. You goin' be dead either way."

"Please, Omari, mi swear it was him. He wait till yuh pull up 'pon di bike and then put di gun a yuh back. 'Im was waiting fa yuh after yuh leff the house dat night."

My emotions were all over the place, but I tried to control them. This wasn't the time to appear weak.

"Yo call 'im 'pon di phone and talk to 'im so mi can hear yo," I ordered.

She scrambled to grab her phone. I stayed close to her, because Angie was a slick bitch and might try to do some slick shit. I was ready to kill that bitch and that fuck nigga.

Chapter 32

Kadijah

"You said that bitch wasn't shit," Nicole said after I had filled her and Tamia in on what was going down. We hadn't really talked since that night at the bar.

It turned out that Imani was with one of the niggas who, my brother had said, was involved in Cam's shooting. When I sent him the picture, he'd been mad as hell, and I'd been ready to kill that bitch. He'd had to beg me not to do anything crazy. My gun had been in my bag, locked and loaded. Imani wasn't home at the time, and Jameel had claimed that he was going to finesse the situation. I knew that he was going to whup her ass, and I didn't give two shits. It turned out that he had.

"Girl, he almost killed that ho, and he threw her out on her ass, buck naked. He said she came there with nothing and that was how her ho ass was leaving. Just like she deserved. Cam is going to be just fine without that bitch in his life."

"So, do you think she meant for Cam to get shot?" Tamia wondered aloud as she signaled for our server to come to the table to refill her drink.

We were eating dinner at the Cheesecake Factory to sort of celebrate my new job. Right after I left the second interview at Pappadeaux, I got a call from the manager of the Café at the Ritz-Carlton. She informed me that I had the job and I was to start in a week. Of course, I took it. That was my first choice, anyway. Still, it was bittersweet, given what was going on with Jameel. My brother didn't deserve to watch his son suffer over his sorry excuse for a mother.

I didn't answer Tamia's question until after the server left the table.

"I don't know if she was just helping him rob my brother, and Cam got caught in the cross fire, or if she really wanted Cam out of the way for good. She's not a good mother, so shit, I wouldn't be surprised one bit if she wanted Cam dead," I said.

"Hmm, in my eyes she's just as guilty either way. I already know how Jameel is, and I'm sure he's gonna deliver some street justice," Nicole said, adding her two cents before digging into her four-cheese pasta.

"He was waiting for Cam to get out of the hospital. They released him yesterday. He's with my mom for now. I told her I'd take him, but she told me that wouldn't be necessary. She and Jameel both claim they don't want to burden me, but my nephew is not a burden at all. I'm sure Meel's gonna do something. Of course, he's not going to let me know what's going on. I just hope he doesn't get hurt or . . ." My voice trailed off.

He should've let me put a bullet in Imani's ass myself, but he didn't want me to risk my freedom. The fact was, my brother, my mother, and my nephew were all I had, besides my two besties. I'd go to the end of the earth for all of them. I didn't know what I'd do if I lost any of them. If I lost Jameel, it would tear me up, because we'd always been so close.

"Meel's gonna be fine." Tamia patted my hand gently and then continued to eat.

Nicole decided to change the subject. "So, any more run-ins with Daryn's crazy fiancée?"

We all laughed, which was needed.

I shook my head. "No. I think he and that ho finally got the point."

"What about Sean?" Tamia gave me a sly look.

"What about him?" I shrugged my shoulders.

"Have you been talking to him?" she asked, digging for information. "Did he get the teaching job?"

"We did talk a few times, and he ended up declining the job. He decided to move his mother to Texas instead," I explained.

"So, what the fuck does that mean?" Nicole quizzed me.

Rolling my eyes, I dropped my fork on my plate and abandoned the juicy steak I was eating to answer her. "It means that I won't be pursuing a relationship with Sean. True, he's a good catch. True, he's fine. True, he can fuck, but . . . it's just not there. Besides, I fucked him that night only because I was drunk and . . ."

"In your feelings about Omari," Tamia said, filling in the blank.

"I was going to say, 'Badly influenced by my best friends.' Why are you bringing Omari up?" I picked up my fork and started eating again so that my mouth would be full.

Talking about Omari was the last thing on my mind. He still hadn't called me, and as much as I wanted to, I still hadn't called him. When I'd sobered up, I'd realized that sex with Sean was empty, although it felt good. There was no passion or feelings there. However, when I thought of Omari, I felt something different. He wasn't even on the same part of the continent as me, and he was still affecting me in every way. I had to get over it, though.

"So, you are just going to ignore the fact that you're really in love with him? Have you checked to see if he's okay?" Nicole asked.

"I'm not in love with him, and no, I haven't."

Tamia sighed. "You're so in denial, bitch. If you weren't in love, your ass wouldn't have jumped on a plane and flown over a thousand miles away just to be by his side. You love him. Face it. Have you heard anything else about the investigation?"

Tears stung my eyes, but I willed them away. "I'm not in denial. I'm just in touch with reality. Okay, so I did go to Jamaica to check on him, but the way he reacted to me telling him the truth about Angela made me change my mind about him. As far as the investigation is concerned, no, I haven't heard anything from Officer Crawley. To be completely honest, I don't want to have anything else to do with Omari and his fucked-up-ass wife."

"You don't mean that. I can see it in your eyes." Nicole shook her head.

"Y'all bitches were just telling me to fuck some nigga not too long ago. Now you wanna convince me that I'm in love with a man that I just met a month ago." With a sigh, I continued. "I just want to start this new job and turn over a new leaf. It's time to concentrate on me. If there's somebody meant for me, he'll find me. I'm not even trying to get involved with anybody anytime soon."

"Understandable," Tamia said.

Nicole sighed. "Okay, well, I'm going to leave it alone. You're a grown-ass woman, and you know what's best for you."

"Thank you," I told her gratefully. Nicole was known to pry, so if she agreed to leave it alone, I was going to take the peace offering.

After wrapping up dinner, we all hugged and went our separate ways. When I got home, it was a little after eleven o' clock, and less than a minute later, there was a loud knock on the door.

Damn. I hadn't even had time to get comfortable. Who the fuck could be at my door so damn late? Nobody had called, and I was hoping it wasn't Daryn. If it was, I was going to shoot his ass, drag him inside, and then call the

cops and claim that he'd tried to rape me. Okay, that
would take too much staging. I'd just have to ignore his
ass until he got the point and left me the hell alone.

But when I peeked through the peephole, I saw Jameel
standing there. He was looking around like he was all
paranoid, so I quickly opened the door.

"You okay?" I asked, taking in his appearance in all
black. It was hot as hell, and he was wearing a hoodie. He
had blood all over him.

He walked in swiftly, without saying a word.

Closing the door behind him, I asked, "Did you get
shot?" My heart fell.

He shook his head. "Nah. I killed them niggas, though.
I need to clean up, sis. I got to your spot before mine
as . . . I ain't wanna risk driving round like this. I left
some clothes over here a while back. . . ."

"Of course . . . Do what you gotta do." Thank God, he
was alive. "Where's the gun?"

"Why?"

I reached my hand out. "Give it to me. You don't need
to be driving around with it right now, either."

He passed it to me, with a nod. "Right."

As I watched my one and only brother walk toward the
bathroom, I could only pray for him. He lived that street
life, and I constantly worried that one day he wouldn't
be walking through my door anymore. Cam needed him
to be a father figure to him, so I hoped one day Jameel
would finally give the streets up.

Of course, my brother didn't stick around long, and I
prayed that he would be okay. Hopefully, there were no
witnesses to the murders and there would be no retalia-
tion. One more devastating blow would be too much for
me to bear. I was just able to grasp what had happened

to Cam and me, so I was trying to move on. If something happened to my brother, I knew it would put me on my knees.

By one o'clock in the morning, I was snoring right there on the sofa, with the remote in my hand. When I woke up, it was a little after six, and I noticed that I had a missed call. It was an international number, but I didn't know if it was Officer Crawley's or Omari's. Then the phone rang again, and the same number popped up on the screen. I quickly answered, and my heartbeat sped up. There were butterflies in the pit of my stomach as I awaited hearing Omari's voice.

"Kadijah? It's Officer Crawley. I know it's early in the States, but I wanted to fill you in on some things."

With disappointment in my voice, I said, "Okay. What's up?"

"Well, turns out you were right. We served a search warrant for Garey Broaden's residence and located di weapon dat was used to shoot di victim. He was arrested with no incident, and after hours of interrogation, he finally admitted that di victim's wife was involved. She didn't pull di trigger, but she will be charged with conspiracy. We have an arrest warrant for her, and it will be served today. Thank yuh for your help. If dis goes to trial, we will need yuh as a witness, since yuh helped solve di case."

There he was, asking me to testify again.

"Why do I have to air my dirty laundry for you to convince a jury that they're guilty? What's the point? You found the weapon that was used," I said.

"Yeah, di gun is di exact caliber that was used in the shooting, but in order for the charges to stick and be valid, mi must explain how I got the information."

"That's bullshit," I told him. "There are many anonymous witnesses who don't have to testify in person. Look,

I'm glad you got him, and I hope you get that crazy bitch Angela. That's all I can do. Unless you can extradite me or something, I say, 'Leave me alone, and job well done.'" With that said, I hung up the phone, relieved that they at least had Garey and would be going after Angela.

At least then their kids would be safe and sound.

A few hours later I was dressed and in my car, headed to my mother's. Seeing Cam was all that I could think about. Once I started my new job in a couple of days, I wouldn't have as much free time on my hands. So, I had decided to spend as much time as I could with him while I had the chance.

My mother greeted me with a big hug after she opened the door. "You heard from your brother?"

"Not since last night. Why?"

She shook her head. "Hours ago, he said that he was coming over to see Cam, but he hasn't shown up yet. I'm worried."

"Don't worry, Ma. You know how Meel is. I'll call him." I walked away from her to place the call, feeling my nerves starting to rattle.

What if somebody knew about the murders last night and had sought revenge on him? What if somebody had told the cops and he was now locked up? What the fuck could possibly go wrong next? Maybe Nicole and Tamia were onto something about Angela. Maybe she had done a root or a spell to make my and Omari's lives miserable.

When I called Jameel's phone, the call went straight to voice mail, and then I heard the sound of my mother's voice.

"No, that heifer is not at my house," she hissed.

I looked out the window and saw that Imani had driven up to the house. She was driving some hooptie, which, I figured, belonged to the nigga she was fucking, since she had left my brother with nothing. She started beating on the door all hard and was yelling and shit.

"Where's Cam? I want my fuckin' son!" she screamed. "I'm gonna get Meel locked the fuck up for puttin' his hands on me, and I'm gonna get y'all bitches locked up for kidnapping!"

The nerve of that ho. How the fuck could she show up at my mother's house, see my car in the driveway, and still be talking shit?

"Cam's asleep. I hope she doesn't wake him up with her bullshit. Where the fuck is Jameel?" smy mother said frantically.

I shook my head. "I'on know, but I'm gon' go outside and handle that bitch. You stay here."

"DiDi, no. You stay your ass in here. That ho will leave. As much as I wanna drag her all over that porch, it ain't worth it, baby girl."

"If I don't confront her, she's just gonna come back. Let me handle it, Ma. You go in the back and keep an eye on Cam for me."

She sighed and then nodded. I could feel her apprehension about me confronting Imani, but it had to be done. That bitch hadn't learned her lesson from Jameel's hands, but she was sure going to learn it from mine. My mother walked off as I walked toward the door.

I opened it and stepped outside.

"You know you don't give a shit about Cam." I stared at her bruised face, feeling no sympathy for the slut.

"I love my fuckin' son, and your brother had no right to put his fuckin' hands on me. I pressed charges on his ass, and my nigga's gonna kill him if the cops don't get him first. Now, you and your mama ain't have no right to take my baby from me."

I got all up in her face. "For your information, bitch, DFCS released Cam to my mother. You are not fit to get him back, because you're the reason he was shot in the first fuckin' place! Now, get the fuck off my mother's property, before I make you leave!"

She took a few steps back before spitting in my face. I grabbed that ho by her neck and did what I'd been wanting to do for so damn long. As my fists connected with her already fucked-up face, I felt no remorse. I was just going to add to her bruises.

"DiDi, stop!" my brother yelled as he pulled me off her. "Stop!"

In the chaos, I hadn't even seen him pull up.

"Fuck that, bitch! She said she pressed charges on you and told some nigga she's fuckin' to kill you. Sorry excuse for a damn mother. I swear." Shaking my head, I lunged at her and kicked her in the pussy.

She doubled over in pain. "Shit! Fuck you, bitch!"

"Go in the house," Jameel demanded. And then he opened the door and pushed me inside.

I took a step outside. "That ho better be glad I ain't bring my fuckin' gun out here! I'd hate to shoot my nephew's mama, no matter how triflin' you are. Beating yo' ass was the next best thing, bitch!"

"Go inside, Di," Jameel said sternly. "I got this."

Shaking my head, I went on inside. I headed to the bathroom to wipe that bitch's spit off my face before checking on my nephew. I didn't know what kind of diseases that nasty ho had. Hopefully, Jameel would go ahead and take that bitch on out of her misery before I did. She had one more time to come for me.

Chapter 33

Angela

My fingers trembled as I searched for Garey's number. I couldn't believe Omari was doing me like that.

"Bitch, call dat nigga and put it on speakerphone!" he yelled.

I pulled the number up and placed the call. I didn't see a way out now. I wondered how the fuck Omari had found out about me and Garey. How much did he really know?

Garey answered on the first ring. "Hey, babe. Tell me you miss mi already."

I wished that fool didn't answer the phone like that. *Shit*. Now was not the time.

"Omari found out sey mi and yuh messing wit' each otha," I said.

"Is about time the bwoy find out 'bout us. Either it was now or him would find out when yuh have mi baby."

"Dat's not all. Him also know sey yuh try fi kill him."

The phone got quiet for a few seconds. I wasn't sure if he was still on the line or not.

"Garey, are you still dere?" I inquired.

"Yeah, mi still here yah. Yuh just fuck up mi medz just now."

"It's not good, Garey. Maybe yuh need fi get yuh tings and leave . . . ," I warned him.

Bap! Bap! Omari punched me twice in my face, knocking me to the floor. He took the phone and ended the call. I guessed Garey was wondering what was going on, because he called back a few times.

"Aye, bitch, I'm going to tek mi yute them from yuh. I should kill yo' ass right now, but I prefer to see yuh suffering," Omari yelled.

I wanted to respond, but I knew that would only anger him more. Instead, I kept my mouth shut. I was hoping he would leave so I could grab my kids and leave from here. I had no idea where I was going, but I would worry about that later.

"Yo, bitch, you better not call this nigga, either," he said before he stormed out.

I remained on the floor, crying. Everything that I wanted was slipping away from me, and there was nothing I could do about it. I stood up and started throwing some clothes in a bag. That was when it hit me: it's not going to be easy to run with these kids.

I grabbed my phone and dialed Mama's number.

"Hey, Mama," I said when she picked up.

"Hey, Mama? Why yuh sound like yuh been running round a track?"

"Mama, mi need yuh," I said in a desperate tone.

"Gyal, wha happen? You okay?"

"No, Mama, mi nuh okay, but mi can't explain nothing to yuh right now. Mi need yuh fi get yo' grandpickney them from school fi mi."

"Angela, wha the rass a gwaan? Yuh sick?"

"No, Mama, mi nuh sick, but mi just need yuh this one time. Please, Mama," I pleaded.

"Hmmm. Okay. What time dem school ova?"

I gave her all the important information she needed. I also told her where I would leave the house key for her so she could get the kids some clothes. I wasn't leaving my kids for good, but I knew shit was going to hit the fan pretty soon.

I took a quick shower and slipped on a comfortable sundress. I zipped up the bag that I'd packed. I checked to make sure I had my bank card, because every dime that I owned was on it. I checked the back door to make sure it was secure. While I walked through the house, I dialed Garey's number. I was trying to see if Omari had made it to him yet, but his phone just rang. I really didn't have time to worry about that nigga. He was grown and should hold himself down.

I picked up my bag and stepped out the grill. I was about to lock the place up when I heard a commotion, and by the time I turned around, police cars had pulled up and police officers were rushing up to me.

"Angela?" said the first officer who reached my side.

"Yes, that is me. What's going on, Offica?"

"You're under arrest for conspiracy to commit murder. You have the right to remain silent—"

"Yo, Offica, yuh have the wrong bloodclaat person. Conspiracy to commit murder? Mi nuh have no idea wey unnu a talk 'bout."

"Please come with us, ma'am." He pulled me by the arm aggressively.

As they dragged me out of my yard, a scene was created, and all my nosy-ass neighbors were standing around, talking and shaking their heads. I hung my head in shame as they led me to one of the police cars.

I knew they were talking about Omari, but there were lots of unanswered questions. I knew one thing: I was innocent of whatever they were accusing me of. There was no way I was going down for some shit that some dumb-ass nigga had done.

I felt a sharp pain in my stomach. I grabbed my stomach and eased myself down on the backseat of the police car. I tried to ignore the pain, but I couldn't. I felt a gush of something between my legs, but I couldn't check what it was, because I was handcuffed.

"Offica, mi need to go to di hospital," I yelled out as the pain ripped through my body. I had no idea what was happening, but I knew it wasn't good.

"We teking yuh to the lockup first!" one of these fuck niggas yelled back at me.

I pleaded with them to get me to the hospital, but all my cries fell on deaf ears. I closed my eyes, said a silent prayer as tears rolled down my face.

"Let's go. Move over," one of the officer said when he came over to close my door.

I scooted over on the seat with the little bit of strength that I had in me.

"Oh my God, there's blood everywhere! We need an ambulance!" the officer yelled.

I looked down and saw blood dripping down my legs. I knew it was a miscarriage, and I couldn't say I felt any kind of way about it. Matter of fact, the way shit was going, I was glad that it had happened. That way, I didn't have to waste my money on a damn abortion.

"Ma'am, how are you feeling?" asked the officer who had said he was taking me to lockup. Now, all of a sudden, he was acting like he really cared.

"Mi tell y'all, mi need fi go to the doctor," I barely managed to say. I was losing blood, and I was too weak to cuss them out the right and proper way.

"God, I need yuh to get mi outta da situation yah," I whispered under my breath.

I wondered if Garey had also been arrested or if Omari had got to him first. I would prefer that Omari got to him first, because then I didn't have to worry about him running his fucking mouth.

Omari

I left Angie's house, feeling like a deranged man. I was on a mission, and no one and nothing could stop me. I had one thing in mind.

I turned on the avenue on which Garey lived, and saw a lot of people outside, which was kind of weird, because he lived in a quiet housing complex. As I approached his house, I saw police cars parked there, blocking the street. I had no idea what was going on, but whatever it was, it wasn't looking good.

I stopped my bike on the side of the avenue, where a couple of ladies were standing. I tried to eavesdrop on their conversation to see if they had any idea about what was going on. Then something caught my attention. A couple of officers were leading Garey out in handcuffs. I was disappointed. I had been on my way to kill that nigga, and there he was, getting arrested. I couldn't help but wonder if they were arresting him because of his connections to the scamming business in Jamaica. There was no need for me to hang around, so I pulled off.

My adrenaline was rushing. I needed to get at that nigga, but how could I when he was in police custody? Shit, I could reach out to a few niggas in the lockup. They would be willing to touch him for the right price, but nah, that was too risky. Niggas nowadays ran their mouths more than bitches.

I stopped at the spot where Don and them were hanging. It had been a minute since I'd been out of the house, but I needed to start getting out again. Shit, getting back into the music thing was a must. My partna had been holding it down, but I had heard I was missed on the scene. I parked my bike, took my helmet off, and walked in.

"Yo, y'all see who just walk in?" a brethren named Mikey said.

The rest of the niggas got up and rushed over to me, then hugged me and gave me daps.

"Whaddup, ma niggas?" I gave each of them a dap.

"Yo, gi mi G a drink of his choice," Don said to the bartender.

I took a seat at the bar, and we all started chilling, drinking, and smoking. It was exactly what I needed to take my mind off things.

I heard Don's phone ringing. He looked at the caller ID, then put his phone down.

"Somebody looking fi yuh?" I joked.

"Paula. She just want to know mi every move. Shit, I ain't even her man."

"Nigga, yuh put dat pipe on har." I took a sip of my Hennessy.

Before he could respond, the phone start ringing again. He answered this time.

"Yo, mi tell yuh sey mi out with the fellas. Huh? Sey wha? Yuh sure?" Don stood up. I noticed his facial expression had changed. He hung the phone up and walked closer to me.

"Yo, mi dawg, di police lock up Angie and Garey fi attempted murder on yuh," he whispered.

I looked at him, but I didn't say anything about being at Garey's house earlier. "Yo, really? Who tell yuh? Paula?"

"Yeah. Sey she on the way to University Hospital. Angie had a miscarriage."

I took another sip of my liquor and took a long drag from the blunt. I looked at the clock on the wall. *Fuck.* I realized my kids should be out of school. *Fuck.* I would have to ride to the house, get my car, and go pick them up. Without saying a word, I got up and walked toward the door.

"Yo, boss man, wey yuh a'go? Yuh good?" Don asked.

"Mi cool, mi G. I'll catch up wit' you niggas lata on."

I dashed out the door and jumped on my bike. The only thing on my mind was my children. That bitch had everything coming to her. I arrived home, got my car, and drove to the kids' school. The school was over for the day, but the principal was still there. He informed me that their grandma had picked them up.

I thanked him and ran out. I swear, I didn't like that bitch, Angie's mother, and it was fucked up that her ass hadn't called to let me know that she was picking my kids up.

I noticed the kids sitting on the porch as soon as I pulled up. I got out of my car and walked through the gate.

"What yuh doing at mi house?" that old bitch asked after she popped up from around the corner.

"Mi come fi get mi yute dem." I turned to my kids. "Y'all ready?"

"They not going anywhere wit' yuh. Mi daughter ask mi to pick dem up and keep them till she come back."

"Lady, yuh daughter is locked up fi trying to kill mi. So mi sure she not coming back anytime soon."

"Tek yuh rassclaat outta mi yaad. Dat is a lie. It's rumors yuh mek up because mi daughter don't want yuh. Yuh is witless, bwoy. These pickney not going nowhere."

I looked at that bitch. She had no idea how crazy my thoughts were at that moment. These were my yutes, just as much as they were Angela's.

"Listen, woman, mi not trying to start nuh war wit' yuh, yuh si mi? But mi come fi mi yute dem." I pulled my gun out and pointed it at that bitch. I knew it was a drastic move, but honestly, I didn't see another way out.

"Lawd of mercy, yuh a guh kill mi? Look how mi treat yuh like mi own pickney, and dis how yuh do me? Lawd God!" she yelled.

"Y'all come on." I motioned for my kids to come with me.

"Yuh is a criminal, and yuh going to jail," Angela's mother shouted.

"You ain't that stupid, bitch."

I tucked my gun back in my waist and walked off with the kids. I put them in the car and pulled off in haste. That bitch was just as evil as her daughter, and she was capable of anything.

"Daddy, why yuh pull di gun 'pon Grandma?" my son asked.

"Son, is a grown-up ting still. Sorry sey yuh si dat."

"Daddy, are yuh teking us to Mommy?" my daughter asked.

"No, babes. Yuh going home wit' Daddy. Yuh will si Mommy lata on."

Even though I didn't feel any pity for Angela, I felt bad for my kids. They were young, and they couldn't comprehend what was really going on. My job now as a father was to step up and make sure they were good, whether their mother was around or not.

I stopped at Burger King to get the kids some food. When we got to the house, I tried my best to make them feel comfortable. I could see on my daughter's face that she was missing her mommy terribly. My son, on the other hand, was more into a video game and really didn't say much. The more I watched him grow, the more I noticed that he was more like me. He loved observing and did less talking. A lot of times, that could be mistaken for weakness. However, I knew my strength was enough to get me and my yutes through the storm.

Epilogue

Kadijah

Two months later . . .

A sigh escaped my lips as I looked at the clock on the wall. There was about an hour left to my shift, and I wasn't rushing it. I loved my new career. It wasn't just a job, and I took pride in that.

When my manager, Robin, called out my name, it took me by surprise. I stopped prepping a piece of salmon to be pan seared and turned to face her.

"Yes?"

"Come here please. Lucas will take over." There was a stern look on her face that I couldn't read. Had I done something wrong? Over the course of the past sixty days, I'd only been complimented on my performance, so I didn't know what to expect.

"You can take off your apron. You are off for the rest of the day. Don't worry. I clocked you out," she told me, her lips still in the same straight line.

Robin was a middle-aged white chick who looked like a younger version of Martha Stewart. She was a no-nonsense go-getter like her as well. As she pushed a strand of her light brown hair behind her ear, I shook my head.

"I don't understand," I said.

She nodded and led me out to the dining area. "Just wait in the private dining area. You will understand soon." With that said, she walked off.

Were they firing me? The thought made my heart drop, because I didn't have the slightest idea why. I was passionate about cooking, and I put my all into it. The food was raved about, and so I was clueless as to what was going on.

As I sat down at one of the dining tables, Robin closed the partition to separate me from the other diners. Was I about to have a meeting with management? She'd even told me to take off my apron. If I was fired, why didn't she just tell me, instead of putting it off?

"DiDi?"

My heart really started to beat fast when I heard that familiar voice behind me. I was so deep in thought, I hadn't even heard the partition open again. When I turned around and spotted him, I had to pinch myself to make sure I wasn't dreaming.

"Omari?" His dreadlocks had been replaced by a close haircut. It looked good on him.

Yeah, the chemistry was somehow still there, but we hadn't talked since I left Jamaica. What was he doing in the United States? My mind was so full of questions, but when he pulled a bouquet of lilies from behind his back, I lost my train of thought.

"These are for you."

After taking the beautiful arrangement from him, I took a sniff before putting them on the table. Then I stood up, and he took me in his arms and held me tight. The scent of his cologne rendered me speechless too. *Damn*. It was like I didn't know what to say. I was thankful that he spoke once he pulled away.

"I know you have a million and one questions runnin' through your head. . . ."

"Where's the patois?"

He chuckled. "I'm in the United States now, so . . ."

My eyebrows shot up. "For good?"

"Yup. I've been here for a few weeks now."

We both sat down.

"How did you pull this off?" I asked.

"Well, I found your girls on your Facebook page, and they helped me."

"Wow. How did those bigmouthed bitches keep a secret for so long?"

We both laughed.

"I begged them to."

"So, how did you get my manager to go along with this?"

"It took some finessing. She loves reggae music, and I got her tickets to see Beres Hammond live."

"Wow. That's surprising. Good move." Robin's white ass was into reggae.

"And she really likes you. Said you're the hardest-workin' chef she got."

"So, what are your plans? Are the kids here?" I asked.

He nodded. "Yeah, they are. You'll get to finally meet them soon. I got a permanent gig. No worries over here. Got a rental spot and everything. I'm finalizing the divorce with Angie."

"Well, that's a given, since she tried to kill you. I figured you'd divorce her. Wow. What a transition."

"Yeah, it's not easy, bein' that I work a lot at night, deejayin'. My sister decided to move here too to help me out. It works out since she doesn't have kids. She'll be gettin' her own place soon, though. Since my mama passed, we figured, why not make a move here?"

"Well, I'm glad you're here." The truth was, I had missed him and had finally accepted that my feelings for him were real.

"I'm glad I'm here too. Now I get the chance to finally be wit' the woman I love." He squeezed my hand.

"So, you think we just gon' pick up from where we left off? I mean, how can you be faithful to me if you weren't to your wife?"

"Whoa. Slow down. Yuh just said yuh was happy mi here."

The patois was back, but damn, it was sexy as fuck. "I am. It's just . . ."

Omari pulled me into his arms. "Mi know yuh 'ave ya doubts, and mi get dat. Mi understand. . . . Fuck it. Mi *overstand*. Mi just know how mi feel, and no time or distance changed that. Now, just enjoy a meal wit' mi and give mi da chance to make it up to yuh. Let mi show yuh, yuh can trust me. Da right woman's in front of me now. Dat's da difference."

Then he leaned in and his soft, warm lips touched mine, igniting a fire that had never even burned out completely. I didn't know what the future held, but I knew that I loved Omari. Deciding to let go of the past, I let the moment take over. Maybe, just maybe, he was my soul mate.

Omari went on to explain that Garey and Angela had both accepted plea deals for twenty-five years to life in prison. It was a good thing she was behind bars, paying for what she'd done to him.

Neither of us had planned to feel anything for the other. Both of us had wanted only to have a one-night stand, and our feelings for one another had evolved over time. Sometimes love just happened, and there was no way to make anyone else understand it. Just knowing that I'd returned to make sure he was okay was enough for Omari to know that I was a different breed than Angie. True, he was wrong for cheating, but she was doing the same thing, and with his friend at that. At least he really did have true feelings for me. There was never an excuse for killing somebody. You just moved on with your life. That was what both of us planned to do. Yeah, I had had my doubts about Omari at first, but I felt that anybody could change. It couldn't be explained in words. That was just how true love went. It just happened.

"Mi love yuh. . . . There's no doubt in my mind," he whispered breathlessly against my lips.

"I love you too."

There was no way I could fight it anymore. Love had won.